Caffein

Frank's Wild Years

Nick Triplow

Fiction aimed at the heart
and the head...

Published by Caffeine Nights Publishing 2012

Published in Great Britain by Caffeine Nights Publishing

www.caffeine-nights.com

British Library Cataloguing in Publication Data.
A CIP catalogue record for this book is available from the British
Library

ISBN: 978-1-907565-14-4

Cover design by
Mark (Wills) Williams

Everything else by
Default, Luck and Accident

Nick Triplow was born in London, 1964. He was educated at Kemnal Manor School in Kent, then later at Middlesex University. He completed the prestigious Sheffield Hallam University Writing MA in 2007. Nick has published several pieces of short fiction. *Frank's Wild Years* is his first novel. He currently lives in Barton on Humber.

www.nicktriplow.blogspot.com

Thanks

I'm grateful to all those who have supported me this far: my family; Jane Rogers; JFNG especially Tina Jackson for wise words of encouragement; Darren Laws and Julie Lewthwaite at *Caffeine Nights*. God bless Mr Zeus & Mooka who kept me (almost) sane.

Wasted and wounded, it ain't what the moon did
I got what I paid for now.
Tom Waits – *Tom Traubert's Blues*

No one likes us, we don't care.
Trad. South London

ROUND ONE

1

You know Frank, he's the bloke who used to line up dry roasted nuts on a bar towel and flick them at Adeline every time he needed a refill. And Adeline, she'd take the hit, usually on the bare roll of flesh between her too-short, too-tight sweater and too-low, too-tight jeans, then top up his pint glass without a word. It was like that for as long as anyone could remember, and that's longer than most of the regulars who think of the John Evelyn as home.

Frank was usually in soon after the place opened. He'd take a slow walk down Evelyn Street, London SE8, and put his money behind the bar if he had it, or make out an IOU on the back of a betting slip if not. Adeline would take it through to the office to get the nod from Carl – he was still the boss then – and he didn't turn down the request more than once in ten years. That was the day last summer, the morning after Diane left him for O'Keefe, the soft drinks delivery guy.

Every hour or so a flicked peanut and a beer, every now and then if someone else was buying, a whisky. Frank could make drinks last with the skill of one born to his art, drawing out the gaps between sips until he felt that to leave it longer would summon up a hex, which meant he couldn't drink at all. Then it was a staring contest: Frank vs. the booze.

As the beer warmed and flattened, a bowl of peanuts sat at his elbow. Although these were intended as communal bar snacks, that particular bowl tended to be Frank's own personal stash, because no one else dared to go near. The last man to try wished he hadn't. Frank's watery-eyed stare fixed him. His lips pulled back from his teeth and his voice – sounding like he'd gargled gravel – was heard to say, 'Help yourself, mate. I always wash my hands.'

Sensing the discord, Carl had stepped out the office, tucking an off-white shirt in the back of his black Sta-Prest, his already hollow cheeks sucked in, a few strands of Brylcreamed hair falling loose like a low rent Buscemi – if Buscemi had been born a stone's throw from the Old Kent Road. 'You alright, Frank?'

'Thought you'd died in there. We was gonna ring Freddy Albin.'

'Just asking.'

In the meantime, Adeline had peeled a pack of peanuts off the display card. 'Have those on me.' She tossed them to the newcomer who seemed satisfied, if faintly bemused.

Carl shrugged and withdrew, back to the books, the sports magazines and the videos of old fights that always seemed to be running on a black and white Visionhire portable in the office. Once they spent a fruitless hour winding him up, asking if he didn't prefer football, game shows, cops shows or talent shows.

'I just like boxing,' he said.

For years he'd refused offers of a new set, a colour TV, a flat screen, wide screen, plasma screen, Hi-def, digital, DVD. You name it, some punter had dropped in with an offer every few months of the latest and best kind of television set ever made. Carl would listen, shake his head at the sheer fucking brilliance of the technology and say for his kind of use he had no need for a new TV. And from the office you'd hear the clunk of a video cassette, the volume notch up, the bell, then body punches' dull impact and rising crowd notes. It was as much a part of the John Evelyn's soundtrack as the clink of glasses, heavy silences on November afternoons and Adeline's occasional Sunday morning fart.

That's the way it was until the day – no one remembers exact dates around here, but they're certain it was between Christmas and New Year – that Frank sent an IOU through and Adeline was gone a while longer than usual. A minute passed, then two. Frank felt his eyebrow begin to twitch, his tongue fattening in his mouth.

She came back, a slow walk and a pause. 'He's not there.'

'Course he is.'

'I just looked, he's gone.'

'Tell him to stop pissing about, I want a drink.'

'Watch my lips old man, he's G-O-N-E gone.'

Frank dropped his backside off the stool, elbow dragged the bar-towel, scattering peanuts. He lifted the flap and went behind the bar which, had it been anyone else, would have been seen as seriously bad manners. Adeline stood aside. The change in perspective altered something in Frank's equilibrium and he held on to the wall for a moment, faced it like a fear of falling. He stepped into Carl's office. 'He's not here.'

12

Adeline was at his shoulder, 'Like I said.'

'So where is he?'

'I don't bloody know.'

Frank looked Adeline in the eye.

She stepped back, 'What?'

He reached behind her and pulled off a note, a scrap of yellow paper taped to the TV screen. *Need to get straight. Got some things to sort out. Back for New Year. Cancel soft drinks order. Take cash from Oxo tin, go to supermarket (not Tesco). Carl.*

They stared at each other for a full minute. Frank said, 'It's unplugged.'

Adeline took it as a euphemism, one of Frank's occasional odd, vaguely archaic turns of phrase. 'Yeah, unplugged – man.'

'The bloody telly.'

'Oh right, meaning?'

'He ain't coming back. Not soon.' There was a long silence. Adeline stripped the varnish from a nail. Frank said, 'You'll have to sign my IOUs.'

She held the door open. 'Out, old man. Go on, back where you come from.'

Frank's dilemma half an hour later, as told to the urinal was, 'I have a choice: bum a drink off a punter, which I can't do, not being a ponce. Ask Adeline and get slagged-off again. Go home. Wait for something to happen. Sit here and eat sodding nuts for the rest of the night.' He zipped up and eased forward, letting his forehead rest on the white tiles until the cold porcelain put a shiver into him. The gents was an ice-box this time of year. Carl never turned the heating on, said he didn't want to make the place too cosy.

There was a whisky on the bar when he got back, a large one. Adeline was nowhere to be thanked. Frank let a sip sit in the well of his tongue, roll around before the swallow. Kev the relief barman turned up and pulled the first few pints with his jacket still on. Some wag in the Public asked if he'd overslept. 'Nah, I got a call, Adeline says it's an emergency. She reckons Carl's done one, run off into the wild blue yonder to get his head together.'

For the rest of the night the talk was all Carl and had anyone seen the signs. Received wisdom took them no further than Carl's extended silences, which had always featured large and not increasingly so since Diane's flit. So why had it taken him all this time to up sticks? Frank just listened, caught the murmurs and ragged ends of conversations. As the evening wound down, the rest

13

of his whisky was still on the bar. The hex was on. He reached out for the glass, but couldn't lift it. There was no sense torturing himself. He shook the nuts from his overcoat and walked out into the night.

2

The switch on the wall in Carl's mum's living room had been painted over so many times it had a magnolia gloss coating which kept it permanently somewhere between off and on. A nudge either way'd do it. Carl didn't bother. It was dark in Mum's flat and could stay that way, he knew his way around well enough. After the three flights up, he was short of breath. He began unloading Asda carriers in the kitchen. Semi-skimmed in the fridge, cream crackers in the orange Tupperware, Bovril in the top cupboard, Ready-Brek, packet soups and instant noodles in the second drawer down. He filled the kettle.

Lauren from next door usually did Mum's shopping – a few bits down the road and a big shop once a fortnight. He and Diane used to take her to the big Tesco's, but one Saturday Mum had one of her turns, stalking the aisles with a holy medal held out in front of her like she was performing a kind of superstore exorcism. Diane walked out. Mum said there was something evil in the place. Carl had carried on wheeling the trolley, ticking groceries off the list. Diane accused her afterwards in the car park, a finger-pointing sideshow for the Saturday morning shoppers while Carl put the shopping in the back of the Astra. Di said Mum was behaving like a bloody kid, trying to show her up. It was personal, she said, adding to the old woman's bewilderment.

Carl filled his mum's cupboards, the fridge and then the fruit bowl. He found a used envelope in the third drawer down in the sideboard, scribbled through Mum's address and put a few quid in to drop into Lauren's before he left.

'I won't need all that lot. I've still got most of me Christmas stuff in.' Mum put the light on. She was standing resolute at the door in her quilted dressing gown. 'I'll only end up chucking it out. There's no room.'

'I've made room.'

'I'll never find anything.'

'It's all stacked together, you know where things are, Mum. It's organised. I wrote it down.'

'I'll open that bloody cupboard and bring the whole lot down on me.' She huffed. 'So what's all this about then, we expecting a flood?'

'No.'

'So it's war, then.'

'Don't be like that, I just wanted to make sure you had stuff in, essentials. Milk and that.'

'Which couldn't wait until the weekend.'

She shuffled into the kitchen. Carl had a flashback of being told to pick his feet up as a kid, copping a clip round the ear for dragging round like a deep sea diver in their boxy little kitchen in the old house in Catford.

'What about them slippers I got you for Christmas?'

'There's wear left in these.'

'They're dangerous. That's what that leaflet said, remember?'

'We don't have to do every bloody thing them leaflets tell us, we're not idiots. Well I'm not. Even if *she* thought I was.'

It was his mum's way, you could call it an opener – dressed up as a dig, which somewhere at its core maybe contained a germ of concern for him. The *she* was invariably Diane and without her, Mum would have been putting the boot into one of her friends or her absent cousin who'd gone 'up market' in Sevenoaks, building to a malevolent peak before settling on Dad, who perhaps deserved it most, having screwed up her retirement plans by dying first, worn out, his guts busted by cancer. Diane was a short-circuit, a cut to the spiteful.

'Bitch never cared much about us anyway. I didn't notice her making much of an effort.'

Was that before you stayed with us for six months when Dad died or after? Unsaid as she elbowed him aside to get to the fridge. 'Mum, I'm going away for a couple of days.'

'You be back for old year's night?'

'Hope so.'

She made the tea, spooned two sugars in his cup and rattled a sweetener into her own. It had always been something for them, old year's night, they'd be together. In the old days a party with the family and Dad's mates and their families. This year it'd just be the

16

two of them if he couldn't persuade Diane to let him bring Grace home.

'I'm still waitin' for you tell me what this is about,' she said, knowing the answer even before he'd said it. Probably even before he'd turned up at eight in the morning with a week's shopping. All the same, she'd make him say it.

'I want Grace with me, with us for New Year.'

Mum said nothing for a bit, just stirred in the milk. 'You're not going after Diane, then?'

'Well I'll 'ave to speak to her won't I? Her and her bloke said I could have Grace for New Year. Christmas with them, New Year with us. We had an agreement.'

'Means bugger all to her what's agreed.'

'It's not Diane's fault, Mum, it's him. This bloke she's with, he's being difficult.' There was a long silence. He could have told her he'd taken a frantic whispered phone call from his nine-year-old daughter the afternoon before begging him to come. He could have told her it was the third in as many weeks, but he didn't. Mum took her tea into the living room and sat in Dad's chair. It still commanded the room nearly twenty years after he'd gone. The best view in front of the telly, little table by the side. Clean ashtray – Mum had packed in the Consulate a couple of years back – glasses case worn down to the metal, Rebus paperback with a leather bookmark halfway through, a souvenir of Broadstairs.

Carl picked up the Radio Times, dog eared, thick with holiday adverts. She'd put little marks by programmes to watch with a green bingo pen. She wouldn't see most of them. 'There's an Albert Finney on this afternoon, Mum.'

'What side?'

'Channel Four.'

She shook her head. 'I don't think so.'

'But you like Albert Finney.'

'Not on Four.'

He put the magazine back on the table. There was a long silence. 'So, you'll be alright for a couple of days then?'

'I don't see why you have to go.'

'I told you, I want her with us for New Year, she *is* my little girl after all.'

'Except she isn't, is she, son? Not actually yours anymore, not in the normal way, not if she takes her away from us when she likes and we see her once in a blue moon.'

17

'All the more reason to make sure she's here for New Year then.' The rest was more silence, tea drinking. The flats waking beneath them, footsteps on the landings. Both of them lost in thought. He came over, kissed her on the cheek, 'See you when I see you. I'll call.'

Outside, Carl sucked in cold air. As he dropped the cash through Lauren's letterbox, she opened the door as if she'd been waiting. Everything she was wearing at least three sizes too big, baggy jeans, a blokes' striped shirt. Tufts of orange hair sprouted from a makeshift headscarf cum turban affair. The last couple of years she'd got enough work off the Council keeping estate kids in art projects to buy paints and keep her afloat, just about. And the rest Carl made up for with the odd bit of cash for cleaning and help around his mum's place. He told her about the trip, and leaving Mum for a few days.

'I'll pop in and see her later,' Lauren said. 'When the dust has settled. I've got some ironing to drop off anyway.' She squeezed his arm. The first flurries of sleet were coming in from the east, settling on the balconies, making the landing slick underfoot. 'Look after y'self,' she said.

Two hours later, Carl was slumped in the corner seat of the last carriage of a train north. He could see a couple kissing a long goodbye on the platform, the bloke attempting a pointless grope through winter coats, the girl pulling away too soon when she sensed someone was watching. Carl looked away. When he looked up again, a mum on her own struggled with two kids, a buggy and half a dozen bags. Carl recognised the panicked look people get when circumstances start spiralling out of control. One kid went too near the platform edge whilst she tried to get the buggy on board. She screamed frantically for him to come away, which only made him cry. The guard, a little Asian bloke in a blue blazer stepped off the train and helped. 'Don't worry love, no rush,' he said. 'They can't go till I say so. We'll find your seats.' The woman looked as though she might cry.

Carl had a paperback, which he didn't want, a flimsy newspaper full of slow news and no news this time of year. Even the sports pages had a warmed-through feel to them. Millwall drew nil-nil on Boxing Day. It was as if they couldn't be arsed. He closed his eyes and a few minutes later he felt the train shrug itself forward.

There was a do he remembered, donkey's years ago – an after-pub knees up at Auntie Chips' flat in Honor Oak Park when he was a kid. They'd all met up for a few in The Ram first and he'd had to stand outside. Dad was away somewhere. Lonnie was there too, Uncle Lonnie he insisted on being called. He wasn't related to Mum or Dad, but he was one of Dad's mates. Lonnie had brought him a Pepsi with a red and white striped straw, and a packet of Golden Wonder as he stood outside the pub. Talked to him about football as if he'd been told to, then gone back inside soon as he could. That song *Back Home* had swelled out as the door opened, Mum's voice singing along louder than all the others.

When they got to Auntie Chips' flat, he remembered Mum still singing, doing the seven-veils bit with those old orange curtains Auntie Chips had in her living room. It was like they'd brought half the pub with them. Big tins of brown beer in dimpled half-pint mugs. Gins, whiskies, towers of ham and cheese sandwiches, tins of salty peanuts, red sweaty faces singing to records on the music centre. Whatever Mum was drinking, she was chugging it back, then someone put that bloody song on and they were off again: *Back Home, they'll be thinking about us when we are far away...* Then Lonnie takes him aside and pulls out this knife. Pearl handled with a four or five inch locking blade. ''Ere son, you can 'ave this if yer want. Little present, just don't tell your mother.'

Carl stepped back instinctively as Lonnie swayed with the knife in his hand.

'Come on son,' he said. 'I spent hours gettin' this sharp.' He dragged the blade across his thumb. Too pissed for pain, he let the first few drops of blood drip into his beer, held it up. 'Cheers everyone.'

The room went watery and Carl felt his legs go to jelly.

His hearing came back first, the noise of the party was the same as before only muffled and distant. He had pins and needles in his hands. He was sweating and thought he'd gone to the toilet in his trousers. His lips tasted something that burned.

'It's alright love.' It was Auntie Chips' soft voice. 'S'only a drop of brandy.' He felt the back of her hand, cool on his cheek. 'You fainted, babe, nothing to worry about. It's ever so hot in there.'

She came back to him out of a blur. He was on her bed, the party in full swing in the next room, voices singing along. Lonnie's was loudest, singing *My Old Man's a Dustman*, his party piece.

Auntie Chips said, 'Between you and me, Lonnie's old man wasn't actually a dustman. He was a boozer and a ponce – the closest he ever came to a dustbin was when they pulled him out of one down The Blue every morning.'

Carl smiled.

'There's a good lad, you want a drop more?' He nodded and she gave him the little red glass. 'Sit up then, just a sip.'

He heard Mum's voice rise above the rest, all slurred and sentimental singing *Two Little Boys* 'For my Carl and my Terry.'

'Your mum's on form tonight, isn't she? You just stay there for as long as you want, love. Put the telly on if you like.' Auntie Chips left him on the bed and closed the door behind her. He ran his fingers along the eiderdown's wavy lines and wished Dad was there.

When he opened his eyes, the train was just leaving the grime-blackened walls of King's Cross and the City behind, then it was the Arsenal stadium, Finsbury Park and Ally Pally rising up out of nowhere. *Back Home, they'll be thinking about us, when we are far away.* The look from the bloke opposite told him he'd said it out loud.

3

Sometime during the night, the wind changed direction. Frank knew this because the Fair-Start Housing Association and their developers on the site over the road had planted company flags outside his window. Which meant that when the wind whipped off the river and up Creek Road, the lanyards rapped against the flags' hollow metal poles, creating an incessant pinking noise, a constant tuneless one note piano. It was like tinnitus. Like Jimmy fucking Osmond.

He drank two cups of Happy Shopper instant, washed the mug. He put the telly on, turned the sound up. In response, the wind lifted and the lanyards pinged louder. Last night's scotch un-drunk on the bar haunted him. Christ, he could drink it now. No Carl meant no more IOUs and Adeline wasn't due back until the evening shift. He put his overcoat on, got back into bed, got out and re-angled the TV. *Self-pity and sobriety, a winning combination – help yourself Frank.*

Later, as it grew dark, he shaved in lukewarm water from the kettle and combed his hair. He put his suit on and was polishing his boots with a pair of boxer shorts more hole than shorts when he heard a key in the door. Hilton, his landlord, the wheezing old shyster was letting himself in. It had become an unpleasant habit over recent months, any excuse and he'd be round there, sticking his oar in. 'You want to put foil on that cooker top,' was one piece of advice. 'You'll ruin the enamel with the fat. I'll bring some with me next time is what I'll do,' he said, giving himself another excuse to come in uninvited.

Frank had actually been trying to get hold of him since the first week in December. Some of the roof tiles must have shifted, because rain was leaking through the bathroom ceiling. The glass globe lightshade had filled up like a bloody goldfish bowl. He'd phoned from the pub and left a dozen unanswered messages.

Frank's hope was that the repeated climb up to his top floor flat would kill the old bastard.

'I just ... wanted ... to tell you ... the rent ... is due.' Hilton's chest heaved up and down with the effort.

'What about the bathroom?'

'Eh?'

'The ceiling, the water. You wanna look? I'm not a qualified electrician, Mr Hilton, but I can't see a lightshade full of water is a safe thing.'

He waved Frank away. 'It's ... on ... the list. Harry's ... getting round to it.'

Harry Singh was Hilton's odd job man – seventy if he was a day. He did the lot, fetching, carrying, shifting, gardening, plumbing, carpet-laying, all with the old bastard standing over him rasping instructions like an asthmatic sergeant major. Harry didn't seem to mind. He just smiled and got on with the job.

'The rent ...' said Hilton.

'Yeah, end of the month.' Frank put his boots down.

'It is ... the end ... of the month.'

'In four days.'

'You'll be out ... if you haven't got it.' He reached into the old vinyl shopping bag he'd modified to go over his shoulder and out came *the book*. 'Frank Neaves, you owe—'

'I know what I owe. I also know you shouldn't be in here without notice. So d'you want to piss off and come back Tuesday.'

Hilton put the book back and waggled a finger, suddenly finding his voice, 'The rent, all of it, or you're out.'

When he'd gone, Frank sat in the one saggy-arsed chair he possessed, reached behind him and pulled out the cushion. He unzipped the cover, dipped into a slit in the foam and pulled out a ten pound note. Attached with a safety pin, a scrap of paper – *Is this really the emergency you think it is?*

By five o'clock it was. First he would pay Adeline back for the scotch, then with a clear conscience he would drink the last ten pounds he had in the world.

*

Adeline was in early the morning after Carl had done a bunk with one thing in mind. She wanted to talk to Linda. Two days a week,

22

Linda came in to 'do' Carl's flat upstairs before 'doing' the pub. Linda was among the regulars in the John Evelyn, but reckoned having a set of keys gave her a stake in the place. It conferred a status, which meant she didn't think twice about jumping the queue at the bar, or helping herself from the buffet if there was a function in the back room. She was also a fearless collector of titbits and Carl was not immune.

Slipping off her coat, Linda hurried through with a muttered 'G'morning.'

Adeline was wrestling with the Gordon's optic and turned too late. Linda was already upstairs, letting herself in with Carl's spare key.

Adeline waited a few minutes, then followed. Not wanting to shout above the noise of the vacuum cleaner, she stood until Linda noticed her at the open door and turned it off. 'What is it?'

'You know he's gone.'

'So?'

'I want to look around, see if there's anything that'd give some idea where.'

Linda raised an eyebrow. 'You know bloody well where, after her.'

'Did he say anything to you?'

'He didn't have to. But if you want it straight, go speak to his mother because he ain't gone anywhere without telling Rose first.'

Adeline entered Carl's living room. Silvery garlands looped from the corners to the central light. He must have done all this. It wasn't like him to go to the trouble. There was a little Christmas tree, its branches weighed down with strings of glittered beads and tinsel and chocolate Father Christmases. She knelt and looked at the tags on the presents; they were all for Grace. And one for her. *Adeline* in neat silver letters. She switched on the tree lights, white and red and then after a few seconds, a slow fade.

Linda sighed impatiently. 'Look love, I need to get on if you want both bars and the lavs doing.'

Adeline carefully placed the present back under the tree. 'I wouldn't have thought he'd go to all this bother, these presents and everything.'

'She made him take it all back.'

'You what?' Adeline turned the tree lights off at the wall socket.

'Diane did. Carl took Grace's presents over the last time she was down seeing her mum and dad, but she never took 'em. Said there'd be plenty for Grace without his, and it wasn't his place anymore.'

'And he told you that?'

Linda shrugged, wound the vacuum cleaner flex once around her hand before flicking it around the dining table leg. 'It's what happened.' She kicked the cleaner back to life and dragged it rumbling across the floor, sending vibrations through the boards. In Grace's room, Adeline found the bed was made; a nightlight glowed dimly in the socket. A miniature tree stood on the bedside table. Soft toys lined up on the pillow, close together as if they were arm in arm singing. By the bed, a few inches apart, the nap of the rug was disturbed, flattened in two patches. Where he'd knelt reading stories, she thought. There were books on the shelf above the bed, a well-thumbed *Paddington* and *Winnie The Pooh*.

Linda came to the door.

Adeline said, 'I shouldn't worry about in here, no one's been in.'

'I clean and hoover every time love, did it Christmas Eve. It keeps the dust down.'

Christmas Eve. That meant that Carl had been in since. Adeline thought of him in there on his own, on his knees. She scuffed Carl's imprint from the carpet. 'I'll see you downstairs in a bit.'

At first, Linda refused to part with the key. Adeline dressed it up; they needed the spare, fire regulations, problems with access, locking up. Someone needed to be able to get in if she wasn't there. She had a flash of inspiration. Or did Linda want the shout at three in the morning if the burglar alarm went off?

'You've known him a long time haven't you?' Adeline poured Linda a small sherry.

'Since he was a boy, ta love.' Linda sipped. 'Still is in a lot of ways.'

'Yeah, but he's old enough and ugly enough to sort himself out, isn't he?'

'If you say so.' Linda slipped her coat on. 'I reckon there's a part of him that's never grown …' She tailed off.

'Go on.'

'Nothing, it's not for me to say. Look love, I'll be in later for my money. Can you have it ready.'

'He pays you at the end of the week.'

'But he ain't here is he, and it doesn't look like he'll be back any time soon and I need some money for New Year.' Linda softened. 'Don't get me wrong, love. It's not that I don't care, just I know where being a mate stops and being a boss starts and it's usually sometime around payday. If you really want to know where he is, like I said, ask Rose. He'll have told her.'

'I don't know her, she don't know me.'

'Lucky old you.' She buttoned up her coat and left the key on the bar. 'I need it back for Thursday.'

Adeline slipped the key in her back pocket.

She found herself taking the narrow stairs up to the flat a couple of times that evening. She practiced the same hollow explanation should she be discovered – something they needed, a mislaid order, the accounts book. It was all in the office plain as day if anyone chose to look. As the punters turned up, she bristled at the gossip, the way Carl's disappearance was explained away and the world closed up behind him. He'd gone up north for Grace. For Diane too, she reckoned, just to torture herself that bit more.

It was dark now, streetlight the only light as she moved through the rooms. Linda had cleaned Grace's bedroom, dusted through and dumped the soft toys in the toy-box. Adeline put them back into bed, tucked them in and cried a bit. She thought about something her dad said once: *the trouble you can get yourself into, it'll look different sober and you'll blame the drink, but it's always just you deep down.*

She heard a noise behind her. It was Frank. 'Kev said you wanted to see me.'

She wiped her eyes, didn't face him, didn't speak.

He waited a bit then said, 'I'll be downstairs when you're ready.'

'Frank, hang on. I've got a proposition.'

4

James Robert O'Keefe watched the TV from his usual place on the sofa while Diane bathed a fresh graze on Grace's knee. Every now and then he muttered, short words and sharp breathy curses. He was drunk.

With each dip in the Dettol water and dab at the knee, Grace grizzled and winced. Diane kept up a stream of soft words, 'Lucky you had them thick tights on love, eh?' Grace managed a nod.

O'Keefe said, 'Can't you do that outside?'

Diane looked up. 'We'll go in the garden shed if you want.'

O'Keefe put his feet up, smeared muddy gravel from his trainers on the arm of the sofa. 'I can't hear this.' He pointed the remote at Donald Pleasence's doomed Great Escape needle trick. Big X stuck his leg out.

'Come on, love, we'll go in the kitchen,' said Diane. Grace put weight on the leg and cried louder, said it hurt and that she couldn't walk.

O'Keefe turned the TV volume up.

'Put your arm around me, that's it.' Diane coaxed Grace to the kitchen, looked back as O'Keefe flipped the lid of the Quality Street and dipped in. He'd been in a pig of a mood since Christmas Day and didn't give a shit who knew it. It started as soon as they sat down to Christmas dinner. She'd just served up and Grace had asked whether her dad had sent a present. Diane brushed it off, but a few minutes later she asked again, where was her present from her dad?

'It's in a skip,' O'Keefe'd said and laughed, speared another roast spud with his fork and helped himself to enough gravy to spill over onto Diane's new tablecloth.

Later, they were alone in the kitchen, Diane washing up and O'Keefe starting on the brandy. He kicked it off again. 'It's not on,

Di. I've put myself out and she's ruined my bloody Christmas. The way she behaves, it's not on. I'm not havin' it.'

'Because she wanted to know if her dad sent her present, *that's* ruined your Christmas?'

'You need to take her in hand or I will.'

Diane plunged her hands back in the washing up water for the last plate.

After Grace had gone to bed, they watched a film. When it ended, O'Keefe beckoned her over to the sofa, but gave her no room to sit. She sat by him on the floor. He said, 'It's just difficult for me, y'know gettin' used to all the changes.' He kissed her, on the cheek, the neck. She had let him, felt his hand pull up her blouse and knew what was coming.

Diane finished dressing Grace's knee and found some clean tights. She was putting her coat on when O'Keefe came through to the kitchen. 'I'm taking Grace back out,' said Diane cheerily. 'She's being very brave and getting straight back on the bike.' She zipped up the coat.

'I don't think so.' O'Keefe wasn't what you'd call a big man, but planted in the doorway, he was an immovable obstacle.

She kept the tone soft, conciliatory, 'Well I've got to go and get the bike haven't I love, otherwise it'll get pinched. Don't want that, do we?' She looked down at Grace, squeezed her pink-gloved hand.

'She left it outside?'

'She was hurt, she couldn't wheel it because the handlebars were stuck bent.'

'So she's broke it as well.'

'Course not, Jim. It'll take two seconds to put it back. Unless you want to fetch it back, get a breath of air?'

'Oh for fucksake.'

'Thought not.' He let her push past.

Then he said, 'Di, gimme your mobile.'

'What's up with yours?'

He came forward. 'Give us it.'

Diane had one hand on the latch. He pulled it away. Grace looked up, wide-eyed.

'I don't want her speaking to him. I heard yous in the kitchen, chattin' away. One of your chats. You'll ring her father.'

Diane knew he'd heard nothing, that the conversation hadn't happened, but couldn't prevent the instant's guilt that flashed across her eyes and knew that whatever protests she made would sound hollow now. He leaned across her, deadlocked the door, pocketed the mortis key. 'S'that simple, Di. Not open for argument.' He went back to the living room.

Diane took Grace's coat off. She was crying again, but silently.

Boxing Day came and went and after she'd made sure Grace was asleep that night, Diane slipped out, leaving O'Keefe snoring on the sofa.

The bike had gone. She walked. The night was cold, sharp and star-filled. A northern sky, she thought. It had been the fresh air and the space that sold the idea of a move to her. In those first few weeks, Jim had been charming, gentle and funny. On the day they came to his house he'd given them a day out and promised them good times, wide horizons, no boundaries. Grace could be a kid for longer and grow up later if they lived up here, he'd said. She'd have a proper old-fashioned childhood.

Away from the house Diane lit a cigarette and phoned her mum, but she and Dad were watching a TV show and Diane had the sense of only being half-listened to. She said, 'Love you, goodnight,' and hung up. She deleted the record of the number dialled and discovered another call had been made – *0208 692* ... the pub. She scrolled down – Grace must have phoned her dad after the row. Diane walked in a wide loop around the deserted streets, finished the cigarette, sucked an extra strong mint and quietly let herself in the back door. O'Keefe was where she'd left him, the room stinking like a brewery.

5

Carl's train was crawling all the way. Every ten minutes came the same pre-recorded announcement: *delays due to industrial action on the East Coast line over the holiday period*. They were an hour late, then two. Periodically he gave into a numbing sleep, which was how he came to miss his stop and wound up at the end of the line in York. As he made his way across the concourse at York Station, deserted except for a skinny girl in dirty white plimsolls, he checked the indicator board and the *how* of getting to Hull began to matter half as much as the *what next*? The night's one scheduled train back to Doncaster was already two hours overdue, and even if it did make it there was no guarantee of a connection to Hull. The woman in the ticket office was sympathetic. 'Trust me, love there's nothing else coming out of here now. It comes down to where you want to spend the night, York or Doncaster?'

Carl shrugged, 'Makes no difference to me.'

'Never been to Donny I take it?'

He'd never been to York either.

She highlighted a couple of hotels on a tourist map and shoved it under the ticket turntable. 'You could give one of those a go. Just out the station and turn left, right at the lights, then down across the bridge.'

Carl needed food in his belly, coffee, time to think out of the cold. He took a punt on the first place he came across that looked like it might have free tables, a bar that did Spanish food. He stood in the doorway and waited to be seated. A waitress walked past with a tray of drinks. A bunch of drunks, young blokes, rugger types at a table roared at her arrival. They asked which one she fancied most. She did well to brush them off, but they pressed her. 'I think of you all the same,' she said with a dead smile, hissing as she turned away, 'Wankers.'

At a table laid for four, Carl ordered. He buttered a bread roll and ate it slowly, then sipped coffee while he waited for what turned out to be grilled sardines and chips. Grace would be expecting him. He'd promised to be there and he wasn't coming, not tonight anyway. On the phone she'd said O'Keefe punished her. When he'd asked how, there was a sharp unbearable silence, which he broke by asking if he'd hit her and instantly regretted it. She said, 'He took Kangi away.' Kangi was an almost furless one-eyed panda with an orange felt waistcoat. Kangi was her comfort, her constant.

'Why did he do that, sweetheart?'

'Because of the presents,' she whispered. 'At Christmas dinner I asked about presents and he said …'

Carl never heard the rest, just made the promise. 'You're coming to me for New Year, babe. You can have your presents then. Nanna can't wait to see you, and Lauren's making one of them cakes with the icing and snowmen on the top. We'll have a right good old time and you can stay up to midnight. I'll make you a special snowball.'

'With a cherry?'

'With two cherries.'

A pug-nosed geezer on the drunks' table was flinging olives across the restaurant. One hit Carl's shoulder and left an oily patch on his jacket. A few seconds later it was followed by another and he realised he was the target. Carl called the waitress over and asked if he could move. The request was met by jeers. Carl saw money change hands on the rugger boys' table.

When he left, they were still in the street outside. He moved away quickly, hoping he wouldn't need to use up the rest of the evening finding somewhere to stay. A couple of streets down, he glanced across at a shop window reflection and saw the lads were following. Pug nose and his mate looked solid; the others were pissed and along for the ride. Carl didn't stop to check the map, but walked back the only way he knew – towards the station, trusting they'd leave him alone. If this was a wind up, it was a tight one. He walked purposefully, but they stayed behind him. When he threw a look back over his shoulder, only three of them still followed. Still, he didn't fancy his chances if they decided to jump him. About a hundred yards ahead was a hotel sign, blue neon. He upped the pace, stepping out just short of a run. Their footfall on the pavement echoed in the street around him as they closed the gap. He jogged the last twenty yards and skipped up the steps. He went to the desk breathless and blew most of the rest of his money on a room.

The drunks argued on the pavement; pug nose came up the steps, then bottled it when an old bill car cruised past.

Carl put his photo of Grace on the bedside table and counted the rest of his money. He made a cup of tea. The rest of the evening stretched out in front of him. He read a few pages of the book but couldn't concentrate. He picked up the newspaper. The quick crossword blurred before his eyes. He turned off the light, kicked off his shoes and laid back on the bed, hands clasped behind his neck. The tap dripped in the bathroom. He went through, turned it tight and closed the door behind him. He could still hear it – every twenty-three seconds.

Grace had been there in the room. At first, she'd been sitting in the chair in a plain grey dress he'd never seen and knew she'd be unhappy wearing. He had other clothes for her, a bright T-shirt and jeans, but when he tried to help her into them they were too small; and then she became smaller, scurrying across the carpet. Carl'd been terrified, crawled into the corner. Then the room seemed to grow and the child/rodent Grace came and sat in his lap. But then it wasn't Grace anymore. It was something that frightened him awake. He came-to with a shameful, tiny moan. Perspiration ran down his chest. The sheets were damp. He lay still until his breathing was near normal. One-fifteen. He'd been asleep for just over an hour. Now he was awake and thinking about his dad.

The first time he'd clued into what his old man did for a living was one of those summers, the long hot ones of his childhood. He was too young to work, but old enough to be left on his own whilst Mum went out during the day and Terry was at playschool – in those days they lived in a terraced house in Culverley Road, Catford. Dad was there, or not there. His presence at the time was patchy in Carl's memory, a few days at home, then gone. Mum's moods went with him, like her sunshine went out the door when he did. She never smiled much when Dad wasn't there and Carl had taken to doing things for her during the day, cleaning up, doing good turns, making little gifts.

On holiday, Mum had seen a small wooden box decorated with tiny shells in a shop in Broadstairs. He'd planned to go back for it, saved enough pocket money to buy it, but it never happened. Halfway through the week, when Dad came back from his daily call to 'the office', he dropped into his deckchair and announced he would have to go back to London. They could stay if they wanted, but Mum wasn't having it and they packed up there and then, left the beach and were home by teatime.

A few days later he was alone at home, sorting through a few small shells he'd collected. Not enough to cover a whole box, but he reckoned he could make the lid look nice. He found some scraps of wood in the shed, old tongue and groove panels Dad had bought to use in the bathroom, but which were still tied in the timber merchant's green twine. That was good, he could glue the sides. But he needed something for a base and a lid and maybe one of those small hinges. Failing that he'd use a piece of material as a hinge and tack and glue it. He pictured the box, glossy varnished seashells across the top. Mum could keep her things in it, jewellery and stuff.

He went out to the shed, cut the pieces to size. He fitted and glued them, two sides, two ends. There was a piece of board he reckoned he could use for the base and lid. The hinge thing nagged at him, though. Using cloth would look cheap and a bit naff, and he wanted it to last. He went through the jars on the low shelves, but there was nothing he could use, so he climbed up on a stepladder to reach the high shelf where Dad kept his big blue metal toolbox. It was heavy, but Carl managed to lift it onto the platform of the steps and from there to the floor, sure that in one of the rattling Old Holborn tins there'd be something he could use. He pulled out the tools: split-handled chisels; paint-pocked screwdrivers; a yellow can of oil with a red nozzle; a bent little toilet brush shaped thing with metal bristles, and a small G-clamp which he set to one side. In the bottom of the box was a string-tied newspaper package. Carl lifted it out and undid the knot. It was like pass the parcel. Inside the newspaper was a piece of grey flannelette sheet wrapped around something. He unwound the bundle and discovered a pistol.

He'd seen something like it before. His mate Daryl had once dredged up an old revolver from the river and brought it into school. It was covered in mud and rusted to shit. They made him take it to the police, who checked it, made it safe then gave it back. What Carl held in his hands that August afternoon looked nothing like Daryl's crappy antique. This gun felt like new. It was blue-black metal, smelled oily, spirit-cleaned, and alongside the other busted wood and scrap metal it was the one tool that looked cared for, ready to use.

He was careful about how he re-wrapped it, making sure the newspaper went back in the same folds. He matched the kinks in the string and tried to replicate the knots as best he could. Everything exactly as it was. And as hard as it had been to lift the toolbox down, he managed to get it back to the same place on the shelf. Mum's shell box never got made; he took the bits he'd already assembled and chucked them in the dustbin.

Carl was awake for a long time listening to the dripping tap. He folded a towel and put it in the sink to dull the sound. He was cold so he put a jumper on, got back into bed on the dry side. It had all fallen into place for Carl as he got older. His dad was a villain. Everyone knew. He ran a protection racket and fed cash through businesses, some of which he owned, some he didn't and were none the wiser. He wasn't overly flash with it and he had as many friends who were straight as were dodgy. He had a wife and two sons who loved him. He kept a loaded pistol in his south London shed. As Carl felt himself slip back into sleep, more than anything he wanted his dad to give him the nod, just let him know he was doing alright.

6

Frank grudgingly agreed to Adeline's proposition, accepting free drinks for an hour of his time. He'd knocked her back for nigh on half an hour, but she wasn't letting go. For some reason – she wasn't saying and he wasn't asking – finding out exactly what had sent Carl on his travels had taken on a dog/bone significance. With his last tenner in his pocket, taking payment came easily. Plus there was logic: before he could lift the hex and have her pour him a drink, he'd have to pay what he owed and to do that, he'd have to go along with this poxy proposition. The deal was sealed with a large Bell's – on the house. It brought them, after a brisk walk, to the landing outside Rose Price's third floor flat in a block of refurbished maisonettes. They should have gone the whole hog and pulled the bloody things down, Frank thought. He turned his collar up as an icy wind sliced through him and a flurry of sleet wet his face.

'He ought to get her re-housed, something a bit lower.' Adeline shivered and pressed the doorbell again. 'Oh come on for Christ's sake.'

'Have a bit of patience. She's an old lady.'

'I'm freezing my arse off.'

He sniffed, 'Should've put a proper coat on, not that bumfreezer jacket.'

'Bumfreezer?'

Frank shut up. This wasn't going to work, not without more of a drink inside him. Adeline pressed again, another two long rings unanswered. She cupped her hand at Rose's window and peered in. 'There's no light on.'

'She's in,' said Frank. 'Listen, you can hear the telly.'

'Well she ain't answering.'

He pushed at next door's bell. After a few moments, a light came on and the door opened a chain's width. Frank pushed Adeline forward, 'Sorry to bother you, we wanted to speak to Mrs Price, but no one's answering.'

A woman, youngish voice with a trace of an accent Frank couldn't place said, 'I'm not surprised this time of night. What's it about?'

Adeline said, 'We're friends of Carl's. Well I am, he's ... a mate, look can you get us in to see Mrs Price? It is important. Please.'

The door closed. A phone rang in Rose's flat and a minute later, the neighbour emerged wrapping a big cardigan around herself. She had keys, unlocked Rose's door and showed them in. 'Wipe your feet, you've got five minutes.'

Frank sized up the room, all focus on the telly with the chair opposite, the prime viewing spot, notably vacant. An absence that Adeline occupied, perching on the edge of the chair. 'Mrs Price, my name's Adeline. I work with your son Carl at the pub. I spoke to Linda who does our cleaning and she thought you'd know where he was.'

Rose glanced towards Frank who stood just inside the door. 'Who's he?'

Frank edged back to the shadows, his coat brushing a couple of Christmas cards off the sideboard. He picked them up. The neighbour folded her arms across her chest, one hand dangled the keys. They weren't going to get long here.

'He's another friend of Carl's. Mrs Price, do you know where Carl has gone? I need to get in touch with him – for the business.'

Rose seemed to look for Frank again, 'He's gone away for a bit.'

Adeline spoke slowly. 'Do you know where?'

'I'm not deaf love. Or stupid, contrary to what you might have heard. He's gone where *she* is, where exactly I don't know, but it's north. He's picking Grace up, she's my granddaughter, and he's bringing her home for New Year. I don't think there's any more I can tell you.'

The neighbour shook her keys, ushered Frank towards the door. 'Come on, then. We won't disturb you any more, Rose. I'll be in tomorrow morning. Put the chain back on after I've gone.'

'What a waste of time that was.' Adeline's heels clicked and echoed on the concrete stairs, the sound flattening once they were out on the wet pavement. They walked all the way without talking, a quick pace for a girl in heels. Stopping at the corner of Evelyn Street to let the traffic pass, Adeline lit another cigarette. 'Any normal person would have a bloody mobile and I could just ring him.'

A 47 bus passed empty heading for Shoreditch Church. Frank said, 'So what is this, you got a thing for Carl?'

'No, not like that.'

'But you like him, right?'

'Mind your own.'

They were yards away from the pub. Frank pulled up short and put a hand on Adeline's arm. 'Look, I think I know where Diane is.'

He expected a demand, a retort, a question at least a *why didn't you bloody say so?* But when Adeline, nearly a foot shorter than Frank looked up, she wasn't far off tears. 'If you do, please tell me. It's important.'

Frank sat at the end of the bar. Adeline leaned across from the business side. It was in the cards, he told her and for a moment he could see she thought he was on about some mystical tarot bollocks. 'One of the Christmas cards, a nice one, not from a box, but from a kid looking to keep in touch with her Nan. I knocked it off the sideboard and when I picked it up, the kid had written the address – *64 Redwood Avenue, Hull, HU10.*' Frank sipped a very large scotch.

'Was there a phone number?' she said.

'Didn't see one.' He paused. 'So now you tell me, what's all this to you if it isn't because you fancy him?'

She moved the damp bar towel across and leaned forward on crossed arms. 'It's no secret,' she said quietly, 'Carl was really good to me when I came back round here. He was a mate when I didn't think I had any. He gave me a job, helped me get back on my feet.'

'And?'

'That's it.'

'Yeah, right.'

'Come on Frank, you've seen it upstairs, he's got the flat all decorated, all Grace's presents an' that. I know what it's like – Christmas and disappointments. This is a big deal for him. I'm just trying to help out.'

Frank's head was clear enough. 'If you don't want to tell me, that's fine but it's not just about a few Christmas presents.'

Her expression changed, grew darker. If they were bartering towards the truth, this was her final offer. 'Last year, a few weeks before Diane left, we had an early morning delivery. Tuesday morning same as usual. Only Carl was out somewhere, Diane was up at the school with Grace and I was left doing the stock check. James O'Keefe and his brother, the younger one – what's his name?'

Frank shrugged. 'No idea.'

'It's Alan or Andrew or something. Anyway, they'd unloaded a few crates, left them round the back for Carl to take down the cellar, so then James comes in for the money. I'm merrily just ticking stuff off against the delivery note and he starts this argument up out of nothing. I thought he was kidding about, going on about what they're owed and being cheated going back months. I checked the books and we were fully paid up. So then I thought he was trying it on with Carl not being around. I told him he'd have to see Carl next time he was down.'

She stopped to pull a pint for a punter who looked like hanging around to earwig. 'Bye,' she said by way of encouragement. The punter sloped off and she dropped her voice, almost to a whisper. 'Then James sends his brother out to the lorry, corners me in the office and starts off on one about how immoral I am, that I dress like a whore, that I use too much make up, then he starts calling me all sorts, really going into one.'

Frank shook his head slowly, the scotch was warming him, that and the fact that he still had the tenner in his pocket. 'Now there's a boy with a problem.'

'He said I didn't know who I was dealing with and tell Carl to call him and he'd tell him to straighten me out or give me the sack. Like he's everyone's boss.'

'What did Carl say?'

'I played it down. Just said there was a bit of a disagreement over the bill, that Jim O'Keefe and me had a bit of a misunderstanding. Carl rung up and smoothed things over with Ewan, he's the eldest one, runs the business side. There never was money outstanding, not a penny. Then two weeks later Diane went off with Jim O'Keefe. What was I gonna do? *Oh Carl, your wife and daughter's gone off with a fruitcake.*'

Frank put the empty glass back on the bar and reached into his pocket. He flattened the tenner and held it under the palm of his hand.

'That's why I need to find him,' she added. 'I don't know what O'Keefe'll do if Carl just turns up out of the blue.'

Frank was sure he felt the lights dim a little, a kind of closing in of things.

'And why I want you to come with me.'

He folded the note, put it back in his pocket. All his remaining un-dulled instincts told him he should tell her where to get off, but he was warm and it was Christmas. 'I don't think so,' he said, knowing it would only take a couple more drinks to kill those nagging voices.

Adeline shrugged, gave a sly smile and stood up. 'Get you another, Frank?' She flicked a peanut and hit him on the chin.

7

Frank didn't ask where the money came from, Adeline had cash and it was a damn sight more than a barmaid's wages. At King's Cross the following morning she asked for two return tickets, her hand flat on half a dozen twenty-pound notes. The dazed and desiccated soul in the ticket office silently finger-punched computer keys then sloped off, returning a minute later to tell them, between sniffs, that there were no available seats. The train was fully booked.

Adeline bit her lip. 'That's no good, I need to be on this train.'

He told her it was Christmas and people usually booked well in advance this time of year, and there was a signalman strike and some were out and some weren't and—

Adeline leant forward to the perforated Perspex, 'So, if I can't get this train, when's the next sodding train?'

He shrugged.

'What, next week, next year?'

'I could check, you want me to check?'

'That'd be a start.'

Frank stood back, shifted from foot to foot – he would help, but only if asked. Adeline threw him an aggravated glance. He looked away.

Ticket office guy looked blankly and tapped a few more keys then, as if he'd been holding back just to deliver a magician's reveal, said, 'I s'pose if you really wanted to be on this one you could do a first class ticket.'

She stuffed the notes back into her purse and produced a credit card, 'Just give me the tickets.'

The train made up for leaving late, arrowing north for half an hour. Then it slowed, crawled for what must have been a mile, and stopped. It didn't moved an inch in twenty minutes. Frank grew bored. 'So, did you have a good Christmas?'

Adeline's eyes were closed. She might have been asleep, but he'd seen her glance out of the window a minute or so back. 'Where are we?' she said.

Frank, his feet on the seat opposite, sipped just enough from a quarter bottle of Bell's whisky to give his throat a coating. He offered it to Adeline who shook her head and did this thing with her eyes, a narrowing from the brow down, the barmaid's mildest admonishment.

'Somewhere north of London, south of fuck knows where,' he said.

'Helpful.'

'Peterborough.'

'Why ain't we moving?'

'Just waiting for your say-so and we'll be on our way.'

This time the eye narrowing came with a nose crinkle.

'You look like a kid when you pull that face, bet you were a right little charmer.'

Her eyes closed again, she rested her head back. 'I was. I was a good girl. Mum always said if she had to sell her kids I'd be the last to go.'

A voice came over the speaker, all the clarity of a 1960s transistor radio. *Due to an unforeseen problem with the points ahead, we will unfortunately be delayed further whilst the problem is being assessed. Engineers are dealing with it and we hope to be under way again in ... er ... soon.* Static crackled, the tannoy clicked off.

'"Sorry" would have been nice,' Adeline checked her mobile.

'Shall we go home?'

'You wanna go, fine. You can get out and walk it though cos I ain't paying for another ticket and the returns are staying right here.' She patted the gold bag on the seat beside her.

'I feel like I've been kidnapped.' Frank stretched his legs out. There really was nothing to do other than watch the steadily falling snow cover the fields until no black earth was visible.

Adeline said, 'I was kidnapped once. For about ten minutes when I was eight.'

Frank turned the flat bottle over in his palm, said nothing but knew he should. As the pause lengthened he felt unable to end it.

'I was fine and I'm over it now, thanks for asking.' She pulled herself up and yawned.

'No, sorry, I just didn't want to if ...'

There was a silence, more snow, more staring. 'He was like this dirty old man, you know, typical geezer in a mac. He got hold of me in some woods near my auntie's house in Beckenham while me dad and me uncle were watching football in the park. I'd just got bored I s'pose and wandered off in the woods. It was sunny and then shady in the trees and there was bluebells in the sunny bits. Anyway this bloke came up from behind and pushed me on the ground and turned me over, put this smelly old blanket thing over me and sat on top ...' She tailed off.

'And?'

'I screamed the place down apparently. He put his hand over my mouth, then after a while he let me go and I ran back to the football pitch, found Uncle Billy and blubbered something about "man" and "woods" and he took off and collared the bloke and called the police. I never knew what happened to him, the bloke. I never went to court or anything.' She looked back out the window.

'So how did they deal with him?' Frank's voice had an edge.

'Told you, the old bill picked him up.'

'But nothing happened – they let him get away with it. Probably did it again a week later.'

She thought for a moment. 'My family's not like that Frank – we don't do lynchings.'

The atmosphere soured, Frank sipped the whisky and went back to staring out. 'You got some snowshoes in that bag?' A lame comment and he knew it.

'I've never told anyone about that, never. Not even my husband, not that he'd have cared less. I wish I'd have left it that way.' She bit at a loose thread on the sleeve of her jacket. 'So, go on, tell me something about you.'

'Nothing much to tell.'

'No chance pal, no way you get away that easily.' She reached over and took the bottle, drank some, put the lid back and swung it between her thumb and forefinger like a sideshow hypnotist. 'You owe me a story now, something you've never told anyone.'

Frank followed the swing and grabbed the bottle back. 'You don't wanna know – my past stays where it is.'

She folded her arms, 'Well that pissed on my chips, didn't it.'

Frank was silent, drifting into private thought as the memories queued up, falling over themselves to be told. 'I'm no good at doing what I should, saying what I should when I should. I'm just out of kilter. I don't fit. It's not you.'

'It is *me*, because I'm the one who's here.' She stood up, took her purse from the bag. 'You want a tea?' He didn't. She went off in the direction of the buffet car. On the ridge in the distance, you could just see a few distant headlights in the gloom, traffic moving slowly. He imagined them, white knuckles on the steering wheel, following in the tracks of the car in front, blokes with home on their mind.

'Fucking Grantham.'

'So you said. That's three times now.'

'Four hours on that train and we're stuck in Grantham. Shit. And you say that bloke had no idea when the next one's due?' Adeline's cigarette butt hit the wet platform and hissed. She flattened it under her heel. Snow gusted under the canopy. Still without a convincing explanation as to why their train had terminated at Grantham, Frank and Adeline had mooched a path between the station buffet and, when she wanted a smoke, a seat on the platform – a red metal fixture that left its perforated imprint frozen on their arses. Frank's enquiries to anyone in a uniform left them none the wiser as to when they'd be on their way.

'You sure he didn't say?' Adeline lit another cigarette.

'He reckoned at least another hour. I told you we should have stayed in that caff.'

'With some pissed up tractor boy copping his free sample. Spotty bastard.'

Frank stood and stretched his legs, felt a twinge in this lower back. He took a few paces down the platform, hands in his coat pockets. Half-three and it was nearly dark. He studied lights from nearby houses picking out something elusive, a suggestion of warmth. 'Here's where you could have been.'

'What?'

He walked back. 'See those houses, take a guess, who d'you reckon lives in there?'

'Who cares?' She huddled into her jacket.

'Families, mums and dads and kids and dogs akip by the fire.'

Adeline groaned. 'Dry turkey, crap telly and rows and money worries and a Christmas full of Chinese tat they'll be paying off till October.'

Frank's turn, 'Whisky Macs, treelights and posh choccies.'

'Family you can't stand, piles of washing up, more crap telly.'

'See down there, that one by the traffic lights, what if that's a flat and inside there's a bloke and his missis having their first

Christmas together, all cuddled up in front of an old film with a drop of scotch and a box of Roses.'

'Or a lonely old biddy freezing her arse off cos she's too frightened to put another bar on the fire.'

He laughed, 'You're a bundle of Christmas spirit, and when was the last time you saw a fire with a bar?'

'You know what I mean.' She shivered.

Frank sat by her and almost without thinking, put his arm around her shoulder and squeezed. 'My little ray of sunshine.'

It was the first time he'd seen her smile since they set off. She shifted her backside along to nestle in a bit closer. He felt her hair, blown damp on his face and brushed it away.

'There might be something nice,' she conceded. 'Maybe a sideboard with a few cards and a bowl of nuts. Granddad snoring after a big dinner.'

'And a satsuma.'

'Just the one?'

'Sat-su-mas.' The word sounded odd the more you said it. Frank looked down the platform. 'Blimey, look it's Nanook of the North.'

You had to give the railway bloke his due, thought Frank, he'd made a special journey out of his heated cubbyhole to find them. With his company tie over his shoulder and his railway blazer blown open so the snow wet his shirt, he marched dutifully towards them. 'I'm off home in a bit, thought you'd want to know, the next train's just left King's Cross. If there's no more points frozen up on the way, it'll be here in about an hour and ten, hour and twenty.'

Frank took his arm from Adeline's shoulders. 'Thanks mate. You off home, yeah?'

'Something like that. Might have a swift one on the way. Got a mate who runs The Cross Keys. You ought to drop in, it's just down from the station a couple of hundred yards. Not far.'

'Tell you what mate, if that train don't turn up we'll see you in there.'

They watched his back as he retreated. Frank felt alone, deserted. Like they could be there all night and no one'd know. He had an image of them found dead and frozen. 'Put another bar on the fire.'

Adeline put Frank's arm back round her shoulders and shivered. 'Maybe we should go back to the caff.'

'If you like.' He pulled her closer. A familiar reflex flickered in his belly. 'We've got an hour though so there's no point in freezing them off here, why don't we see if we can find that pub?'

He walked on the outside, so that as they made their way down the platform, she was sheltered from the worst of the bitter wind.

Frank and Adeline's quick drink with the railway guy – his mates called him Rooney, except a dark-eyed bloke in stained beige Farahs with dandruff on his shoulders who called down from his bar stool, 'Oi, Spud, get us a round in.' Spud, as it turned out, was Rooney and he duly got a round in. Frank was reluctant to take the drink and said they'd buy their own as they'd be off soon, but Rooney insisted. Frank's pint and Adeline's Jack Daniel's and Coke were sipped slowly enough to knock back further offers of drinks. It looked like it was turning into a session for Rooney and his mates. Frank and Adeline were along for the ride, finding themselves the butt of an hour or so of mostly good natured banter, ribbed as southerners and cockneys. Neither Frank nor Adeline fulfilled the required Bow Bells criteria, but the distinction was lost. Adeline leant over and whispered to Frank, 'Where are the women?'

Beige slacks heard her.

She had a point, thought Frank. Here they were, boys at the bar, with the women – a group of about five – confined to a table in a dim corner of the room. As round after round went down, the atmosphere became noticeably prickly, the chat taking on an offensive edge. Frank picked up comments, half-jokes with bitter undertones about him travelling with a girl young enough to be his daughter, about her red lip-gloss and cock-tease tight sweater. Fair enough, he thought, they're just words. But Adeline bristled. There was a visible straightening of her back. From that point he noticed, her drink, untouched on the table, went flat.

Frank tried to move things along. 'Rooney, can you try your mate at the station, see if that bloody train's got past Watford?'

The still affable Rooney pulled his mobile and speed-dialled work. Frank figured they'd have time to get back to the station – twenty minutes max with Adeline in impractical shoes linked into his arm to avoid slipping on the frozen pavements. It was plenty of time. Rooney announced that the train had just left Peterborough.

As they got up to go, beige slacks made a comment that they'd not bought a round. Frank doubted he had the cash to front the half dozen pints and shorts that the last round had been. He offered his hand to Rooney, 'Mate it's been a pleasure, we've got to make tracks or it'll be Shanks's pony back to King's Cross.'

Beige slacks wiped the back of his hand across his mouth, repeated his complaint, 'So you're not getting us a drink in?'

The others were strangely quiet, only Rooney saying, 'Come on Pat, they're with me – guests of the management.'

No one laughed. Pat said, 'Y'gonna get us a drink in before y'go or are you another tight cockney wanker?'

Frank felt Adeline behind him stuff a note into his hand. 'No mate,' he said. 'Never that.'

'I'll get you another, Pat. They've got to go, got a train to catch.' Rooney already had his hand in his pocket, a note on the bar.

'I want one from him.'

'We have to go.' Frank turned his back, steered Adeline between the tables to the door.

Pat shouted at their backs, 'I 'ope you get cancer.'

Frank gave Adeline back the money and they walked without speaking. This time she didn't try to take his arm.

8

The only cab at the Hull station taxi rank had its engine running. Diesel fumes caught in Carl's throat. He took off a glove, tapped on the driver's side window and held up the *xyz* page he'd torn from Mum's red telephone book, the one he'd scrawled Diane's address on. The driver lowered the newspaper he'd been reading, squinted, scanned the address then gave a slow shake of the head. Carl tapped again. This time the driver dropped his window, spoke through the four inch gap, 'There's no chance, I'm not goin' out there in this fuckin' weather.'

'So what, is it far then?'

'Yeah, it is.' The window went back up.

'There's a drink in it, a big drink.' The driver ignored him. 'Come on mate, I need a ride.'

'Get a bus.'

'Which one and where from?'

Carl's question went unanswered as two girls with shopping bags pushed past and got in the cab's back seat. The driver pulled away.

In the time it took Carl to find the nearest bus stop with an intact timetable, the snow had started falling again, whipped down the street by a bitter wind. It was mid-afternoon and almost dark. He zipped up his jacket. The bus numbers, place names and destinations meant nothing. He chucked his bag down and leaned back against the bus shelter. Mum always used to tell him they'd invented the saying *a fool's errand* just for him. Over the years he'd come to realise that where Mum was concerned, that meant anything she hadn't personally sanctioned or that didn't in some way benefit her; a favour for a mate or going out of his way for a girl and the tutting and sighing'd start. At his age he shouldn't have given it a second thought, but it had eaten away at him all the way from London and half the night listening to that tap drip. In the end, he'd folded up a towel and let it catch the drips and managed a few hours' kip. Mum hadn't actually said those words yesterday morning, she didn't need to – the disapproval was written into the slow shake of her head; the disappointment in her tone of voice. She reckoned he was wasting his time, being taken for a fool, and for what? She just didn't want him to go.

As kids they would do anything to keep her out of the doldrums. She'd even give Dad the deaf and dumb treatment. But he had this way of taking it for so long and you'd see him getting more and more wound up and you'd think he would explode but then, picking his moment, he'd sing back – *don't laugh at me 'cos I'm a fool.* Clowning about with granddad's old cloth cap on backwards until she broke and that thin little smile passed her lips, and then he'd won. She got away with murder and Dad let her – they all had.

The cold sent an ache down his spine. He picked up his bag and walked towards a row of shops. A dodgy looking burger bar next to a dirty bookshop looked like his best shot at a warm and a cuppa. Maybe they'd have the number of a cab company who'd show a bit of sympathy for a bloke on his fool's errand.

From the front, the house was in darkness. Carl stood in the street ankle deep in settled snow waiting for movement, knowing he'd be seen by the neighbours and not caring – let the curtain twitchers ask him what he was doing and he'd lay it on the line: he was there for his wife and his daughter, to take them home. He'd tell O'Keefe the same – he had presents for his girl and he was making sure she got them.

In the alley at the side of the house, Carl navigated between over-stuffed wheelie-bins. He tripped, kicked an empty beer can and found himself in the full glare of a security light. He retreated into the shadows and waited to be challenged. There were voices, but they sounded distant and unconnected, the conversation terminated by a car door slam. He squeezed past the garage to get a view of the back of the house. There was a light on in one of the upstairs rooms. He made his way back down the alley, working up the courage to ring the doorbell. A thousand times on the way up he'd planned what he'd say, but his head was empty, his thought processes hampered by the need to piss.

The first thing he noticed was that Diane was pale, which made the bruise on her cheek stand out all the more. Carl felt himself move towards her, the instinct to embrace, the sudden need to hold her.

47

'I thought it'd be you, I was waiting,' she said.

'You were supposed to call,' he said.

'I couldn't. Carl, it's not right for you to be here. It's bad for me, for Grace.' A car turned into the street, skidded on the snow. Diane fidgeted, shuffled from foot to foot, sniffing until the car cruised by. She wiped her nose on her sleeve.

'You got a cold, babe?'

'Don't call me that.'

He shrugged.

Diane's hair was tied back, loosely. She pushed a strand off her face, 'You can't be here when Jim gets back, it's his home, his property. You've no rights being here.'

The words didn't sound like Diane's and they stung him. 'I want to see Grace. She called me and I told her I'd come.' He paused. 'She wants her Christmas presents and I want her with me for New Year like we said.' The need to relieve himself was becoming overwhelming. 'Look Di, can I come in a minute and use your lav? I'm breaking my neck here and it's freezing. Please.'

'For crying out loud, Carl.' She thought for a moment, sniffed again then opened the door a little wider. 'You'd better not be here if he comes back.'

'Cheers, Di.'

'Use the downstairs, it's through there.' She motioned towards what was essentially a cupboard under the stairs, a cramped space shared with coats and boots: Grace's pink flowered wellies next to O'Keefe's steel-toecap riggers.

The warmth of the house permeated as he pissed, his feet thawed slightly and once relieved, he felt able to think straight.

Diane whispered from outside, 'Carl, please hurry up.'

When Grace had told him her mother had been crying a lot and had gone all funny and weird, he'd found it hard to believe. She'd always been strong, a tough girl from an even tougher family. Seeing her again, things seemed plausible that hadn't before. She was a different person. He zipped up. 'Just finishing.'

As he came out, Diane tried to usher him towards the front door and back into the street, but he stood his ground. 'I've come all this way – I want to see her.'

'No Carl, please.'

But Grace must have heard his voice. Diane's face fell as the sound of feet light on the landing came before Grace's wide awake smile as she tiptoed down the stairs. 'Hiya babe.' Carl moved to the bottom of the stairs and she launched herself at him, burying her head in his shoulder.

Diane went to the window, looked out.

'When are we going home, Dad?'

Diane threw him a glance, shook her head sharply.

'Me and Mum have got some sorting out to do so nothing's definite yet, we'll have to see. Soon.'

The answer was unsatisfactory. 'But you said I could come after Christmas. It's horrible here, isn't it, Mum? ... Mum?'

Diane's face as she turned from the window had drained of what little colour it had. 'Grace, get upstairs now.'

Carl had expected Grace to argue, but when he put her down and kissed her lightly on the forehead, she scurried back upstairs without a word. The tone of her mother's voice did most of what was needed, the key turning in the front door did the rest. Carl's stomach took a dive. O'Keefe stumbled in, appeared not to recognise him for a second, then his eyes blazed. He looked to Diane. 'Well?'

She pinched the bridge of her nose, 'He came to see Grace, to take her back for New Year as we agreed.'

'I never fucking agreed nothing. I wasn't consulted.'

'I know. I wasn't sure how to …' As her words faded then failed altogether, Diane shrank into the corner, said to Carl, 'You've come up here, you sort it out.'

'Look, Jim,' Carl opened his hands, 'I didn't mean to drop by this late, should have been here hours ago, but the weather – the train was delayed so I came straight here.'

'How did you know where I lived?'

Carl realised, too late as it turned out, that the card Grace sent to his mum should never have had the address printed on it, she must have given it back to Di with the envelope sealed. 'We had it written down somewhere, must have been to do with the pub, maybe when Ewan was off last year he let us have it for—' It was a lie, a transparent one.

'Y'take me for a fool – my brother never gave out my address.'

'I just want to give Grace her Christmas presents.'

'She don't want 'em and I don't want 'em in my house. You're not welcome here, Price. Grace is going nowhere with you so get out my house and fuck off back to London.'

O'Keefe crowded him and churned out abuse. Carl felt flecks of spit on his face, winced at the stink of stale whisky on O'Keefe's breath. O'Keefe grabbed him by the collar and threw him at the door. Fucks and shits and bastards rained down before one almighty shove over the step threw him on his heels. He jarred his back as he skidded in slush against the wheels of the black BMW X5 parked in the drive. O'Keefe slammed the door.

Carl came to his feet slowly, the seat of his wet trousers clinging to his arse. As he looked up at the house, a front bedroom curtain moved. Grace. He coughed and felt a pain in his ribs. He could still hear O'Keefe ranting. And then there was a silence, which was worse.

The night cold cut through Carl's wet clothes. As he paced the pavement outside the house, he caught O'Keefe watching from behind his curtains, a low light behind him. He raised his glass in a self-satisfied toast. Grace would be watching too, waiting and hoping for his next move, but there wasn't one. He bit his lip, dropped his gaze to his boots and started walking towards the main road. Halfway down he stopped, this wasn't what he wanted. None of it. If there's anything to be had from being on a fool's errand, he thought, it's that a fool never knows when to pack it in and go home. He turned and made his way back down the middle of the road, footprints making a third hard line between the tyre tracks in the snow right back to O'Keefe's front garden.

O'Keefe was still at the window, glass in hand. Carl went to the bins, dragged out the bottle box and pulled out a handy-weight whisky bottle. He mule-kicked at the front door, his heel hard on the bottom panel. Then, to irritate the pig, he gave the doorbell two businesslike rings.

He would have been caught cold by O'Keefe coming from the back alley if it hadn't been for the kicked can skidding past him. He was ready, but not for a swinging baseball bat. He ducked, swerved left and the first blow caught him across the shoulder.

'Yeah? Yeah? You want it?' O'Keefe was swinging. 'Yous people never know what you're dealing with, think you're a hard man, takin' me on in my own house.'

Carl, who had never felt less like a hard man in his life, moved inside O'Keefe's frantic swings. The bottle was useless that close and he wouldn't have used it anyway. He dropped it and drove forward, feet skidding behind him, but somehow forcing the momentum to knock O'Keefe off balance. They both went over. Carl landed two low punches inside without having much idea what they connected with, but O'Keefe let out a gasp and seemed to slow down. Carl broke away just enough to land a third punch, a short uppercut. Then there was a pause, blood on O'Keefe's lip, a smile showing blood discoloured teeth, then he grabbed Carl and jerked him onto a headbutt. The world went vague and warm, everything bent slightly out of shape.

The next thing Carl remembered was a flashing blue light across the snow-covered lawn. He got to his knees just as one copper was picking O'Keefe up, an arm around his shoulder. His mate was dropping the bat in the boot of the squad car. Another black X5 pulled up. O'Keefe's brothers got out. Ewan pulled on a dark overcoat over his roll neck sweater. He told a reluctant Adam to hold off, stay by the car. A custody van pulled up, more police. Carl was certain he was about to be arrested for assault or trespass or whatever they'd cook up. He got to his feet. After a word between Ewan and the Sergeant, the van pulled away. Ewan O'Keefe joined his brother. He looked over at Carl, lit a cigarette and turned his head to one side before exhaling. Adam O'Keefe walked across, leaned his backside on the police car, swept back a lank fringe and bit his nails, didn't take his eyes off Carl until the copper told him to piss off.

The police drove away. Carl was walking, his back rigid and pain down his right side every time he took a step. Ewan gave a sharp whistle. Adam O'Keefe headed him off, walking alongside. 'Where ya going? Eh? Nowhere *to* go, nowhere for you now. Ewan says you're with us. He wants to talk.' Carl shook off Adam's hand on his sleeve, but let himself be turned and steered to Ewan's BMW. Adam shoved him in the back seat and got in beside him. Carl tried the door handle, felt himself pulled back. Adam O'Keefe punched him on the cheek. Ewan got in behind the wheel.

Adam said, 'Where we going?'

'Put Mr Price on a train home.'

'An' that's it?'

Ewan turned round, 'What do you reckon, Mr Price, is that it?'

Carl looked up, shrugged.

'It'd better be.' Ewan started the engine, a burst of warm air came over Carl's feet, the radio played on the police frequency.

When they got to Hull Station, there was a change of plan. No more trains. A bus service could take him as far as Doncaster, but Ewan wasn't keen to let him travel solo. 'Looks like you've got a lift to Donny, Mr Price.'

'Ah, fuck it.' Adam kicked the back of the seat.

'What's your problem, something better to do?'

Adam folded his arms. Carl allowed himself a smile.

It was like hyperspace in one of those old arcade games as the headlights picked out snowflake galaxies hurtling towards the windscreen. Carl was feeling warmer than he had all day. It wouldn't have been a half bad ride if every now and then Adam O'Keefe hadn't given him a sly dig in his already aching ribs. For the third time he asked his older brother, how much longer to Doncaster?

'Fuck should I know, I'm not breakin' me neck to get there.' There was a long pause, then Ewan said, 'Mr Price, you should count yourself lucky tonight. James has a temper and left to him, you'd have been in a far worse state than you are. It's a silly thing you did.'

Curled in the corner, Carl didn't feel much like talking.

'He was easy on ya, for the kid's sake I guess and Diane's too. In a way, I can understand why a man like you would want to give something like that a go. It's an emotional time of year. But really, take my advice and don't try it again. He'll do time for you and we none of us want that.'

'I just want to see my girl, I've got a right to see her.'

'Not if James says otherwise. He's master of his own home.' As Ewan accelerated to join the M180, an artic thundered past, sprayed the windscreen with gritty black slush and they drove blind for a few seconds.

A few miles down the road Carl said, 'So you think it's alright that your brother knocks Diane about?'

'That's between them.'

'So fucking what?' Adam delivered another stiff poke in his side. In the half-light in the back of the car, his cheekbones stood out as he chewed on his lip. There was a resignation about him that reminded Carl of Terry, his own brother. Another one-track fool who picked fights, a bigger bloody fool by half for being a dead fool. For the umpteenth time, Adam's bony elbow dug into Carl's ribs. Already sore and beginning to stiffen, he let out a groan. Adam dug again.

'Ewan, can't you let him sit in front with the grown-ups?'

Adam jumped all over him with knees, elbows, fists. Carl, belted in and cornered, was unable to fight back or even block the punches. Ewan pulled into a parking area, opened the door and pulled Adam off. He helped Carl out. Frozen air hit his lungs in short gasps and he felt the damage. Something wasn't right; the hurt was too sharp, unrelenting. He dropped to his knees with Ewan standing over him. A slow pain sent hotwire fingers around his chest and in a lay-by in the middle of nowhere, he thought about dying and blacked out.

9

Frank's only thought was to put space between him and Adeline and the Cross Keys. He didn't look back once.

'Frank, what happened there?' Adeline pulled gently on his arm. Frank shook his head and refused to slow down until they were in sight of the station. She asked again, 'I said, what happened?'

'You were there, what do you think?'

'It just turned, we were alright and—'

'I just saw a bloke who had a shit Christmas and took it out on the new folks in town. That's all.'

'But what he said—' She danced up beside him, her shoes slipping.

'Was a bad joke.' He stopped as they entered the station. 'Buying the nasty sod a drink wouldn't have made a blind bit of difference. Let's just get on with it, we're not on bloody holiday here. Have you got the tickets?'

'I've got everything just here.' She patted the bag and took his arm again. This time he let her. 'Come on Frank, I'll buy you an ice cream when we get there.'

His face didn't crack.

'With a flake.'

And then he smiled. A day out in the pissing snow – to Hull for Pete's sake, what was he thinking? But now they were out in the open and on their way it did feel better. And he couldn't help thinking how good it was to have a girl on his arm.

Passengers were milling around the concourse. Others emerged from waiting rooms and station snack bars and took their place on the platform. A tannoy announcement that the train was due in seven minutes raised a few weak ironic cheers at the sudden recourse to precise timings. There was a shuffling of feet, expectant glances down the track where only the two red signal lights were visible in the darkness. They switched amber and soon after the train's own lights came into view. Two men in long overcoats positioned themselves on marks close to the four carriage stop sign. To Frank it seemed the train was coming in too quickly, but it was impossible to gauge its true speed in the darkness with no reference points. People picked up their bags and edged forward; there was one almighty race for a seat in the offing. The track whined, then hummed before the sound of the train itself took over. Frank looked again, this time certain its approach was way too fast. He drew back, pulling Adeline with him. She looked up, but as she was about to speak the engine noise exploded into the station. A blistering slipstream threw people back; carriages fired through with flashes of yellow light and glimpses of blurred white faces. The train did not slow, let alone stop.

The litter settled. Noise echoed under the canopy.

'Shit.' Frank watched the last carriage disappear into the night.

You had to have some sympathy for the station staff. One poor sucker mooched out to face the pissed off crowd of punters. A ticket office attendant with a grubby shirt and several chins held his hand up for quiet. He had no information because there was no information, no explanation, he was in the dark just as they were and could only apologise. He blustered, of course he accepted the mistake. It may have been an unscheduled service, but yes he knew it should have stopped. It didn't, he knew that too, he'd been there. No, there was nothing he could do. Would he call ahead? There was no point, the train wouldn't stop and he couldn't bring it back. A bloke with his wife and kids began to make his way out, swearing and dragging his crying daughter behind him. He left the girl with her mother at the fringes of the crowd then shoved his way back in, went up to the railway bloke and lamped him. Full face. He went down to a mixture of cheers and gasps from the crowd, hands up to his nose, blood between his fingers.

Old bill arrived. Two uniforms, that night not loving the job. They treated the whole thing like a full scale bloody riot, shoving people around, making noises about public order offences, threatening arrests. Half a dozen more turned up with batons drawn, fronted by a sergeant, a hard-faced woman whose calls for quiet were met without argument. The police cleared the station and blanked any further protests. Frank and Adeline were carried along. Once they were all outside freezing their nuts off, another company man came out. He gave an apology, but had no explanation. He told them to keep their tickets and apply for a refund. The shout went

55

up, they didn't want refunds, they wanted to make their journeys. He couldn't promise anything. It probably wouldn't be that night, but what he could say was that a train back to King's Cross *would* be stopping in fifteen minutes. Yes, he could personally guarantee it would stop. Otherwise he advised them to go home and come back in the morning.

Frank looked to Adeline. 'What d'you think? We could be on our way home in quarter of an hour.'

'If you wanna go, go.' She looked away.

'We won't get there, not tonight.'

'Like I said.'

He told her to wait while he went for a piss. He knew she didn't think he'd be back. There was a part of him that longed for home, even after a day to be back at the John Evelyn with nothing lost and a story to tell. But as he thought the idea through, it didn't carry quite the appeal he thought it might. He straightened up. A copper stood in his way at the main entrance. 'No one's to re-enter station premises until we get the all-clear.'

'I just want the toilet.'

'Do I look like I give a fuck?'

Frank looked him up and down, 'No, you can 'ave that one, mate. Well done.'

There was no other way in, he'd just have to hang on.

By the time he'd worked his way back to Adeline the crowd had thinned. He wanted to tell her he'd made his decision, affirm his commitment, but she was talking to two men – the blokes in overcoats who had been standing close on the platform. She lifted her face to him, gave a smile. 'You can get your train back if you want. I've got a lift. These guys are going to Hull.'

Frank sized them quickly, made a judgement. 'You sure?'

'Yeah, course.'

'Just the three of you?'

'Yes,' she said.

'You'll have room for one more then.'

Frank sat in the back of the Overcoats' silver saloon, a Jap model with grey plastic trim and a soft-rock compilation in the CD player. Adeline was in beside him, the bag between them. She gave his knee a pat, seemed satisfied with the outcome, happy he was still with her. Overcoat One sat behind the wheel and introduced himself as Andy, then introduced Overcoat Two as Graham. They worked in reclamation, 'Some call it trash, we call it cash.'

'Rolls right off the tongue,' said Frank.

They drove for about twenty minutes before Andy slipped into the conversation that they'd actually be going well out of their way to drop them off.

'Oh, yeah.'

Graham chimed in, saying how good it was of them seeing as how the trains had messed up their schedule and now they had other stops to make.

'Where are you heading for?' said Adeline.

'York,' said Andy.

'Thirsk,' said Graham, adding quickly, 'If we get finished in York on time.'

'Which doesn't look likely,' said Andy. 'The York job looks like it might run over – some old dear with an inheritance and a fireplace that's worth a few quid. Might take a bit of persuading.'

'You'll never get it in the boot,' said Frank, wondering where the hell Thirsk was.

'Oh, you'd be surprised what we've had in that boot.' Andy adjusted his rear-view. Frank guessed it was to give him a better view of Adeline. 'And then we're off to an old school that wants shot of some antique radiators. We'll get the van up if the price is right.'

Graham said, 'See, that's what we do. Don't matter when or where, we'll get it first. It's a competitive market, which is why we're shit hottest.'

Andy chipped in. 'I've got a bloke who's doing up some apartments in Fulham. Them radiators'll be painted up and we'll have 'em sold on inside a fortnight.'

Graham opened a bag of salt and vinegar crisps, offered them around, but there were no takers.

Conversation dried up for the next few minutes, just the sound of Graham chomping rhythmically over some flabby rock ballad. He twisted the empty packet into a tight knot and licked each of his fingers in turn, then dropped the packet into the ashtray.

'Don't do that,' said Andy.

'What?'

'The crisp thing, not in the ashtray, it'll undo and chuck ash.'

'No it won't.'

'It did the last time. I opened the ashtray and it sprung up and chucked ash all over the console.'

'Only because you put fag ash on top.'

'It's an ash tray, a tray – for ash.'

'Fine, whatever.' Graham rescued the crisp packet and looked for somewhere to put it.

'Just put it in your pocket.'

'After it's been in the ashtray? No chance.'

Andy turned the music up, whistling between his teeth to REO Speedwagon.

Frank bit the inside of his lip. For all the Mr and Mrs squabbling, he had the feeling they were being played to. Each time he looked up, a rear-view glance from Andy caught his eye. They'd been on the A1 for what couldn't have been more than a dozen miles when Andy indicated and pulled off. 'I need to get some juice.' He added, 'Donations gratefully received.'

Frank could see the petrol gauge and Andy must have known it. There was still half a tank left. As they drove onto the Esso station slip, cars sped past on the main road, slush spat against the windows. Andy leaned round. 'So is this a free ride or are you on the team?'

Adeline said, 'How much d'you want?'

'Twenty quid. S'fair.'

'Fare's fair,' said Graham.

Frank thought otherwise, but Adeline's hand went to the bag. She stopped before opening it. 'Well I haven't got the cash on me, if there's a cashpoint—'

'There will be,' said Graham.

'No problem.'

Andy pulled into the pump. 'I'll fill up, why don't you go in and I'll wave when I've stopped pumping, then you can pay.'

'I need a piss,' said Frank and followed Adeline into the shop.

'You should have stayed with them,' she hissed. 'What if they piss off once I've paid.'

'Just let me go to the lav and don't pay for anything till I get back.'

Frank was quick, but she was nearly at the front of the queue by the time he got back. Andy was outside, waving – a wink and a gun. She pressed a wad of notes into Frank's hand. 'Put that away, hold onto it. I don't want it in the bag. And here's the twenty for the petrol.'

'Where are you going?'

She was halfway to the door. 'I'm getting back in, guarding my investment. I want that ride. Hurry up.' She ran back and kissed him on the cheek which for a split second threw him completely.

He let her go.

He watched her walk to the car, saw her slide into the back seat.

There was a problem with the customer in front – something to do with a new card. 'It says January,' said the girl in the Esso sweatshirt. 'We're not *in* January.'

'They said I could use it. It's been activated.' The customer fingered through his wallet for another card while the Esso girl tried to void the sale, only succeeding in locking up the whole system. She pressed buttons, which made bleeps. The supervisor appeared at her shoulder, shoved in a key, pressed another series of buttons which made longer, more emphatic bleeps. Frank glanced out the window. The silver saloon pulled away from the pump, accelerating towards the exit. He moved fast, knocked a display of sweets flying, knew there would be CCTV, knew that if Andy and Graham didn't give a shit about that, they didn't give one about the car being identified, which meant it wasn't their car. He ran, Jesus Christ, he ran. But the car had gone, away up an unlit side road. He kept on as it slowed for a car in front, then swerved violently. Frank kept running, his lungs burning, legs turning to water. He was fifty, then a hundred yards away with the tail lights disappearing when suddenly the brake lights came on. The car stopped dead. The engine idled then a door opened and Adeline stepped out, cool as fuck. She put the bag over her shoulder, slammed the door shut and walked back towards him as the car drove away.

He went to her, met her, said nothing. Put an arm around her shoulder and they walked a few paces in the dark. She stopped and buried her face in his chest. He held her close until she stopped shaking.

There were no trains at Newark, wasn't even worth trying. The cab driver who picked them up asked did they want somewhere to stay? He could call ahead find out where there might be a vacancy.

'That'd be well appreciated, mate,' said Frank.

The driver had someone in his office ring round a couple of hotels on their way in. A woman's voice came through on the radio with a list of possible places. They chose the nearest and cheapest. The driver took them straight to a travel inn. Adeline went in while Frank paid over the odds for the ride with Adeline's twenty quid, then checked them in. Adeline stood aside, hands deep in her pockets. When they got to the room with the door closed behind them, she sat on the bed. Frank put the lamp on, turned off the overhead light.

'D'you want to talk about it?'

'No.'

He scratched his head, took his coat off and threw it over a chair. 'Can I get you anything?'

She thought for a moment. 'Ten Silk Cut, a packet of Rizla kingsize papers, a small bottle of brandy, a bottle of Coke – full fat, some crisps, a few bars of chocolate, a Ripple if they've got one and whatever you want. Use some of the money I gave you. There's a Spar down the road, I saw it on the way in.'

'So what, we having a party?'

'If you like. And Frank …' He'd picked up his coat. 'Don't be long and when you come back, just give me a cuddle and forget this afternoon happened.'

Adeline had melted chocolate on her chin. They'd watched an episode of *Porridge* from Christmas past and some crappy celebrity special Christmas game show on the even crappier portable in the room. 'Same as Carl's telly,' Adeline said.

Frank hadn't touched his whisky. He lay on the bed. Adeline had got in and was sitting up surrounded by spliff mess, sweet wrappers – he'd bought Quality Street – and celebrity magazines. 'I'm having a Christmas time.' She laughed, threw her head back and banged it on the headboard. 'Ow, shit.' And laughed again. 'So Frank, you still owe me from this morning – tell me one thing, just one thing about yourself that I don't know. Entertain me, man of mystery.'

'You'll have to tell me what you do know.'

She gave it some thought. 'Honestly?'

He nodded.

'You drink too much, you're a loner, bit of a miserable git most of the time. I think you're smarter than you let on. It's like you see all and say nothing. And you can be a moody pain in the arse, but I'm finding you're actually quite a nice man to be with.'

'Thank you.'

'Your turn. One thing, you owe me, remember, so make it good.'

He thought about it, all the secrets that had been lining up since the morning, since forever. 'I went to prison once.'

'Frank Neaves, a fugitive, hunted like a dog and sent down for a crime he didn't commit.' She laughed and swept her hand over the duvet, brushing off a storm of loose tobacco.

'It was fifteen years and I didn't do what they said, as it goes. I did other things, but not ...' Frank stalled.

'I'm sorry, you don't 'ave to.'

60

'I was hanging around with some people. Wide boys really, not full on gangsters; there weren't any round our way by then, most of it was just paper talk. But there were a few blokes – I mean I never got into all that shit they did, all that mohair and flash. I used to come out of Ladywell Baths with my kid when she was little and watch 'em pulling up in their Jags and acting like they'd worked for it. Not just scammed it or nicked it off some poor sod lower down the food chain. They could never have done what I did.'

'And what *did* you do?'

'I dunno, just tried to look after people I s'pose, me mates, family.' He went to the bathroom and closed the door behind him. He put the lid down and sat on the lav, chin in his hands.

Adeline called from outside, 'Frank?'

'Yeah?'

'What's your kid's name?'

'Kate.'

'That's nice.'

There was a long silence.

'Frank?'

'What?'

'Have you ever met Michael Caine?'

'No.'

'Frank?'

'*What?*'

'I'm cold, come and keep me warm.'

The lamps were off, the murmuring TV gave the only light. The smoke alarm panels were open, battery wires hanging loose. Adeline licked the Rizla and rolled. Her voice was a little rougher, a whisper fraying at the edges. 'Some nights, when I was a kid, I used to say my prayers and pretend I was holding onto Jesus's hand.' She giggled to herself, propped up on the pillow. Her joint rolling was a credit to her in the circumstances. 'How stupid was I?'

'I've heard stupider.'

She twisted the end and lit up.

Frank declined the smoke.

'Come on Frank, you know what it's like to drink alone.' She offered the spliff.

'I prefer it alone if I'm honest.'

She leaned over for the makeshift ashtray. 'Anything else you do alone?'

He raised an eyebrow.

She laughed, then kissed him. And it didn't feel like pity; there was no shame. And he didn't feel like an old man kissed by younger woman. It just felt warm, soft-lipped, then a little harder, a show of intent. God help him, he kissed her back the same. Only this kiss was clouded with old man anxiety. She sensed it and pulled away. 'So?'

'So what?'

'Exactly.'

'I'm older than you.'

'By what, twenty years? And mister, if you wait till the morning, you'll see my thirty-two year old face looking a damn sight nearer forty, so get over it and see what happens if you kiss me again.'

The way she touched him, anywhere her hands went was warm, real, gentle. Electric. She stroked at the back of his neck, then gripped his hair. 'You need a haircut, old man.' She picked a hair off her tongue and sipped his scotch. 'S'better.' The next kiss was spiced and she pressed herself closer. The one after that tasted of Coca-cola. Then she stopped, for no reason.

'Sorry Frank, I don't think I can. So, so sorry.'

She curled under his arm and he held her with a sense of relief. For a moment he'd believed, kidded on by the long lost thrill of intimacy, but it wasn't right. Not for him now, not ever. For him there was the sunset, the long walk and the next town. He was John Wayne in *The Searchers*. He was Clint fucking Eastwood with no name. For him there were bad decisions made for the best of reasons. For him there had only ever been Carol.

10

By the summer of 1971, Dave Price was well known in the streets around Lewisham and Catford – on the up you might say – and for the third time in as many months he found Frank in a quiet moment in the Black Horse. He put a pint in front of him and laid a thickish brown envelope across the top. Frank removed the envelope, which he knew to be stuffed with used blue fivers – he'd looked the first time – before handing it back. 'Cheers for the pint Dave, you can keep the chaser.'

Price sat down and gave him *the talk*. He wanted Frank to work for him in an unnamed capacity that had the word 'driver' in it somewhere. There were plenty of other drivers, Frank argued. Drivers who were faster, better suited, more ready to make the moves and take the risks he would demand of them. Besides, he already had a job chauffeuring for a big city type: Mr Schiller was the Swiss-German Managing Director of an EC3 commodity brokers. And of course he had Carol, who he probably wouldn't have for long if she found he was employed by an out and out chancer like Dave Price.

'Thing is Frank, the blokes I could use are too full of themselves, too flash, no discretion. I wouldn't ask you to take risks, I can find a dozen getaway racers. This would be a private arrangement between the two of us, no one need know if that's what you wanted, just me and you – someone I can trust.'

Frank was under no illusion as to what lay behind the offer. Dave already had strong-arm men, cruel and ruthless men who worked for him. What he was missing was intelligence, someone who could think ahead and near as dammit guarantee he'd be in the right place at the right time. It was to his credit that he'd made it this far without an up-front reputation for nastiness. But there was no getting away from it, to keep what he'd got and stay free of the law, same as you needed accountants and lawyers, you needed people you could trust, and not just for the rough stuff. Frank knew that if he were drawn in there would be no turning back. Once more he refused.

'You tell me what you need, Frank. How long have we known each other?'

'Too bloody long.'

Price took it on the chin. 'Years, right? So give me some credit. It ain't like I'm asking you to sit outside Barclays with the engine running while some half-arsed firm with stockings on their 'eads grab a few hundred quid. I swear on Harry Cripps' life you'll never see your pretty face on *Police Five*.'

Frank smiled.

'So, why not?'

There were a few more punters in the pub, drinks coming over the bar, fags lit up. Frank felt the weight behind the question and knew whatever he said, Price would have an answer. They could carry on going round in circles half the bloody afternoon. Even at school Dave had always been a persistent sod. They'd gone on to start their national service together, taken the train down to Aldershot on that bastard cold Thursday in November, did their basic together, then a tour in Cyprus. Received wisdom was that if you didn't know how to drink, fight, shag, smoke and swear before you went in the army, you would by the time you came out. Dave had already had his fair share, but in his two years' national service added thieving to the list. He bailed as soon as he could, but not before he'd relieved the stores in Akrotiri of enough NAAFI cigarettes to give him a start back home. Frank signed on for another three years and another three after that. He was a good soldier, learned more in a few weeks as a regular than eighteen months of spud-bashing, drill and latrine duty. He got out and about and grew to love the island and its people. And when he finally came home there was Carol. She'd loved him since they used to meet up down Deptford Broadway after school. Now she'd waited for him and he wasn't putting that on the line.

'Let me think about it, Dave. It ain't as if I don't appreciate the offer. I'm flattered, but I'm straight and staying that way, and whatever I do for you, it's …' The words left hanging, his gesture, open-handed.

'Just try it. One job, cash in hand, nothing to piss Carol off even if you choose to tell her. My absolute word on it – I need you to keep straight as much as you do. And if you don't want it after that,

I won't ask again.' He slid the envelope back across the table. 'Keep that as an up-front gesture of goodwill. I'll give you a couple of weeks then I'll take what you say one way or another, okay?' He gave Frank a pat on the shoulder and left him to his pint.

The moment Frank stuffed the envelope away in his jacket, he felt the burden that came with it and knew something of consequence had shifted.

For the next few weeks on and off Frank checked Price out, sometimes coming closer than he'd have liked, but making sure he kept himself out of sight. In the Black Bull, he watched through cigarette smoke at the respectful space around Price made by friends and associates; easy smiles and routine group dynamics shifting to accommodate the boss's presence. You sensed the lull, the long exhalations of breath when Dave stepped to the gents. Same at the club, Price buying drinks, leaning over tables to shake hands and whisper a word here and there between rounds of housey housey, blue comics and brassy wannabe cabaret singers.

On the second Saturday evening, Price and his crew were in The Ram with their families. A bunch of lairy bits of kids, pints in hand, spilled their beery offence into the Price tables – three had been moved together to accommodate latecomers. Wally Patch and Roy Wills stood up sharpish. In the public bar Frank bit his lip, willing the kids to back off. There were words, no more. Then Wally and Roy peeled away unnoticed by the kids. Minutes later after a quiet word with the guv'nor, the kids were asked to leave. Dave's boys were waiting outside.

Frank had the measure of Price's weekday routine. He'd leave home around nine-thirty, drive to his office at the back of the bookies on Brownhill Road where he'd stay until mid-morning when Wally turned up. They'd make their rounds, two or three in-and-out visits before lunch and a couple after. Then back to the bookies. Nothing like working for a living, he thought. Frank picked up information discreetly and along with what was common knowledge, put the pieces together. Some of the businesses were legitimate customers who simply shoved Price a few quid for a quiet life. You could call it protection, but there wasn't much evidence of any threat Dave's stake was protecting them from. Other pick-ups, among them Pete's Motors, Jacqui's Launderette, Ron Morris's cabs and Baldwin's Turf Accountants, were strictly Dave Price investments, set up with his own cash. The brown envelope came weekly. But it was small beer. Frank was intrigued, there couldn't have been more than fifty or sixty quid a week coming in between them.

When he made his rounds, Price was to all intents and purposes the same as any other moderately industrious businessman. His visits, for the most part in an inconspicuous mid-blue Vauxhall Viva, were brief. The exception being Friday, when a solo lunchtime drop-in to Jacqui's ran long into the afternoon. Frank waited, his car parked at a discreet distance. Price was still there at three o'clock when Frank left for the drive back into the City. He was driving Schiller to Heathrow; an extended business trip to Hong Kong and Singapore and hopefully a bit of breathing space.

On the Monday morning, Frank was up, shaved and getting dressed for work.

'I thought you said you'd have a bit more time at home with the boss away.' There was still a sleepy growl in Carol's voice. 'You could always get back in.' She lifted the bedclothes.

He sat on the edge of the bed, 'I know babe. Thing is, every other bugger who thinks it might be nice to turn up chauffeur-driven wants me to drive 'em. I'm up and down like a blue-arsed fly.'

She lifted the bedclothes a little higher.

Frank stood in socks, boxers, shirt and cufflinks, making a half-arsed protest. 'I'm nearly dressed.'

Carol reached out, grabbed the waistband of his boxers and pulled him towards her, 'Nearly undressed, though, depending how you look at it.'

It wasn't until Thursday of that week, Frank lifted the lid on the true extent of Price's empire. He nearly missed the show. After Monday's love-in, him and Carol had made the best of the bright, warm spring mornings and the absence of the need for Swiss punctuality hanging over them. When Frank parked down the road from the bookies just before nine, Price's entire crew were waiting. A dozen blokes, suited, booted, stood smoking on the pavement. They went inside in twos. Like Noah's bloody ark, he thought as the pairs came out and drove away. He stayed with Price.

As the morning wore on, it appeared – and Frank rarely found appearances deceptive – that Dave Price had a stake in pubs and clubs across the whole of South East London. From Tooley Street to Downham, Surrey Docks to Peckham, and pretty much every point in between. The visits were quick, strictly no boozing. A walk in the saloon and out through the same door, five minutes at most. Instead of the usual leisurely two or three pick-ups, by lunchtime, Dave and Wally had made eight pick-ups. When they met back at the bookies later that afternoon, each pair walked in with a sports holdall, Adidas, Puma, Slazenger. Either they were the best dressed pub football team in history or these were strictly cash transactions.

Looking back, Frank was never certain what swung it for him. It might have been the buzz he hadn't had since leaving the army; the chance to make a few quid tax free, or the fact that him and Carol were making love like they had when they were kids, but the end of the month when Price sat down, put the pint in front of him and offered the job, Frank said yes. 'Bit of advice though Dave ...'

'What's that?'

'You need to vary the routine. Same places, same pick-ups, same days; you're making it too easy. Anyone with half a mind to take you down, it's a piece of piss. All they have to do is get a service wash at Jacqui's half-one on a Friday afternoon and they've got a guaranteed result.'

Price's smile dropped. Frank realised too late, this was the wrong example. 'What do you know ... *how* do you know?'

The reaction was unnerving, but Frank had set his stall out. This was the way it would be, no bullshit, no holding back. 'You go to the same places at pretty much the same times every week, and I know because I've seen you. And if I've seen you and you didn't know, then you haven't been looking and if you haven't been looking—'

'Yeah, yeah, I get it.'

It looked like it might turn out to be the shortest job he'd had. Frank felt a chill; even if he got the bullet before he'd even started – metaphorically speaking – he didn't want to piss Price off. 'Thing is Dave, you're on your way up, right? You must have already thought of it this way, surely. It could be the old bill, could be anybody, especially if you're a *somebody*.'

'No one's gonna have a dig at me.' The protest had a whiff of conceit. The thought that he might be a target flattered him. It gave him status, which gave Frank a second piece of insight: not only was Price bloody careless, he was bloody vain with it.

'Just change the routes, alter the days, the times, that's all I'm saying. Otherwise the minute whoever gets a sniff, they'll have your routine off pat in a fortnight.'

'Well it ain't gonna be our old bill round here, won't happen.'

A third piece of knowledge: Price was paying someone locally to keep him up to speed with the local plod's shopping list.

'As long as you're sure.'

'I'm sure.'

'Flying Squad, what about them? Other firms? Come on Dave, there's always someone.'

There was a long silence. For a full fifteen seconds Price stared through him. 'So how d'you want to play this?'

'The way I see it, we're old mates. As far as anyone's concerned we've got no business connection, no involvement in each other's affairs. This has to be a very private arrangement.'

'Fair enough.' Price tried to light a cigarette. The flint on his lighter sparked, but didn't take. Frank tossed over a book of matches.

'And I'm straight, Dave. You want me to drive, I'll drive. You want me to tell you honestly what I think, I will. Anything else, you've got Wally and the rest of 'em.'

Price lit the cigarette and pushed the matchbook back.

'Keep 'em,' said Frank. 'My phone number's written in the flap. Call me when you need me.'

*

Frank lay still for a long time after Adeline unfolded herself, scrunched the pillow and turned away. He was at home with the dark, with his thoughts, and the memory of the look of satisfaction that used to come over Dave Price's face any time he got his own way.

11

Carl came to and shielded his eyes. A string of orange streetlights unwound overhead. There was a blinding pain-filled minute with the smell of upholstery in his nostrils before he knew for sure where he was, bent horizontal on the back seat of Ewan O'Keefe's BMW. When he eased himself up, his head was swimming. They were driving along a wide dual carriageway lined with low lit car showrooms and darkened warehouse stores.

'You with us, then?' Adam turned round from the front seat. He sounded vaguely contrite. Ewan must have had a word.

'You're a fucking idiot,' said Carl.

Adam threw a punch that fell short as a combination of Ewan and his own seatbelt pulled him back. 'You fucking say sorry for that.'

Ewan slowed for a red light.

Carl looked out the window. On a street corner were two houses side by side overloaded with Christmas lights; a reindeer towed a *Merry Christmas* sleigh in flashing white. 'I'm sorry you're a fucking idiot.'

Adam's mood didn't improve when they pulled into the station car park. Some poor soul in a high-viz anorak was waiting to tell them there would be no more trains.

Adam leaned across, 'You could've told us that at Hull.'

High-viz looked confused.

'Alright mate.' Ewan shoved his brother back. 'Any ideas when the next one's due?'

'Not till morning.'

Adam kicked out at the dash, the glove compartment dropped open. 'Shit!'

'There's a bus service operating between here and Newark. They're expecting a train through from there …' he looked at his watch, 'I dunno, sometime later tonight. I'm sorry I can't be more precise than that. With the weather an' that it's all gone to shit to be honest.'

'Cheers.' Ewan buzzed the window up and pulled into a parking space. He turned to his brother. 'You want to tell me what your problem is, apart from the fact you owe me for a new dashboard light? Come on, if you need to be somewhere sometime soon you better tell me, otherwise we're driving Mr Price to Newark.' Adam stared back at Carl. 'Don't worry about him, talk to me.'

'I need to be at the docks. The night boat's in from Rotterdam in an hour and I'm s'posed to meet a bloke.'

'Rudi, right?'

'Yeah.'

'After I told you I wasn't happy doing business with the prick.'

He shrugged. 'It's personal, for a mate.'

'Is it bollocks. You haven't got any mates.'

He turned to Carl. 'Jesus, you look awful. D'you want a painkiller?'

Carl nodded.

'Adam, pop in there and get a pack of Nurofen for Mr Price.'

The car shook as he threw his anger into a door slam.

'Going to have to put you on the bus, Carl. Sorry we can't take you to Newark, but it seems my pinheaded brother's got a date to keep with a bloke I'd rather not blow out. I'd let him go on his own, but he's not quite the full shilling when it comes to business.'

Carl was silent.

'So, I've got to trust you here because the alternative is just a bit unpleasant, especially if you're not feeling too good already. I want your word you'll go to Newark and get yourself home, and not go back and bother James.'

Carl peered into the darkness where the only light was the glint in Ewan's eyes.

'A promise,' said Ewan, 'on your daughter's life, and I'll have a word about him letting you see her properly once things have calmed down in a few weeks.'

Adam opened the passenger door. 'They've only got Anadin.'

'So get Anadin. And get him a bottle of water.'

There was a commotion over by the coach, smokers sucking up last drags, shuffling feet on the tarmac, kicking off the snow before boarding. The driver climbed into his cab. The engine turned over with a diesel gurgle and a thick cloud of fumes.

'Sure,' said Carl. 'I'll get the bus. But I want my daughter for New Year.'

Ewan found him a seat near the middle, where the bounce wouldn't be too bad, make sure he didn't do any more damage to his ribs. Considerate bastards, he thought. The bus rumbled out into the streets around Doncaster, snow piled at the roadside. Once the overhead lights went out, the murmur of conversation dwindled. Carl flipped open the Anadin and took three.

He'd never been a fighter, not one of those blokes who'd bring it on for a Saturday night with a skinful if they hadn't pulled by closing time. Or the lads at school who had gangs and gave themselves names, carving their 'turf' in playground skirmishes that rolled out into the street come half-past three. It just wasn't his way.

He ached, waiting for the Anadin to kick in. How could you touch a man like James O'Keefe?

He remembered Donny Trew.

Donny was a wiry old man with Old Holborn yellow finger ends who ran Bellingham boys boxing club. Carl pictured him strolling across the gym to meet him and his dad one Saturday morning when he was about thirteen and as he did, barking instructions to two lads slapping each other around for fun in the ring. 'Do it right or bugger off.' They shaped up, instantly.

Donny shook his dad's hand, put his arm around Carl's shoulder and took him to a wall of bill posters and black and white portraits. 'See that photo, the big one, know who that is?'

Carl nodded. 'Uncle Henry.'

A knowing smile, 'That's right, son, Henry Cooper. He come here, started out boxing with his brother. You reckon you can do what he did?'

The gym was like a machine fuelled by sweat and energy. A place of bare boards and worn leather and skinny lads with hard faces and cruel smiles.

Dad said, 'Find him some kit, Don. Might as well now we're 'ere. And I need to talk to you in private.'

Carl sensed something between Donny and his dad, an unspoken disapproval. Donny looked him up and down and said, 'He don't look too sure, Dave. Maybe needs to build himself up a bit.'

'Just get someone to show him how to punch the bag.'

Carl shivered as he pulled on the shorts and sweatshirt Donny gave him. He listened to every word the old man said, how to jab and hook, how to feint and move, to plant his feet to push his punches through, to put combinations of punches together. Donny said a kid his size was going to have to have fast hand-speed to score, good leg strength to keep moving, and plenty of heart to stay the course. Carl's body responded; it let him make the moves. He punched the heavy bag, made dents in its cracked red leather. In the mirror he could see he was making shapes like the boxers in the photographs. The two hours flew by. Donny's gruff front never fell away, but there was no cross word as long as you tried your best.

As some of the other lads were warming down and others putting the skip-ropes and medicine balls away, Dad told Donny to put him in the ring. Rain battered the windows and Carl was cooling off quickly. 'Best way to learn, Don. Three minutes, give it a go.'

They gave him a gumshield and put him in the ring with a bony kid called Miller. As Donny laced up his gloves he whispered, 'You use your feet, son. He's got a longer reach, so don't let him pick you off easy, make him work for it. Watch his eyes, and don't be frightened.'

For the first few seconds, Carl moved and Miller followed, pacing around the ring. Then he took his first punch, Miller's long left, a jab that was little more than a sighter. He took it on the nose. It made his eyes water. He glanced across at Donny and his dad standing ringside, arms folded. The lapse in concentration was all Miller needed. One minute he was standing, the next he was on his arse in the middle of the ring. He picked himself up quickly, brushed his gloves off on his sweatshirt and didn't dare look across to his dad. He heard Donny's voice, 'Box him son, don't give it 'im easy. Make the bugger work.'

Carl thought about Ali, about Conteh, Finnegan and Alan Minter, about his shape. He brought his guard up and threw a couple of punches, air shots that wrenched his shoulder. Miller came in close and connected again, this time Carl was thinking – the punch opened up Miller's right side. He connected with a good left of his own that must've hurt and followed up with a right to the body. Miller got serious, covered up, chased him down and made three or four punches count, but Carl stayed in the game, kept moving and counter-punching each time Miller left himself open. By the time Donny rang the bell, Carl was reading Miller, making him miss and making his own shots count. Miller cuffed Carl's head close, said, 'If I see you in the street, you ain't getting' off so easy.'

Dad said nothing on the way home. He didn't have to, Carl knew he'd impressed him by sticking at it, giving as good as he'd got and going back for more. He never minded the hurt, the sting of the gloves or the burn in his muscles. He was tired.

Mum looked at his face when he got home, put witch-hazel on the bruises. She never said anything to him directly, but she didn't talk to Dad for a week and Carl never boxed again.

A year or so later when Dad took Terry down the club, his brother turned out to be a brawler, a whirlwind who blew himself out after three minutes. When he came home banged up with rope burns on his back, Mum told him he wasn't to go back either. He told her to get stuffed and went anyway.

12

Adeline dressed in the dark and put Frank's coat around her shoulders. She went to the window and lit a cigarette. The snow was coming down heavily, layering the deserted streets. Frank kicked the duvet away as he slept and she turned back; the light from the street showed scars, two of them, long and straight down the back of his thigh.

When she met Frank, that first ever shift behind the bar, it had been a slow summer lunchtime, the streets thick with petrol fumes and her asthma playing up. It was her first full week back in south London since the lost, lonely weekend in Crawley that lasted five years. It was called a marriage, but not by her. It had stripped her of confidence, faith, humanity, laughter. In return she'd got frown lines and the wardrobe of a fifty year old woman. Gordon – she could still barely say his name – had dressed her like his mother. That morning in the John Evelyn as she got used to where things were, busying around the bar, conversations rolled on. She wrapped herself in their voices and when they wanted serving, she noticed one or two who had smiles in their eyes. In those days, Frank was one of them.

She heard him before she saw him, his low growl saying, 'I never said I had a thing about shagging black women.'

He stopped when he saw she was listening. 'Sorry, love.'

She threw the damp tea towel over her shoulder, planted her feet. 'Go on, don't let me stop you.'

Frank's mate Gary, second generation Deptford via Kingston, was having none of it. 'Come on then, explain – bearing in mind I will take offence.'

'Sometimes a bloke just wants to be held. Like if you knew you were about to turn your toes up and you knew it was the end, you'd want it to be in the arms of a woman, right? Agreed, yes?'

Gary nodded. 'So you'd want it to be a woman ...'

'With ...'

'... soul and big tits, you said. That's what you said. So she'd have to be black. If she was white, she'd be a fat bird.' Gary, whose Jamaican mother hadn't missed a Sunday service at St Nick's in thirty years, would have kicked his arse from here to Kingston and back again for what he said next. 'You just wanna shag Aretha Franklin.'

Frank considered his response for a moment, 'No, see you're not listening. It's not about sex, not if I'm dying in her arms. And probably not Aretha as it goes.'

Gary sipped whisky and sucked his teeth. 'Billie Holiday, she'd be one sweet-voiced angel.'

'Who'd have it away with your wallet and spend the contents on a nice little bag of class As.'

'Small price to pay if you're on your deathbed.'

They nodded. 'True.'

Adeline wanted the conversation to carry on; it felt like a hug.

'Got it.' Gary slapped the bar, looked up to the heavens. 'Lord, let me die in the arms of Mavis Staples.'

'Yes, yes, yes.' Frank downed his drink. 'Exactly. Mavis, that voice – she'd soothe you, bit of gospel singing on the way so it's a double hit. You wouldn't even notice you'd gone.' The day's business resolved, they downed their drinks.

'Same again?' said Adeline.

'Amen,' said Frank.

From the hotel room, Adeline watched as a bitter wind tore across the street and carried the snow in drifts up against the shop fronts.

'Amen,' whispered Adeline. She shivered, wondering whether Frank was still sleeping and thought probably not. She drew on the cigarette, flicked the ash on the carpet and trod it in. 'You awake Frank?'

'Apparently.' He pulled the duvet round himself.

'D'you think we'll get there?'

'Tomorrow.'

'Sorry, about earlier.'

'Don't worry about it.'

'You sure?'

'It's fine, forget it.'

There was a long pause. 'I always used to miss London when I was with Gordon,' she said. 'He never let me go back. Said we had

75

all we needed in Crawley with his people, squash club, golf club, quiz league. Jesus, what was I thinking?'

'You were thinking Crawley.' He yawned. 'I'll drink you under the table when we get back. We'll have a happy New Year.'

'I don't really like drinking. You do stupid things.' She watched a shambling pisshead in the street, stumbling in the snow. His legs went from under him, an involuntary slip. 'Just to prove my point there's some poor sod on his hands and knees out there.'

'Insulated from the inside,' said Frank from deep in the duvet.

The drunk tried and failed to get to his feet.

'He's in a right state.' She reached across to the chest of drawers and stubbed the cigarette out in a makeshift ashtray. When she looked back, the drunk had moved out of the shadows and fallen on his side. He managed to sit up and then was still for a minute, maybe longer. 'Can you die sitting up?' Adeline couldn't take her eyes off him. It was a moment before the impossibility shifted into possibility. 'Frank, this bloke …'

'Yeah?'

'He looks like Carl.'

Frank kept his voice low, his hand stroked Adeline's shoulder like he was brushing off fluff. 'He goes to casualty, no question.'

'Casualty.'

'Casualty, A and E whatever they call it. Look at the state of him.'

Carl sat shivering on the edge of the bed, the duvet around his shoulders, a pug ugly bruise under his eye, a cut over it, grazes on his face and neck and hands. He'd only made it up the hotel's back stairs with them both lifting him stair by stair. The bloke on reception took a twenty from Adeline's handbag to keep his mouth shut. Every move seemed to rip Carl's breath from him. He wouldn't let them take his shirt off and he wouldn't lay down and, so far, he'd refused hospital. 'I *can* hear you,' he said, dry voiced.

'You want a glass of water, babe?'

'Cuppa tea'd be better.'

Adeline rinsed a cup, set the kettle to boil, tore off the foil on a UHT milk sachet. 'Oh Christ, that's rank. Frank, go down to that Spar will you, this milk's got a slick on it. And get some more paracetamol, I've only got a couple left.'

The shop was closed. What were they thinking, it was two in the bloody morning. Frank took his thoughts for a walk in search of milk. The snow was barely falling. A gritting lorry belatedly sprayed its load across the street. A transit-load of police cruised by on the home run. They slowed for an eyeful, but didn't stop. So he'd be finding the nearest all-night garage without help from the law. Frank buttoned up and turned his collar to the cold, took off and let his instincts lead him. Up ahead he clocked a lad in a bloodstained shirt smoking and shivering on the corner. Frank took his hands out of his pockets as he got close. 'Bit under-dressed, mate.'

The lad moved towards him. 'Lost me coat. D'you know where Stanley Street is?'

'Can't help you son.'

'I've got an interview tomorrow, for a job.'

'In Stanley Street?'

'Nah, Stanley Street's near where me girlfriend lives, I can find my way from there. We had a row. I've got … blood …'

'I'm looking for an all night garage. You know one?'

The boy shrugged, or twitched, or shivered. It was hard to tell. 'The Shell on the main road might be all night. Might be, dunno. Couldn't lend us a tenner could ya?'

'Walk with me, son, warm yourself up a bit.'

The lad gave a sideways look.

'Or don't walk, fucked if I care. Sooner we find a garage, sooner we get a look at a map.'

'For Stanley Street, yeah. Nice one.'

The snow lay thicker as they approached the edge of town. The lad stomped along, hands shoved deep in his pockets, telling Frank the cracked narrative of his night: vodka and a few lines at his mate Skink's; beers and shots in Mixers, a club; a row with Leanne over a shit Christmas present she hadn't even wanted, and her going on about her mate Caz who'd had a gold chain from her bloke; losing his jacket – Leanne's present to him; getting knocked about by some chav bastards who were off their faces at the taxi-rank. Frank was only half listening. He'd lost himself in the certainty that Adeline had wanted him out the way. If it hadn't been milk or painkillers, it would have been something else. Against the odds, it pissed him off.

'I mean it ain't right, is it?' said the lad.

'No it isn't,' said Frank. 'You've been hard done by there, son.'

At first, they weren't certain the garage was actually open. The light inside the kiosk was dim and a couple of the forecourt lights were out over locked-off pumps, but there was definitely a body slumped over at the desk. The automatic door didn't open. The

77

lad's knock on the glass woke the attendant – a balding Asian geezer in a garish red corporate fleece. He waved them to the window, miming locking a door. The Anadin Extra and carton of semi-skimmed UHT were straightforward enough and he had a supply of late night staples and junk food essentials laid out on the counter. But persuading the guy to find a local map and then show them Stanley Street took some communicating through the Perspex. As it turned out, it wasn't far and Frank walked the lad round. He left him knocking gently at a door, whispering, 'I love you, Leanne,' through the letterbox.

On his own again with his feet feeling the chill, Frank upped the pace the best he could. His thoughts raced. Forget him and Adeline, this had to be about Carl and what he needed, and what the O'Keefes had done to him. Frank had seen James O'Keefe in the John Evelyn, short-arsed, loud-mouthed, over-playing his Mick heritage for the sheer hell of having something to justify the chip on his shoulder. Sometimes the O'Keefes had hung around in the bar after a delivery, drinking, not paying, and fucking up the evening for everyone else. Nights like that, the regulars looked to Carl, but he never came out.

Frank began to recognise the streets. The hotel was around the corner. He stepped it out. It bothered him they'd done violence to Carl. There was no need for it. They could have warned him off, maybe. But not like that. An old feeling gnawed away and Frank stopped, reminded himself Carl was not his to protect.

13

To begin with, Dave Price had been as good as his word. The first job was a straightforward pick-up. A large brown envelope from an office near Gatwick one September Saturday afternoon. Dave was along for the ride. Frank felt like he was on his driving test. They used Dave's new Ford Escort, which he made great play of claiming was as clean as a whistle. As Frank drove back up the A23 he wondered why he couldn't have taken the bloody train. The second job a couple of weeks later was more the sort of thing he'd expected. A trip over the river and a meeting in a Tottenham pub a stone's throw from White Hart Lane. Strictly opposition turf as far as Dave Price was concerned. It was a dirty, drizzly October evening, growing dark as they pulled up outside.

'Comin' in?' Dave turned the rear view to check his tie.

'Less I know the better, cheers. I'll wait here.' Frank turned off the engine and reached to the back seat for his Evening News. Price went in, but came out a few minutes later and gestured with his thumb for Frank to join him. Frank felt a sinking feeling in the pit of his stomach. He stalled a moment before turning off the radio, 'Sod this.'

Sitting quiet at a corner table flanked by a couple of handy looking blokes was a man Frank knew from the papers. Danny Georgiou was a protection and fruit machine merchant who'd come up smelling distinctly of roses when the Krays went down. In that respect he was Price's North London equal in luck and judgement – Dave having made the most of his chances when Eddie and Charlie Richardson went inside.

Frank took what he considered a respectfully distant seat at the bar and refused a drink. He said nothing for the duration, just listened to what amounted to negotiations over pubs and clubs, and reaching 'understandings'. He tried to look like he was tuned out. It would have helped if he'd brought the paper.

Price lit up a Dunhill Kingsize as soon as they were back in the car. 'Danny don't like smoking, he gets asthma. So?'

'I think he's very sensible.'

'The meeting.'

'I wasn't really listening.'

'Like fuck.'

'I don't know, Dave, I'm the bloody driver remember? I liked his cufflinks, matched his tie-clip which I also liked, they were very nice, smart.'

'Says he wants to do business.'

Frank was silent.

'D'you reckon he's serious?'

'You mean was he taking you seriously?'

Price raised an eyebrow at the distinction. 'Either.'

'I'd say no, not at first, but something you said about Eddie seemed to catch his attention, which I'm guessing is the reason why you said it. But I reckon he knows a bloody sight less about you than you think. Oh and his bloke, his *driver*, was armed so I'm guessing he doesn't exactly trust you.'

On Dave's directions they drove on through the shady wet streets of Stoke Newington and into town. The streetlights down through King's Cross threw a sickly yellow light on the girls and punters alike. 'One day they'll bulldoze the lot of this,' said Price. 'Take a left down here, I want to drive down by the river so's I can think.'

Frank had the impression that the meeting with Georgiou had been a trial run. A week later Price called him at home. 'We're over the river again tonight.'

'When?'

'Pick me up half-seven.' He hung up.

Carol asked who'd called. Frank figured she'd overheard so he told her. She turned away. 'What the bloody hell are you doing getting phone calls from a man like that?'

'He wants me to drive him, bit of cash in hand.'

'We don't need it. Tell him to get a bleedin' bus.'

'Last time, I promise. I'll tell him I'm not interested.'

Whatever Price was paying, it wasn't enough. Now Carol knew, Frank had a reason to back off, but the conversation on the way over to Tottenham didn't leave room for his resignation. Price checked the chambers of a revolver, then stuffed it in his coat pocket.

'You never could stand to be one-upped could you?'

Price ignored him.

Frank knew he should have stopped the car there and then. But at the meeting, from the moment Price invited him to the table as 'an associate' and Georgiou and his people stood to shake his hand, he was involved, like it or not.

'Kali spera, Mr Georgiou,' said Frank.

A broad smile spread across Danny Georgiou's face 'David, you brought a good guy with you. A Greek speaker.'

Frank held his hand up, 'Just a few words, phrases an' that.'

'Pos se lene?'

'Frank, Frank Neaves.'

'Come and sit Frank, let's get you a drink.'

'I'm driving.'

'Coffee then, have a coffee and we can sort this thing out, right Dave?'

Dave was stony-faced. 'Let's talk.'

'He likes you,' said Dave as they drove back across Tower Bridge. 'And I trust you. It doesn't look good if you come and go. I want you there.'

'That mean you ain't gonna shoot me?'

Price smiled. 'Can't afford to be at a disadvantage. Especially with foreigners.' The Victoria Embankment rolled by. 'It's good business we're doing with these people. Safe.'

Frank nodded, eased into Lower Thames Street.

'It's gotta be better than lackeying for some rich City tosser.'

'I'm not complaining.'

'Yeah, but this is management.'

Frank smiled.

There was a long pause.

'So, d'you want to make this a bit more formal, come on the payroll?'

'I don't think so.'

Another long silence. Frank thought about Carol.

'We can keep it quiet, Frank. I just need to know I can rely on you. Georgiou liked you, yeah?'

'Anyone else finds out, I'm gone.'

Carol was still awake when Frank got home, waiting. 'You told him?'

'Yeah.'

She put her arms around his neck, pulled him onto the bed and unbuckled his belt. 'We don't need 'em, love. Not now, eh?'

14

When Frank got back to the hotel, Carl was in bed, propped up by pillows and the spare blanket. If anything, he had a little more colour.

'We 'ad a little smoke, just to relax things, take the edge off,' said Adeline.

It seemed Carl had won the A and E argument and was staying put, for now.

'Spar was shut.' Frank put the milk and Anadin on the dressing table, dropped into the chair and wrapped his coat around himself, yawning. 'So, we going home tomorrow?'

The glance between Adeline and Carl said not. She re-lit the half-smoked joint. 'Carl wants to take Grace back.'

'Which we know, which you tried and which earned you … this.' Frank opened his hand. 'See, the thing is Carl, we came to find you and now we have. Grace is with Diane, she's alright, yeah? You gave it a go. So the best thing'd be to get you home, get your own doc to look you over, and get a decent solicitor to write to Diane and sort out some sort of access.'

'And that'd be best, would it, Frank?' He tried to lift himself higher on the pillows. 'That's what you think, your considered opinion?'

'Yes, it is.'

Adeline chipped the ash and passed the spliff to Carl. 'O'Keefe's been knocking Diane about, Frank. Grace is terrified of him. She phoned on Boxing Day begging for her dad to come and get her and take her home. We can't leave her, or Diane if she wants to come.'

'Carl, you feel shit now. Trust me, in the morning when you've had a couple of hours sleep, you'll wake up too stiff to move. If you've cracked a rib, you won't be able to walk half a dozen steps without stopping to breathe. That eye's already almost closed. You're not up to going another three rounds and is O'Keefe likely to let you have it any other way?'

A silence.

'Is he?'

'We could try,' said Adeline. 'You and me.'

'Let it go.'

'You did it for Dad,' said Carl. 'You could do it for me.'

Frank got up, threw his coat over the chair. He put the kettle on. Made a mess opening a coffee sachet, spilling half in the tray. Picked up a few granules, gave it up and opened another. He poured in the boiling water, gestured to the scotch at the bedside, 'Give us that, will you.' Adeline reached over, handed him the bottle like he was a stranger. He slugged a large one into the coffee and drank half. 'One, I don't work for you. Two, if I did, I'd be telling you the same thing. Three, I'm thirty years older and stupider and slower. People say never regret anything. Bollocks. Regret what it's right to regret. And with all due respect, I do seriously regret ever getting involved with your father. And you're out of order bringing it up.'

Suddenly, the room felt crowded.

Adeline got up. 'I'm going for a walk, this is way over my head.'

Carl raised his hand. 'Please, stay.'

She excused her way past Frank, shoving him aside anyway, then edged round to the window, folded her arms and looked out.

'My dad was a smart bloke.'

Frank gave a tight little laugh.

Carl didn't push it further, but Frank could see him stirring up ghosts and re-framing them. He had every right to smooth off the edges. His voice choked a little. 'Frank, this isn't me, is it. Look at me. I can't even talk to these people. I've got no – no *status*. They don't respect me. I need some help.'

Frank nodded. 'Agreed. From a solicitor.'

'From *you*.'

Adeline chipped in acidly, 'Don't you fancy giving your street cred a boost, Frank?'

'Which fucking street's that then? Carl, they ain't gonna respect me I'll tell you that for nothing. For a start they'll 'ave seen me propping up your bloody bar.'

Adeline exploded. 'Jesus Christ, Frank, put yourself out for once. Come out of Frankworld. This pisshead self-pity, it's ... it's boring. It's like you're in quarantine in that pub. Ever since we left it's like you can't wait to get back there. He's asking you to help. Just pull your head out of your arsehole and go and speak to the bloke. If you don't I will.'

Frank refreshed the cup, scotch only this time. He held it in both hands. His finger tapped a rhythm gently on the handle. Carl closed his good eye, the other was barely more than a slit. He might even have dozed for a couple of minutes as his breathing grew steadily deeper, but then he coughed himself awake. At the curtain Adeline watched a seedy corner of the world go by and fingered a drawn game of noughts and crosses in the window condensation. It was as if the room had sucked up their energy, absorbed it into its shitty furniture and threadbare pastel fabrics. There were no arguments left.

Frank whispered, 'I'll go in the morning. Carl stays here.'

The following morning, Adeline took herself into a betting shop to keep warm while Frank went in search of a map, train times and tickets. She'd grown up with a steady stream of her dad's gamblers' logic and wayward justifications for the hours he spent in Baldwin's, the High Street turf accountant – *Bookies are the working man's library* he'd say. *I'm off to study.*

Adeline claimed a corner and read the form for the afternoon's races. There was no harm in putting on a few quid for the old man's sake, but she couldn't find anything on the English card that looked worth a few quid. She felt the carpet under her feet, the warmth of the place creeping into her toes – that was different from the patchwork lino of the old days. She processed runners, riders, numbers, comparing form the way Dad taught her. If it thawed, the going would make the distance a right slog; if it didn't, chances were most of the meetings would be off anyway. She ran her finger down the list again, gave it up and moved to the Irish card at Leopardstown, scanning the Racing Post pages pinned to the wall, the betting slip under her thumb. On a day like this she needed a winner, a stayer.

She sensed someone behind her. Frank stood for a moment. 'We're sorted. I got hold of a map.'

'Did you get tickets?'

'We're sorted.'

The pen hovered over the slip. She couldn't write with Frank watching over her shoulder. 'Just give us a minute, let me do this.'

'What for?'

'For the hell of it,' she said.

'I'll wait outside then, don't hang about. Oh, and I'd have a look at *Tipsy's Kiss* in the two-fifteen if I was you.'

'Thanks. And you're not me.' She held on to the moment, hearing Dad's voice. *You wait outside love, shan't be a tick – I'll put one on for you.* He'd come out and make her look after the betting slip. Then when she was older and there was no money for new shoes, school bags, dinner, the gas meter, and Mum'd had enough of trawling charity shops for clothes, he'd kicked the habit – nearly. *Thing is love, places like this soak into you, so whatever happens you still think you can throw your bad luck over the counter, turn it good, but you can't.*

There were whispers as she got to the counter to place the bet. A bloke with last night's grubby A and E dressing unstuck and flapping over one eye stopped chewing on the end of his pen and looked up.

'I'll take the board price,' Adeline said. 'What time d'you close?'

The counter-hand, an anaemic looking woman with split fingernails, took the cash and nodded to the Christmas and New Year opening times on the door. She handed over the slip.

Frank was waiting. He took her arm and propelled her towards a parked Ford Focus. There was a *B&D Motors of Newark* £1895 price card on the back seat.

'Trains are still up the creek,' said Frank. 'Get in.'

'You stole it?'

'Get in.'

She hesitated.

'Alright, don't get in. Station's that way, best of luck.'

She got in. Frank produced a key and with a few sharp movements over the ignition, the engine turned over. He looked over his right shoulder as they reversed enough to make it out into the traffic in one easy sweep. They accelerated, Frank taking the revs up before changing gear. He drove steady, fast but not flash. Easy and in control.

'Thought you said you couldn't drive.'

'I said I *didn't* drive. Now I do.'

She folded the betting slip and handed it to him. 'Can you look after this for me. It's bad luck if I keep it.'

'Might be worse luck if you don't.'

'Then I'll just have to take my chances won't I?'

ROUND TWO

15

On the mornings he went to work for Dave Price, Frank always took extra care not to wake Carol. She seemed to find a way of posing awkward questions and leaving a lie as the only way out. He dragged on a cigarette, balanced it on the ashtray and knotted his tie, one of three Pierre Cardin silk stripes in different colours he'd bought from Selfridges at the weekend. The first time he'd ever gone further than Monty Burton's in the High Street. He turned his shirt collar over – a crisp white double-cuff Van Heusen – made final adjustments to the knot, slipped his suit jacket on and spoke to the mirror, 'So Frank, tell me, where did it all go wrong?'

Dave had told him to make it smart: *look the business to do the business.* Frank needed no second bidding. He pulled his shirt cuff down so there was an inch or two showing under the suit sleeve, the flash of a gold link.

He went downstairs, made Carol's cup of tea and put it on the bedside table with the saucer on top. Her hair, fine and dark-blonde, fanned across the pillow. He risked kissing her lightly on the cheek. She didn't stir and he closed the door quietly behind him.

As Frank pulled in, Dave was waiting on the pavement outside the house, tapping at his watch. He got in and put his briefcase on the back seat. 'I said seven-thirty.'

'Which is what it is.'

'I make it twenty-five to.'

'You want to synchronise watches or what?'

Dave gave him a sideways look. If he wanted things timed to the second, Frank could do that. If Dave wanted military precision, a soldier in a suit and tie, he could do that too.

They made slow progress along Tooley Street and across London Bridge. A steady flow of human traffic moved densely together then scattered into the City's narrow streets and alleys. Dave punched buttons on the radio, listening for a minute then changing his mind. That didn't bother Frank half as much as when he clocked the gun again in Price's waistband. 'D'you want to cover that up? Only wants a copper to look in.'

'And stare at my cock.'

'You know what I mean.' Frank sliced through the backstreets, avoiding the Holborn traffic.

'Just concentrate on getting us there on time.'

This was to be their last face to face with Danny Georgiou – Dave had taken to calling him 'Gorgeous'. They were en route for Hampstead and another open-air meeting for the sake of the Greek's nerves. Over the winter, two of his people, one his wife's nephew, had been arrested and he'd convinced himself all sorts of spooks were listening into his conversations. He reckoned the Flying Squad or Special Branch or MI5 had him marked down as their next big target. Dave said he was kidding himself, but went along with holding meetings in open spaces to keep him sweet. They'd walked in Alexandra Park in November, drunk frothy coffee from a Borough Market caff just before Christmas. A one-off as it turned out – Gorgeous complained about having to come south of the river. Frank hadn't minded. He'd come to like the bloke and you couldn't fault him for taking precautions. This last meeting was planned for Hampstead Heath. It was a bright March morning. A nice day out, as Dave put it.

As they hit clear road on Haverstock Hill, Dave issued instructions. 'Stay close today Frank, just keep yourself sharp. Christ knows he's taken his time deciding, but I've got a feeling he'll want more, just at the point you think you've got it done. You know what I mean, just squeeze us a bit harder. Well I'm not having it. It's ten grand and sorted. That's all I've got, that's all he's getting.'

They drove into the car park of Jack Straw's Castle, just on the fringes of the Heath. Dave made some lame comment about bare arses and maybe Gorgeous had his own pitch booked on the Heath. Frank was hardly listening. The Greeks would be waiting across the road in a clearing between the trees, out of sight of the passing traffic.

There were introductions and greetings. Georgiou had his boys with him, the same two silent types who'd been there every time, plus one other – a squat silver-haired geezer in a Gabicci top, smart suit and handmade shoes. He was new.

'This is my Uncle Costas. He's here to make sure I do good business.'

Uncle Costas flicked a cigarette from a Disque-Bleu soft pack. One of the lads stepped forward and lit it for him.

It was staged. Frank knew it from the off. Just as Dave said, they got to the point where all there was left was the deal-closing handshake and Uncle Costas piped up – in Greek. Frank caught, 'Po so ka nei?'

'It's ten grand, as agreed,' said Frank.

Georgiou's boys tensed a little, fingers flexed, shoulders squared.

Uncle Costas said something else, Frank didn't understand.

Georgiou translated. 'David, Frank, my uncle must have the final say on this, and he thinks perhaps, because you will be making ten times this money in the next three, four years, we could do a little better. Another couple of thousand, a goodwill gesture. Just to seal things.'

Dave paused, turned to Frank, 'What'd I tell ya?'

Frank shrugged. He thought they had a point, a sweetener wouldn't go amiss all things considered.

'Mr Georgiou, you can tell your uncle I just don't see it that way. We've been pissing about for months and now we've agreed ten grand. That's what I've got here. That's how we do business. You want it or not?' Aside to Frank, but loud enough, he said, 'Old man's a fucking peasant.'

Uncle said something and one of the boys made a move, his hand went to his pocket. Frank was closest and went for the arm, locked it behind him and reached in his pocket, pulled out an automatic. 'No need for that son.' Dave had levelled his gun point blank at Uncle Costas's forehead.

'You want the deal, or not?'

Frank turned the radio off and drove in silence. The briefcase was on Dave's lap. He was in surprisingly good spirits, flicking through one of the stacks of ten pound notes. 'Well that was a complete waste of time, weren't it?'

Frank said nothing.

'I mean, what does he gain out of that, tell me? He's got pubs and clubs he can't handle, fruit machines spilling cash he can't collect and he knows he hasn't got what it takes to keep 'em. Jesus, we could have taken them off his hands, looked after 'em and he'd still make a load, no risk.'

'He'll come back, give it a few weeks to settle.'

'Nah, bollocks. I'll find another way. I can walk in and take 'em anytime.' He paused. 'I was right about you though, keeping on the level. My lads would have turned that into a bloodbath.'

'No need, Dave.'

'And I liked the thing with the bloke lighting his cigarette though, how comes you don't do that for me?'

Frank stared ahead. 'Cos that would make me a bit of a cunt.'

Dave started a laugh somewhere deep in his belly. Every time he looked at Frank keeping a straight face, the laugh grew until Frank couldn't help himself either and had to pull the car over.

Dave said he wanted to drop the money off at Jacqui's. Frank didn't ask questions. On their first drive past a couple of coppers were dealing with a car smash, looked like a Mini had pulled out on an old Hillman Minx. It was all shattered headlights, bent wheel arches, notebooks out and serious faces. Frank drove on and parked a few streets away. There wasn't a lot of chat as they walked back.

The faint whiff of vinegar mixed with the usual soap-powder and damp pants smell suggested Jacqui had been to the chip shop. She came out of the back room, wiping her hands on a tea towel. 'I wasn't expecting you.'

'No, well, I wasn't expecting to be here.' Dave closed the door behind them.

'Problems?'

'Nah, we're alright. Things didn't go as planned so ...?' He thumbed in the direction of upstairs.'

'Help yourself.'

Frank shoved his hands in his pockets.

'Wait here,' said Dave, and disappeared through the office. They heard him take the stairs two at a time.

'Want a cup of tea?'

As well as the usual Friday afternoon liaisons, it seemed Jacqui's served as a drop off for whatever Dave couldn't or wouldn't take home. 'How long's he likely to be?'

'Long enough. He'll probably just make himself at home. He's got this thing for bacon and egg sandwiches and Rose doesn't let him have 'em.'

Frank gave a quizzical look.

Jacqui shrugged and led him into the office. There was a kettle, half a pint of milk on a small fridge. A newspaper was open on the table along with the last few chips in their wrapper. 'What can I say, if he wants his bacon and eggs here, he can 'ave 'em.' She screwed up the chip paper and tossed it in the bin. 'Dave's kids call me Auntie Chips. Rose brings 'em round sometimes on a Friday after school so's she can get an evening out with his lordship. Not so often these days, I s'pose they're getting a bit older now.'

The kettle boiled. As she poured, Jacqui pulled her hair behind her ear inadvertently revealing a pale scar, a thin line that ran from under her hairline across her neck. Frank wondered how she'd earned it, but couldn't bring himself to ask. The hair fell forward. Dave's voice could be heard upstairs.

'Who's he talking to?'

'He's on the phone.'

Frank tried to listen, but one of the washers went into its spin cycle and made ear-wigging impossible. Jacqui smiled. 'Trust me, you're better off not knowing.' She put the mug of tea down in front of him and sat the other side of the table. 'Dave's talked about you.'

'Has he?'

There was a long silence. She laughed. 'You are allowed to ask, or don't you want to know?'

'It's between you and Dave.'

'Fair enough.'

Another long silence.

'So what went wrong this morning?'

Frank smiled. 'That's between *me* and Dave.'

'I've known him for years, Frank. We're old friends and he trusts me and he trusts you. He's changed since you've been around, for the better. Not so edgy, y'know, a bit more thoughtful about things. I've got nothing to do with his business other than having a safe upstairs that he uses once in a blue moon. Now *I* trust you, so what happened this morning?'

When Dave came downstairs. There was egg yolk on his shirt. Jacqui sponged it off. 'For Pete's sake, Dave, how old are you?'

He smiled like a ten year old.

Back in the car he opened the glove compartment and tossed in half a dozen or so folded tenners. 'Call it a consolation prize.'

Frank looked over. 'How do I explain that to Carol?'

'You don't. Or you could tell her you've been selling your arse on Hampstead Heath.'

Frank wondered whether that might be preferable to the truth.

16

Adeline was hungry so they pulled in for a mug of tea and a bacon roll. The lay-by snack wagon flew the Polish flag alongside a tattered St George's Cross. Frank hadn't wanted to risk parking up in a service station, not that B&D Motors were likely to miss the car from their forecourt until New Year, by which time he'd have it back. It was too cold to eat at the roadside so they got back in the car and ate in silence. When they'd finished, he slow-walked the length of the lay-by to chuck the rubbish in a bin, taking in the traffic. One lane, slow and steady, the other coned off for broken down and abandoned vehicles.

They'd been back on the road for a couple of slow miles. 'Under the circumstances,' said Frank, 'D'you want to forget what happened or didn't happen last night, what we said?'

'Under the circumstances, yes.'

A three-mile silence.

'Adeline. Don't think I've ever met anyone called Adeline.'

She licked a ketchup spot off her finger. 'It's not my real name.'

'I gathered. So if not Adeline, what?'

'Hasn't it occurred to you that by changing my name I've made an effort to get rid of the old one? Can we talk about something else?'

The next silence was interrupted by intermittent local radio squawk. Until then the radio had been obstinately knackered. Flat vowel sounds crackled and *The Fairytale of New York* went out to Sez and Alex in Rotherham for a few bars then went dead. Frank turned it off, then on. Nothing. 'Loose connection. Remind me to have a word with the manager when we take it back.'

No response.

'You really not going to tell me?'

'What?'

'If not Adeline ...' Frank whistled between his teeth. At the roadside, two trashed cars, bent and ditched. One on its roof, burnt paintwork, melted tyres and chips of windscreen glass in the road. 'Doris? Daisy? Peggy-Sue? Sammy-Lee? Penelope? Norman?'

'Piss off.'

'Tyson? Whiskers? Butch?'

She folded her arms. 'It's Brenda, that's all. Plain old Brenda.'

'Nothing wrong with that, s'a good name. It's a—'

'A fat name, alright? The name I had at school. And it's the name the husband and my outlaws insisted on calling me, which is another reason I can't stand it. "Is Brenda coming to dinner? Why doesn't Brenda come shopping in town? Brenda was a bit miserable today. Gordon, tell Brenda we'd like her to make a bit of an effort to look smart this time." I got hauled over the coals after that one, for being a less than perfect wife. So, Brenda is my real name.' She clicked the radio on-off, on-off again.

'Why Adeline? Come on I'm interested.'

'You never know when to leave it alone do you?' She waited a few moments, took a deep breath. 'When I was about fourteen I was big, really overweight. At school and out of school I was Big Brenda, Buxom Brenda, Brenda Balloon, Bren gun, Brendover it's a total eclipse – and it went on, I had years of it. I started smoking and starved myself sick to get somewhere near a size twelve, but I still copped a packet every time I saw someone from the old days. Still Big Brenda.'

Frank slowed, 'Get a look at that road sign, just make sure we're on the right road.'

'Yeah, we're fine. Goole, Scunthorpe, Hull. So this one Sunday, I must have been about nineteen and I'd been waiting for me mates to pick me up to go out and they didn't show, which wasn't unusual. Dad came in my room, just put his hand on my shoulder and gave me a tatty paperback book. See, he used to like those old western novels. He'd find them in charity shops or jumble sales. And when he'd finished, he'd pass them to me and I'd read them and we'd have something to talk about. And when we got a video player, we used to watch films, old westerns, John Wayne, James Stewart, Robert Mitchum. Don't look at me like that.'

'Like what?'

'Like you just pictured me in cowboy boots and a Stetson.'

He risked a smile.

'So my mates didn't turn up and I read the book. It was called *Sweet Shootin' Adeline* and she was like a Calamity Jane type character. Pretty, but deadly when crossed. So I took the name, cut my hair, dyed it blonde, bought some new clothes. My mates all thought I'd flipped or gone butch but I didn't care.'

'So now you're Adeline.'

'S'right.'

'Sweet Shootin' Adeline.'

For a few miles the traffic picked up speed. There was distance between the daytime tail-lights until the wide open spaces, muddy fields and snow-dripping trees gave way to the city's outskirts. As the daylight faded, they slowed through suburbs into narrow terrace-lined backstreets. Pulling up at a red light, Frank shook his head, 'You have to wonder ...'

'Sorry Frank, you have to wonder what?'

'What on earth possessed Diane to leave home, shack up with a bloke like O'Keefe, put her kid through all this bollocks. This ain't her home, is it? I mean, look at it.'

'Green light.' It was raining. Adeline rubbed the window mist away with her sleeve, watched wet streets and shabby shuttered shop fronts pass by. 'She probably wanted something better.'

'Northern rain instead of London rain.'

They were through the city and out into the suburbs. Adeline looked back. 'Is that it?'

Frank cruised past O'Keefe's house, checked the address and clocked the BMW in the drive as Carl had said. Adeline had flatly rejected his first plan for what next – her to go in, play the sympathy card and soften him up. She refused point blank to go anywhere near the man. 'He hates me, remember, thinks I'm some evil pox-ridden harlot.'

'P'raps you remind him of his mother.'

'Whatever, I'm not going. You go. I'll wait in the car.'

He drove round the block one more time and pulled in. He walked up the drive, planted one foot on the step and pressed the bell.

O'Keefe came to the door looking like shit warmed up. There was a yellowness to his complexion, unshaven for a day, but with tufts of three or four day bristle around his chin. His eyes set deep, bloodshot, shadowed. His checked shirt, partly unbuttoned, gaped at the belly. Frank offered his hand.

O'Keefe ignored it. 'Who the fuck are you?'

'My name's Frank. Carl Price asked me to come and sort out this misunderstanding that happened yesterday. I wondered if we could have a chat?'

O'Keefe shook his head, 'And you're what, Dad's Army? Jesus, he's a bigger prick than I reckoned. No we can't have a chat. There's nothing to chat about.'

As he went to close the door, Frank stepped up. 'That's what I told him. I told him, I said, "Carl, you'll never get anywhere just dropping in on the man, you need to do these things properly." But he's taken it, y'know, not so well with the kid. Christmas an' that. Look, it ain't gonna cost you anything, just give me two minutes and I can at least go back and say we spoke, right? Don't make a liar of me. As a favour. Come on mate, it's Christmas.'

O'Keefe might well have told Frank to piss off, which was pretty much what his body language was conveying, but at that moment he put his hand to his mouth and disappeared into the house. The door swung back in time for Frank to see him dive out of sight into a downstairs room. It also brought Diane into view down the hall to the kitchen. Frank stepped in, carefully avoiding pre-puke spatters on the mat. He nodded. Diane seemed not to recognise him. He heard Grace calling, 'I've finished, Mum, what do I do now?'

Diane wiped her hands on a cloth. 'Be with you in a minute, sweetheart. Just roll it out nice and thin.'

O'Keefe was retching. Frank pointed to the living room. Diane nodded. He went in. The telly was on, an Alka Seltzer ad, holiday ad, then a monotone commentary over a race meeting. He walked to the window, waved to Adeline who sank down in the Focus's passenger seat.

Diane came in, 'You want a cup of tea or something?'

'No, love. I doubt I'll be staying.' He kept his voice low. Knockabout bruises were visible under her make-up. 'Carl asked me to come – for Grace, you as well if you want. Take you home.'

Di's hands worked, twisting the tea towel. 'I don't think so.'

'No strings, he just wants to spend time with Grace. Carl's worried, Di.'

'I know. Is he alright?'

The toilet flushed.

'He'll be fine. Just say and we can go.'

'It ain't that easy.'

O'Keefe came in carrying a pint of water. 'She wants you in the kitchen.' Diane left the room and he turned his attention to Frank. 'Look, can y'just piss off. I'm ill. Tell him he's not seeing his kid,

96

tell him they left him and they're not coming back. There y'go, we've chatted. You don't have to lie.'

'Oh he knows that, Mr O'Keefe. It's for his mum really. Have you ever met Rose? She's not got long and seeing her grand-kid for the New Year's been keeping her going. I think that's probably the thing that drove the lad to come up and see you like he did. I know he regrets it.'

'Too right he regrets it. Y'seen him?'

'Yeah, I've seen him.'

'So what d'you make of that?'

Frank shrugged, 'It's not for me to make anything Mr O'Keefe. It's not my place to judge what goes on between people. I could, with your permission of course, just take Grace down with me today, bring her back tomorrow. You could have a bit of time to yourselves and—'

O'Keefe was looking out the window. 'Who's that?'

'What?'

'In your car, is that *him*?'

'No, she's a friend along for the ride, keep me company.'

He put the water down, some sloshed on the table. 'A woman?'

'Yeah.'

'Who?'

Adeline's reluctance to go face to face with O'Keefe made him hesitate. 'Her name's Brenda.'

'Bring her in. I want to see her.'

'She's—'

'Bring her or we're finished here.'

As Frank went to the car, he felt O'Keefe's fuckwit stare at his back. Adeline wound the window down. The radio was on, a sports commentary. 'You got it working then, the radio. Look, he wants to see you.'

'No way. He'll flip.' Her hands gripped the seat.

'Come on, I reckon he might let us work this. If we can get Grace away, Diane'll have no problem getting past him. He just wants to see who I've got with me. I'm close to a result, I know it.'

She tutted, 'Me and you both. It's a bad idea, Frank. Trust me.'

'For fucksake, I'm here 'cos you wanted me to come, all that bollocks you spun last night about getting off my arse, so will you just get off yours?' He stood back, waited as she opened the door. 'Don't show me up.'

He heard her feet drag behind him up the drive. 'We're screwed, you do know that?'

Frank led them back into the living room where O'Keefe was still staring out the window. 'I thought it was you. Got some front y'fucking bitch.' He looked at Adeline, then at Frank. 'You made a mistake. Your mate Price made a mistake, *is* a fucking mistake. And anything *she's* involved in is a total fucking mistake. It's worth shit to me.'

Frank took a full hit of O'Keefe's vomit-stink breath and swallowed. 'All I'm asking is just let the little girl see her Nan.'

'Leave, now.'

'We'll bring her back tomorrow.'

'Go, or I will lose my temper. And on the way back to the shithole you crawled from, get her to tell you why yous were never gonna take that little girl back, even though I know it's the right thing to do.'

Adeline glanced behind Frank, trying to catch a glimpse of the TV.

O'Keefe's voice went up an octave. 'Are yous watching my telly? I don't believe you. You piss-taking slag. You people, come up here and fuck up my Christmas.' O'Keefe pulled the plug. The screen died. 'Get out.' He moved towards Adeline, his hand raised.

Frank put himself between them. 'Alright mate, we're going.' There was a push at his back as he was half out the door. He stumbled, but kept his feet. The door slammed behind him. Halfway down the street a dog-walker looked up as O'Keefe went full volume from inside the house, gabbling like a Smithfield auctioneer. Frank steadied, straightened his coat and walked back down the drive without looking back.

Adeline dropped into the passenger seat. He started the engine. The radio came to life. Tipsy's Kiss came in at 18-1 and Frank had the sure and certain feeling he'd backed a wrong 'un.

They parked on the almost empty fourth floor of a car park in Hull city centre and sat in silence for five minutes. Frank had no recollection of the drive there, just the burning sensation in his gut and a vague knowledge that where the road had been signposted back south, he hadn't taken it. 'So?'

'So what?' Adeline sniffed.

'So what next?'

She shrugged. 'Dunno.'

'Oh you *should* know, Brenda. You should have that well covered. A woman with your gift for foresight should be looking way down the road. Three, four moves ahead.'

'Don't call me that.'

'See, what we've got as far as I can see is you chasing after Carl who's walked into Christ knows what. I've got no idea what this is about for you, but it's got sod all to do with Diane and Grace has it?'

'It has for Carl.'

'But not you.'

'Not really.'

'*So?*'

The explanation was a long time coming. At first there were fragments. Half stories and names remembered that made no sense. It took them from the car park down to a cafe called McCoys, a couple of rounds of cappucino and a warm room and eventually she told him.

The husband, her husband – she bit back from saying his name – had taken his young fiancée from her home and married her, never once hiding his belief that he had pulled her from the gutter-life of her upbringing and she ought to be thankful. And she, back to being plain Brenda again, the boots and buckskin fringed jackets packed away, was duly grateful. So that when he chose her new clothes, her new friends, and started to dish out an allowance and demand receipts, she smiled and kidded herself it was a kind of love. An unkind kind of love.

Adeline blew gently across her coffee cup. 'One night after a dinner party he accused me of flirting with one of the blokes from his work. I was a bit drunk, not hammered, just ... relaxed. When everyone had gone, he started. Then he hit me, he'd never done it before. Just a slap, really. But he must have liked it because he did it again a couple of weeks later, and again, and again. He never really beat me up ... we never had those balls-out domestics blokes like O'Keefe dish out. This was a slap here, or a sharp word when we were in company to let me know I'd stepped out of line and he'd be dealing with it later at home. Sometimes he did and other times I'd be waiting, dreading the moment we got through the door and no more would be said.' She laughed. 'I'd be so relieved, I'd make him cocoa and toast, do the whole perfect wife thing.'

'You never thought of getting away?'

'How could I? Where? What to? You don't understand ... I had *nothing*. He used to buy me cookery books – Jamie Oliver, Gordon Ramsay, Gary Rhodes – whoever was on the telly at the time and tell his friends it was my new hobby. And I'd cook him these meals to taste first and he'd have a mouthful and push his plate away. I'd get myself so worked up at dinnertime I couldn't bring myself to eat with him, so I'd save a bit to eat in the kitchen later. And then I stopped bothering and he'd ask why wasn't I eating? I'd say it was because I didn't have much of an appetite. And he'd say he wasn't surprised with the shit I was cooking and tip his plate over the tablecloth.' She shrugged. 'That's what I was living with, Frank, day in, day out. First time in my life I was thin, living with him. It ... it reduced me in ways I never knew. No-one knew what it was like, not my family, maybe some of our friends had an idea, but they didn't give a damn, they were his friends anyway.'

'What was it made you leave in the end?'

A memory played across her face as the waitress cleared away the cups. She choked back and looked away, shaking her head. Then she left the table and was gone for some time. Frank looked around, took in the mud and mocha walls and dusty artificial greenery. When Adeline came back, composed, the story was straight.

'I got pregnant and I never told him. And one day he slapped me, caught me off balance and I fell awkwardly and I had to go to hospital and all the way there I knew something was wrong and ... when I got home, he knew. One of the doctors told him and that was it really. Next time he went out I got away with nothing except a bag with a few bits and pieces, some clothes an' that. I knew Carl a bit, used to know his brother Terry more. So that's where I went and he helped me. Him and Diane let me stay over a couple of nights and he subbed me a month's deposit on a flat. And he gave me a job. But you can't live on that, can you? Not barmaid's wages. Not these days.'

Frank nodded.

'So when the O'Keefes turned up and I realised that Adam was doing a bit more than dropping off the Schweppes, I made a point of talking to him. Once I got to know him, he asked me to sell the odd bit of blow and whatever on his behalf. I'd got to a point where I didn't feel like I could turn it down.' She bit her lip, tried to gauge his reaction, but he gave nothing. 'So I did it, Frank. It was just between me and him, a sideline. Never anything more than a bit of hash and a few pills, just Saturday night keep-me-ups, y'know.'

Frank nodded. 'Sold over the bar.'

'No, not over the bar, round the back. Carl never knew. I felt like I was letting him down as it was, but Adam reckoned there were half a dozen other punters who'd do it for him if I didn't. At least that way, I knew what was going on. I could make sure it didn't get out of hand.'

'Looking after Carl's best interests.'

'Yeah, I guess.'

'And you and Adam?'

There was a long pause. 'Deep down I always felt it could so bite me on the arse. Thing is, Adam O'Keefe's not the brightest, so I was upping prices by a couple of quid, then flogging stuff to some of the smart lot that started coming in the pub. And it was around the time I got that other job waitressing at that new bistro place in Greenwich, remember?'

Another nod.

'For them sort of people it's way safer than taking a chance with some backstreet dealer. I'm safe and they don't mind paying a bit over the odds. Sometimes a lot over the odds if you're in the right place at the right time. But I never passed on the extra cash to O'Keefe. It went straight in my pocket. It was alright for a while, six months, a year maybe, then Adam started coming onto me. I knocked him back two, three times. Then brother James overheard this argument we had, stuck his oar in. I don't know what pissed him off most, that Adam was dealing and he hadn't been in on it. Or that I'd broken his idiot little brother's heart and he was making a prick of himself.'

Frank raised an eyebrow.

Her voice rose. 'That's what James said. It was bollocks, but that's what he's like. All moral and dramatic when it suits him. Anyway it got very spiteful, really ripping into each other, and James said using me was spoiling a good business thing they had going and Ewan'd be really pissed off. Adam just laughed and said what about him carrying on with Diane behind Carl's back? So I knew. Before Carl, before anyone. And I kept it to myself. I had to, otherwise ...' She tailed off and met Frank's eyes pleading for a reaction.

He sat in silence trying to make sense. 'How much did you make?'

'In all, about ten grand.'

He nodded. The café hadn't seen a fresh customer for a good twenty minutes. The waitress and one remaining girl behind the counter had washed up, swept up and mopped up around them. Frank sniffed, pushed his hands deep in his pockets and leaned forward. 'It's late, we'd better go. You need to give Carl a ring, let him know we blew it.'

'We can't just go home and leave it like that Frank. It's all fucked up.'

'It was that before I ever got involved, love. It sounds as though O'Keefe had nothing to lose.'

'You think I should have told Carl about Diane?'

Frank shrugged. 'You could have done him that courtesy.'

She shoved a stroppy arm in her jacket. 'And you sit on your arse at the end of that bar watching the world go by. Mr see-all, know-all, do-nothing. Would you have told him the truth?'

'Maybe.' Frank said goodnight to the counter girl as he walked out, leaving Adeline behind. He felt the biting rain like a smack in the face. Adeline came out and slipped on the wet step, ending up on one knee, her ankle twisted. She yelped in pain. He stalled for a moment before he went to help her up. She threw his arm away.

'Piss off.'

He left her in the street as the lights in McCoys went out behind them. He walked and wanted to keep on walking.

17

In the weeks after the failed meeting with Georgiou, Dave's calls became more frequent. Usually he wanted to talk, chat like old mates. More and more Frank was treated like a trusted adviser, with Dave making him feel like he had the inside track, a knowledge that none of the others had.

What Frank knew he had was insight. He could read people, suss out their motives, and because he wasn't involved in the shadier parts of Dave's little world, he had nothing to lose or gain by being honest. They took to meeting early mornings before work, in caffs usually. Or over lunch in Manzies in the High Street, or Blooms, which was handy for Frank as he could nip down from work on his lunch break.

As far as Frank could tell, Carol never knew. As time went on, keeping it from her became less a big deal for him. Dave wasn't taking liberties with his time; they were discreet, and the occasions he had to spin a white lie were rare. He came and went and Carol was none the wiser. Only Wally Patch of Dave's usual crew knew about their arrangement and Frank made sure their paths crossed as little as possible, taking Carol out to country pubs in Chislehurst and Bromley rather than the rat-holes the boys called home. For the most part he lived comfortably with the arrangement, but occasionally his conscience pricked. He succumbed to an attack of the guilts one night, when a pissed-up Dave had him cornered in some private drinking dive just off the Old Kent Road, spilling his own guilt and self-recrimination on everything from his failings as a dad and husband to how Georgiou had taken the piss and how he'd let him off too lightly. Stone cold sober, Frank wasn't in the mood to humour him. 'For what it's worth, I reckon you missed a trick there. That was a deal worth doing.'

'You saying I screwed it up?'

'I'm saying if you don't do it, someone else will.'

'Ah, bollocks.'

Dave announced he was off for a piss and stumbled out the back. When he sat down again he said, 'He would have to come to me, and it would be the same money on the table, maybe a grand more. I can't see him going for that, can you?'

Frank nodded, 'Leave it with me.'

A couple of weeks later, Dave got a call from Georgiou. Frank got the call from Dave straight after. 'You'd have thought we were best mates. He's up for it, wants to put it back together.'

They met over steak and chips at the Tower Hotel and shook hands on the deal. Frank wondered if Dave even remembered their conversation. If he did it was never mentioned.

To celebrate, Dave took Frank to this place he'd become a member of in the West End, a not altogether legitimate Mayfair casino, the sort of sleazy pit that sold over-priced booze and welcomed punters with cut glass accents and cash to burn. He called it The Zoo and something about the down-market fucked-upness of the place appealed to him.

They had a good dinner. Dave was pouring the wine and chatting about old times. Afterwards, as they stood at the bar, he asked Frank to join him on a more permanent basis.

'What, pack in work? I couldn't. Anyway, what's wrong with the way things are?'

Dave stacked a pile of five quid chips in four columns on the bar in front of him. He evened them up. 'But I could really do with you onside on the inside.'

'I am onside.'

'More involved, you know what I'm saying.'

A bloke, late forties, booze-flushed complexion, blue velvet jacket and matching bow-tie, swaggered up and threw his arm around Dave's shoulder. 'Now then young David, are we going to be taking a slice of your ill-gotten gains this evening?' The accent was plummy and slurred. The atmosphere suddenly grew tense and Frank noticed a few heads turning in their direction.

Dave peeled the hand off his shoulder. 'So speaks a pillar of the aristocracy. Frank, this is James Weatherall, his family owns half of Dorset, or less depending how long he's been here. James, I want to introduce Frank Neaves, a friend and associate. Frank keeps me honest.'

'Ah, and one finds so few of those sort these days.'

'You'll be looking in the wrong places, then.' Dave slung the ice around his glass and downed his drink.

'Quite. Well, yes, I do hope you'll be joining us for a few hands later, Mr Neaves. David did rather well out of us on his last visit.' He raised a beckoning finger to the barman who supplied a large cognac.

Dave put his glass on the bar. 'Frank's not a gambler, are you Frank?'

'Not at these kind of odds.'

'Well, if you do change your mind, I recommend baccarat.' Weatherall took a sniff of his drink before weaving a surprisingly precise path between the tables.

Frank picked up the conversation. 'I wouldn't be here with you if Carol weren't down at her mum's for the weekend. She trusts me and I promised. All those years when I was posted overseas, she waited. That's a big deal. I think the world of her and the money and ... these places, I can take or leave it.'

'Oh, cheers. Well you can just sod off down the Black Horse for a pie and a pint next time.'

'You know what I mean. I appreciate it, it's a good night out, but I'm not bothered about it. I don't need it.'

'And you reckon I do?'

'I'm serious. If it came to a choice between Carol finding out and me having to stop being involved, I would have to back off.'

Dave slid two of the stacks of chips across the bar. 'Well before you skip back to your slippers, see if you can spend that. And stay away from the baccarat, that table's bent as a nine bob note and so is Weatherall.'

Frank didn't play baccarat and he didn't lose. Keeping to relatively low value bets on the wheel he managed to come out about eighty quid up. He cashed in and on the way back home in the car he gave Price back his original stake.

'It's yours.'

'Nah, mate. I didn't earn it.'

A week later, on Sunday evening, Frank got a phone call. It was Dave and there was a stiffness in his tone from the off. 'Time to start earning. I need you Friday night.'

Frank pulled the living room door to, muting the sound of the telly. Carol was well into *Upstairs Downstairs*. He kept his voice steady, conversational. 'It's gonna be difficult this week, can't someone else drive?'

105

'Yeah, they could. And if all I needed was a lift, I could get a bloody cab. Meet me tomorrow morning first thing and I'll explain. Luigi's in Smithfield, you know it?'

'Yeah, I know it.'

'There at seven.'

The line went dead.

Frank hung up. He slumped back in the sofa more heavily than he'd intended.

'Everything alright?'

'Yeah, well, no, as it goes, it was Denise. Schiller wants an early pick up from Oxford.'

Carol glanced at the clock on the mantelpiece. 'Not like Denise to leave it this late on a Sunday night.'

'She says he's been entertaining this weekend, only just looked at his diary for the week and something's lined up he wasn't expecting. He wants to be in first thing, you know what he's like.' Frank put an arm around her shoulders and squeezed. 'And he wants me to pick him from Heathrow on Friday at some ungodly hour as well.'

'Oh well love, can't be helped.' Carol sighed and snuggled. Frank felt the sting in his conscience.

Luigi's was one of those cafes that felt like it had an instant line to the past. You could have been in any decade of the last five if it hadn't been for the steamed up Gaggia handling a mix of eager office workers, meat market porters and medics on their way home from shifts at Barts. Dave was waiting. 'Got you a coffee.'

'Ta.'

'We've got a problem. Nothing we can't deal with, but it'll take some proper planning. That's why it needs to be you.'

'Go on.'

'You know the Salisbury up on Green Lanes?'

'I've driven past it, why?'

'It's one of Georgiou's and I've had word there's a bunch of hooligans from Tottenham, bits of kids mainly, looking to make a name for themselves with a hairy bastard called Louie Stafford. They're planning a visit on Friday to make themselves at home. I want us to be there and make sure the line is well and truly drawn. If we do this one right, it should go some way to keeping chancers like these off our backs.'

'Where's the info from?'

Dave sipped his coffee. 'It's reliable, that's all you need to know. I want you to have a bowl up there. Have a quiet look around the place. I want the layout an' that so's we can work out the best way to handle it.'

'What's Danny Georgiou say?'

Dave put a hand on Frank's arm. 'Just check the place over. Today or tomorrow is fine, then come round my place and we'll work it out. Don't worry, it'll be okay. I'll have the names and numbers by tomorrow.'

Frank didn't wait. With Schiller busy after lunch, he told Denise he had a delivery to make and headed north out of the City.

The Salisbury was one of those grand old Victorian boozers in need of a guv'nor who gave a toss or a brewery with a few quid to splash about. Outside it was all arches and pillars. A 'Saloon Bar' sign flaked rust in wrought iron scrolls over the entrance. Inside was shabbier still, the paintwork stained yellow, dingy alcoves, dark even on a sunny afternoon. It could have done with a few blown bulbs replacing and something more than forty watts in the ones that were working. Frank walked through the bar, ignored by the half dozen diehards supping solo at tables. A barman looked up, then went back to a conversation with an old soldier stood at the end of the bar. The row of medals on his outsize blazer was probably worth a half of bitter now and again. Frank checked the downstairs exits and fire escapes. Upstairs at the front was an unused function room: stacked chairs, a dusty orange squash machine on the bar, and an upright piano in the corner. He lifted the lid and picked out a couple of low notes. The hollow clank echoed in the empty room. He looked out into Green Lanes, traffic snaking past. You could cover the entrances and most exits from here. He memorised the layout, took a look out the back and called Dave from the payphone downstairs outside the gents. Then he made a second call, to Danny Georgiou.

When Frank walked into Dave's living room on the Friday night, the buzz took him instantly, an air of anticipation. In a fug of fag smoke and conversation were Dave, Wally Patch and his brother Stan, Ruby Barratt, Roy Wills, Tony Wicks, Tony Conroy and Lonnie Chambers. A bottle of Bell's was half empty on the table. Lonnie was helping himself to a healthy stiffener. 'Easy, Lonnie.' Dave took the bottle and poured Frank a couple of fingers in a tumbler.

'I'm driving,' said Frank.

'So's Ruby.' Dave gave him the glass.

Wally chipped his cigarette. 'Copper pulled him over pissed last week in the High Street, right Rube?'

Ruby waved him away.

'On the way home from the Arms. Tell 'em.'

Dave cut in. 'Frank, can you give Ruby directions, just show him the route so's if we get split up, he can find it alright.'

'He couldn't find his own arse if it weren't for the 'ole.' Roy Wills dodged a cuff round the ear.

Dave rapped his knuckles on the table. 'Listen, if you lot have got *any* questions, now is the one and only chance you've got to get it straight. So ...'

They crowded round the dining table and Frank opened up the A to Z. He took them through, stage by stage. First the route, up through the City, King's Cross, Stoke Newington, Stamford Hill, Seven Sisters, then across to Green Lanes. Then he went through the plan. Each man talked through his own job. The what ifs and whys all dealt with, Dave let them have another drink. He checked his watch. 'Give it another quarter of an hour and we'll make tracks.'

'And remember,' said Frank, 'once we're in, no one speaks except Dave, unless you're in trouble and it's unavoidable. No one speaks.'

They nodded.

The conversation picked up. Ruby pulled out a pack of cards and laid out a game of patience. Tony Wicks, then Stan Patch went up to the lav. When Stan came back, Roy disappeared upstairs. He seemed to have been gone a long time.

'D'you reckon he's alright?' said Frank.

'Probably fallen down the 'ole, he's only little.' Ruby put a black eight on a red nine and shifted the column over. 'Nah, the thing with Roy is, he has to 'ave his lucky wank.'

Frank looked up. 'What?'

Ruby flicked three cards off the pack, then another three, put an ace of diamonds up top. 'You know what a superstitious bunch his lot are. Before we go on a job, Roy has to knock one out. Apparently it gives him good fortune.'

Frank looked around the room. There were respectful nods from the others.

Finally, from upstairs came the sound of a toilet flushing, then Roy's feet on the stairs. He came back in rubbing his hands. 'Right, that's me. We off?'

There was a moment's silence before the room lifted with laughter. They got up, still laughing, stubbing fags and emptying glasses, Roy was backslapped as they went out. 'What? What did I do?'

The others were out the door. Dave and Frank were the last to leave. 'You alright, mate?' said Dave.

'Yeah.' Frank put the A to Z under his arm. 'I'm fine.'

Frank had known a sergeant in Cyprus, a tough, intelligent Geordie with years of soldiering behind him. He reckoned he'd never known one battle plan that didn't head down the Swanee the minute they'd come up against the enemy. That night, Dave's firm came close. From the moment Louie Stafford's mob steamed into the Salisbury beered up and found Dave at the bar sipping a Pepsi, it was almost exactly as Frank planned. 'You don't know me, son. My name's David Price and I look after this pub for Mr Georgiou.'

Stafford pulled out a machete. His crew of maybe a dozen were likewise tooled up. Baseball bats, pickaxe handles, an assortment of nasty looking blades. 'You gonna throw us out, then?'

Dave nodded and Wally Patch wrapped a heavy duty chain around the door handles and padlocked it.

'No mate. You're staying.'

Stafford took a broad swipe at Dave's head. Dave stepped aside. Ruby caught Stafford by the wrist and used the momentum of the swing to wrench his arm around his back. The machete hit the deck. Stafford's face hit the bar. Dave shoved a gun in the nape of his neck. He stayed put. A couple of Stafford's boys went for the door through to the gents and the fire exit, one swung a cleaver at Roy Wills. Roy dodged and let the fag machine take a hit, then followed them through the door, bringing a sawn-off out from under his coat. Moments later there was a single blast. They walked sheepishly back through the bar. Stan took a couple of whacks across the shoulders from a pickaxe handle before Frank kicked the bloke's legs from under him. Once down, Stan's boot made sure he stayed down. A hefty looking bloke made a run for the stairs. He rolled down on his arse a damn sight quicker than he went up and landed sitting, a stunned expression across his face and an ugly gash down his cheek. Tony Wicks followed him down. One by one, the others dropped their tools. A hard-faced geezer in a denim jacket spoke up. 'Alright, you've made your point, mate.'

'And what point is that?' Dave pushed the gun barrel deeper into Stafford's neck.

'This place is out of bounds.'

'Too fucking right.' Dave stood up, turned the gun on the hard-faced geezer and shot him below the knee. He went backwards, clutching his leg and spilling a table full of drinks in one of the alcoves.

They lined Stafford and his boys up on their knees, hands behind their heads and one by one, Tony Conroy walked down the line with an instamatic camera and took a picture while Dave gave the lecture. 'I know who you are. I know where you live. Stafford, 28 Landsdowne Road, right? And I've got these snaps. These are going to every landlord of every one of Mr Georgiou's pubs. If you as much as drop in for a Sunday lunchtime pint, you'd better 'ave a bloody good disguise.'

The lads cracked open a crate back at Dave's, but Frank didn't stay. He drove home, parked up and turned the radio off in the car. All he could hear was the engine and the sound of his heart racing.

Carol stirred when he got into bed. 'You smell of pubs.'

Frank lay on his back, eyes wide. 'Stopped for a swift one on the way home.'

'That's nice.'

He kissed her, she turned and was asleep in seconds. He put two fingers on the pulse at the base of his wrist and counted as the adrenalin left his body and his heart rate slowed.

18

Watching the rain trickle down the window, Carl felt like he was wasting time. He checked Adeline's phone again, the third time in as many minutes: there was no message, no missed call. The clock read 3.22. He worked out that they should have been there and on their way back by now. Adeline should have been in touch. He popped more Anadin from the pack and lifted himself long enough to swallow before the soreness in his ribs pinned him back to the bed.

The day had slipped away in the hotel room. Sleep, rain, painkillers and circular memories of his route into this rotten situation. Remembering Grace kept him going. Birthdays, holidays, how he'd battled through Oxford Street to John Lewis's last Christmas to buy the red shoes she wanted more than anything. Red shoes, like Dorothy. He wouldn't let her be O'Keefe's, but the possibility burned. He reached for the phone again. Still nothing. There were raised voices along the corridor. A door slammed and the drunken rant continued, muffled. He flicked the radio on. The pills were beginning to take the edge off the pain. He threw back the duvet and gingerly swung his legs round, steadying himself for the half dozen steps to the tiny bathroom.

He let the shower run until it was as hot as he could stand, left the mobile in view on the cistern. He soaped himself, went easy over the bruises. Adeline wasn't going to call. And if she did, he couldn't see it being good news. But then there was Frank …

Carl had his first proper introduction to Frank Neaves, a bloke who, until then he'd known only through Dad's soldier stories, on a drive over the river one hot Sunday when he was a kid, barely into his teens. What came to mind mostly about that day was the car. Frank picked them up in a blue Mark III Cortina with a black vinyl roof.

As they cruised under the lights in Rotherhithe Tunnel, he felt like he was in Starsky and Hutch.

Dad had directed Frank to Joey Silverman's.

Joey had been tailoring Dad's suits since the '60s. The business was one of a string of small concerns that had been grateful for a Dave Price investment. No questions asked. The premises, on the frayed edge of the City off the Commercial Road, stayed one of its best kept secrets.

Carl pictured his old man leaning against the cutting table, winding Joey up.

Joey had bristled at the piss-take that he was nothing more than an East-end schmutter merchant. 'I've got the best cloth and I cut the best of any tailor you can afford.' The finger pointed.

Dad said he'd heard good things about a cutter at Dege and Skinner.

'Let me tell you, David Price, them Savile Row blokes make suits for lords, poof guardsmen and Yank tourists.' A tap of the nose and the point was made. 'Go there if you want, but mark my words, son, you'll get better, cheaper, here.'

The two-piece, midnight blue, single-breasted suit Frank was measured for that Sunday should have been a gift from Dad. A little extra for a service rendered, but he wasn't having it. 'Last time I had someone buy my clothes for me was my mum. I'll sort myself out, thanks.'

Dad smiled, 'I just want to make sure you look right.'

'Like I need that from *you*.'

Joey's tape measure flicked out. He muttered numbers under his breath like incantations, pencilled notes in a brown pocket book in which he kept, '… the measurements of every man it's been my pleasure to have known.' The borrowed line came with a quick smile. 'Final fitting Sunday week, Mr Neaves. Pick it up a week later.' He offered his hand.

'Cheers,' said Frank. 'What do I owe?'

Joey glanced at Dad as Frank shook his jacket back on. 'Fiver on account. The rest if it fits.' He snapped an elastic band over the brown book. 'I'll throw in a spare pair of strides 'an all for an extra fiver, you won't get that up bloody' Savile Row.'

The Cortina cruised through the City's backstreets, windows down. Dad slipped a Motown Chartbusters tape in the player. *Nowhere to run to baby, nowhere to hide*. The City was empty that Sunday and Carl felt like they owned a piece of it.

Around Dad in those days, you could usually perm any from Roy, Lonnie, the Tonys, Stan and Wally and sometimes Uncle Ruby. Their faces were imprinted on Carl's memory, flushed with booze at late night card sessions, at the pub at Christmas, or round the table at Nan's with their wives and kids. These were the 'uncles' and 'aunties' of his and his brother's childhood. Little brother Terry, talking back and blagging sips of beer whilst Dad looked on and he was in the kitchen playing beggar my neighbour with Mum and the aunties.

But it changed on the afternoon Terry had a fight with a kid near Loampit Vale. Carl remembered it clear as day. Terry wasn't about to let some kid with a dark brown fuzz patch on his face ride his bike, no matter how big he was or how many mates he had with him. There was a stand-off. Carl stood back, uncertain.

'I'll bring it back,' said the kid, his fist closing around the handlebars.

Terry gripped tighter. 'You won't cos you ain't taking it. It's my bike.'

'You calling me a thief?'

Terry's eyes lit up. 'No, I'm calling—'

Carl stepped in, knowing Terry's new favourite word would spark the fight the big kid was after. 'Just leave him alone and leave his bike alone. Have a ride of mine if you want.'

'He reckons I'm gunna take his poxy bike. I just wanta ride of it.'

'He says no.'

The big kid threw a haymaker. Carl surprised himself by moving away from it easily. Terry let the bike go and launched himself. He tripped over the pedal and went sprawling, got a hand out, but couldn't stop his face connecting with the pavement. He wiped his mouth, smeared blood from his cut lip. Then he was up, eyes blazing indignity as they laughed at him. He rained punches on the big kid, rocking him back on his heels.

It looked like the others might wade in. Carl said, 'Our Dad's Dave Price.'

They all stopped. The big kid held Terry. 'Bollocks is he.'

'It's true,' said one of the others. 'I remember you,' he said to Carl. 'You came down boxing once with your old man.'

Carl recognised the skinny kid who'd roughed him up in the ring. He pulled Terry off the big kid and picked up the bike.

The boy from boxing said to his mate, 'Leave 'em. They ain't worth it.'

As Carl and Terry walked their bikes away, the boy shouted after them, 'I only said you was game that day 'cos Don told me to. We 'ad a right laugh about it after. And we ain't scared of your dad. Gary Stack's gunna do 'im anyway.'

The parting shot hadn't registered with Terry who was more concerned with his chipped front tooth. 'You should never have said about Dad. Made me feel like a right cunt.'

There was Terry's new word, tested for its shock value. Carl could see he was pleased to have used it.

Carl's legs were shaking all the way home. Odds on he'd get the blame from Mum for letting the fight happen, and from Dad for not steaming in on his brother's side soon enough. But when they got home, Mum barely fussed, just pulled down the old Oxo tin with the Germolene and plasters from its shelf in the kitchen where the two Tonys were sitting drinking tea.

'Where's Dad?'

'Out looking for you two. Soon as he phones I'll let him know you're safe.' She took the cotton wool pad away from Terry's split lip and winced. 'We'll have to get you to the dentist tomorrow, won't we love?'

Carl asked Mum what was up.

'Nothing,' she said.

Terry made the Tonys look at his lip, wanted to go over the park to show his mates the broken tooth.

'There's a corned beef sandwich in the fridge,' said Mum. 'Get some milk and go and watch telly. You're not going out again. Not tonight.'

Later, Dad came back with Roy and Uncle Ruby. They went straight into the kitchen and closed the door. When Carl went in to say goodnight, the air was smoke-heavy. The conversation stopped and there were no smiles, even the usual bedtime backchat from Uncle Ruby was missing. But as he closed the door, for the second time that day he heard the name Gary Stack.

Carl towelled himself down and checked the mobile again. He eased back into his clothes, shivering, but better for the shower. He tidied the room, made the bed, put the litter in the bin. It took him a long time, a slow process testing his body's sore limits. He sat down and combed his hair in the TV screen's reflection, propped himself up on the pillows, turned the telly on and waited, and dozed.

It had been a long time since Gary Stack found his way into Carl's dreams and there was no abiding image, just a sense of him in his place as one of those static childhood fragments that occasionally flashed out of his subconscious. Gary Stack had always resisted being built into a whole truth. Carl woke and as the hotel room came into focus, for a moment he was unsure of his surroundings, muddled and a little frightened. He found he could only settle on the memory of a shirt, one of those bits of 1970s chain-store schmutter that time would make ridiculous with its flapping round collar and penny-farthing print. Fine if you were twelve and your mum had bought it for you, but Gary Stack had to be close on thirty when he was released in the summer of 1978. One afternoon a few weeks later, he persuaded Carl and Terry into his car. The seatback in front of Terry had a rip in the vinyl and he was picking out crumbs of yellow foam. Carl remembered the reek of the car. The smell of vomit rising out of the carpet. Stack shouted when he tried to wind the window down. He knew they weren't being taken home. There were two of them. He tried to pull the passenger's features together, a bent smile that didn't reassure, a lipless mouth. Then it slipped away.

Gary Stack was a faceless man in a room in a flat wearing a stupid shirt.

First thing Terry did was show him his broken tooth and ask for orange squash.

'You'll be here for a while, lads, hopefully not too long. There's some comics an that.' They were put in a room and the door locked behind them.

Carl couldn't believe he'd been dumb enough to allow him and Terry to climb in the back of a stranger's car. Looking back, that part still bothered him. Even as a kid, surely he'd had more sense. But then he remembered, the face in the front seat came into focus: the driver was Lonnie, Uncle Lonnie, Dad's mate Lonnie, *My Old Man's a Dustman* Lonnie, penknife and piss-take Lonnie. Lonnie who he now realised for the first time had a thing for his Mum. Lonnie who was always the last to leave and always had an excuse to be around when Dad wasn't.

Carl had no idea how long they'd been kept in that room. It had a single window, boarded up. He hadn't been able to see out, but then he might not have tried. Lonnie brought them a carton of milk and half a pack of McVitie's Digestives. Carl heard the key turn in the lock behind him.

When Terry wanted the toilet, Carl told him to hold on. He'd crossed his legs, walked around. But he had to go. Carl banged on the door and shouted for Lonnie, but it was Gary Stack who came and took Terry to the lav. Carl listened at the door. There were raised voices, Terry defiantly spewing his swearwords, then Stack shouting back louder. Then a smack. Terry was shoved back in the room, a red mark coming up on his cheek. He said nothing, just stared at Carl. 'Don't worry, Dad's coming soon,' he said, wishing he believed it.

When it got dark, Lonnie brought blankets. He told them to make a bed out of the sofa cushions. Carl wanted the toilet by this time and he wanted Terry to go with him while Lonnie was there. But Stack was waiting outside the room and showed them to the toilet one at a time. There was something not right about the way he took Terry's hand. 'You be a good boy this time.'

Terry yawned and just nodded.

He should have looked after his little brother, like he should have looked after Grace and Diane. Carl sat on the edge of the hotel bed and sobbed.

A faceless man in a room in a flat wearing a stupid shirt with blood down the front. The rest was blurred. He remembered they were in the back of Frank's Cortina with Dad between them as they made their way through the darkened streets. He remembered feeling ashamed that when Frank glanced in the rear-view mirror he'd been crying.

The following morning, the police came to the house, the only time he could remember them being allowed in without a slanging match at the door. But this time their voices were low, respectful almost. Mum took him in the kitchen. Terry was allowed to stay. Carl wanted to be part of it, to stay and hear what they said. 'Just let your Dad deal with it, love.' She made ham sandwiches that went dry on the plate.

Some days later Terry was inspecting his re-built front tooth in the hall mirror and making a pain in the arse of himself so Mum took him out. Carl went to sit with his dad, 'Dad, this bloke Gary Stack, is he coming back, do I have to look out for him?'

Dad hugged him hard. 'You don't have to worry about him, son.'

But he did. Every hot sleepless night that summer, listening to the house cool down, the crack of floorboards, the cats in the back garden. They were all Gary Stack coming for him. One night he went to the window and could have sworn there was a figure in the shadow of the garden shed.

Dad never mentioned it again and the only time he ever tried to speak to Terry, he said he couldn't remember and if it was stuck in the past, that was where it belonged.

What did happen was that Terry was allowed to get away with murder after that. There were always excuses, Mum let him off and moved the world around him to keep him sweet. Carl never thought anything other than being taken by Gary Stack was his fault and no one ever thought to tell him otherwise.

*

Carl wiped his face on his sleeve and checked the mobile again. There were no calls or text messages. More than anything he wanted to talk to Grace. He knew what Dad would have said, especially where family's concerned. *There's no sense sodding about, son. Just get on with it, do what you have to. There's only room for one guv'nor. Front up or don't bother.*

Carl straightened up with some discomfort. He spoke to the empty hotel room, to the old man's ever present echo. 'Thing is, Dad, that doesn't take any account of a mess like this.'

He pulled his shoes on, just about managed the laces with a rest between shoes. They might have gone back to O'Keefe's for another try like Adeline said, but deep down he knew Grace wasn't coming and Diane wasn't coming. He couldn't just sit and wait any more. He got his stuff together, threw down the last of the painkillers and made his way past the dozy desk clerk. Stupid to think Frank could bring them back.

At the station Carl slid his credit card into the chip and pin machine, bought a one-way back to London. The bitter wind that tore down the platform cut right through him, only sharpening the sense of failure.

19

Frank kept his walking pace easy, thinking Adeline would catch up. She was behind him, then she wasn't. He started to double back, thinking he saw her in the shadow of a bus stand. But as he came closer he could tell it was the reflection of a Primark window display on the bus shelter adverts. She wasn't following. He felt an almighty shiver, an involuntary rasp in his breathing. He stopped for a moment, coughing, which only made him more breathless. He found his way into a memorial square, a soldier statue blank-stared across the main road. A gaggle of girls in short skirts, skimpy white shirts and schoolgirl ties teetered past. He looked back for Adeline, his skin pricking as shivers came down his arms, his back and his legs. When he coughed again, palpitations fluttered in his chest. It was karma, fate taking a final swipe at him for not seeing Grace and Diane safe, for letting Carol and Kate down, for letting Adeline lose herself in the empty city, for leaving Carl beat up and alone in a hotel room, for a lifetime of fuck ups. He grew dizzy and tried to control his breathing, keep himself steady. A group of rowdy lads approached, dressed for a night out. They crossed the road, ignored him. Voices echoed and died in side street piss-takes. Frank managed a few more steps, giving himself easy to reach objectives: to cross the road, to make it to the next street corner, to get back to the car. He had to rest, propping himself up in a department store doorway as another wave of dizziness and nausea crept over him. The numbness seemed to come up through his legs. His knees gave way and he slid down the window in a dead faint.

Adeline's voice came through the darkness. 'Frank, come on babe. You were out cold. Jesus, this is all we need.' She pinched the skin on the back of his hand, 'Come on, Frank, wake up. You can't stay here, there's some old bill hanging around here and they seem pretty keen.'

He felt himself dragged into a sitting position and tried to help. The street was swimming in front of him. 'Oh shit.'

He had no recollection of arriving at the pub. Adeline put a scotch in front of him at the bar. He drank it down and it almost came straight back. She bought him another, which he took away to a spot near the radiator and nursed.

Paint-thickened, brown-stained wallpaper peeled away from the wall in spite of a half-arsed sellotape repair job. Dampness seeped through the plaster and black mould edged the ceiling. Faded prints of sailing ships, whalers, and trawlers clung to the wall, not one on the level, but that might easily have been his eyesight.

As he settled into the corner, Frank began to feel the blood circulating in his feet, his body warming. His breathing, which had been coming in shallow gasps, relaxed and grew steady. After a few minutes his eyelids grew heavy. He felt himself nodding and napped, maybe for a few seconds, maybe longer. Adeline prodded him. 'Hey, you.'

He jerked awake. 'I'll be fine, I'll be fine.'

She held his arm. 'Come on Frank, come back to me.'

'I'm sorry.'

'It's ok.'

'It isn't, I left you.'

She moved in closer to him and for a while neither of them said anything, adrift with their own thoughts, and the need for each other. Gradually, the head fog cleared. He took long even breaths, filling his lungs and exhaling slowly.

She took his hand. 'Frank, I hate it that you think badly of me and I want to explain. Is that okay?'

He nodded. 'Yeah, course it is.'

'Y'know, when I moved back to London, that was the first time in my whole life I'd ever been alone. I didn't have a clue, about anything. My husband had been in my ear every day, *every day* for years Frank, controlling me until I couldn't have felt more useless. I didn't know what was left of me or what I was going to do.' She fiddled with the zip on her bag and moved it between them. 'In those first few weeks I'd have gone back, easy as anything. How stupid is that?' She looked at him directly for the first time.

'I just wished you'd told me earlier. I knew it wasn't just a jolly, a favour for a mate.'

'If it wasn't for Carl putting me up and giving me the job, I would have gone back to my husband.' She hesitated. 'And then the money I got from the O'Keefes. I'm sorry Frank, honestly. I know it's my mess, but …'

'I shouldn't judge.'

'I made bad decisions, Frank, but when you're out on your own … I wasn't looking six months down the road, or six days come to think of it. So I leaned on Carl and that was alright. And I couldn't bear being alone so … Adam O'Keefe.'

'And that wasn't alright.' Frank sloshed the scotch around his glass.

'No, it wasn't.'

He drank up.

'You want another?'

'Yeah, d'be nice.'

She fished a tenner from the bag. 'I phoned Carl. I told him Diane wasn't in when we called and we were going back to give it another go.'

Adeline waited to be served while the barmaid chatted to her mates at the pool table. When the girl finally sauntered behind the bar, making it clear she resented doing so, Adeline picked up the coffee jar which was decorated with a couple of tacky foil bows and a hand-written gift sticker: *Happy Christmas from the Staff.* She gave it a shake. When her change came she dropped in a ten-pence piece and gave an angelic smile.

'Priceless,' said Frank. 'You making friends again?'

She kept her eyes down, stayed silent and then gave him a look as if she expected him to tear her off a strip. 'So, are you okay with going back to give it another go?'

With the chills turning to sweats, he would have gone back to the car and driven home there and then. He'd have left her sitting in that pub, chasing after Diane and Grace, bullshitting, guilt-tripping and telling the world what it wanted to hear. Except this once, Frank couldn't bear the thought of being alone. 'And if she won't come?'

'Then we tried.'

They walked back to the car slowly. Adeline held onto his arm. There was a police car at the multi-storey entrance. As they drew level, two coppers strong-armed a kid in handcuffs through the shopping centre fire exit. They opened the car door, bent the kid's head down and shoved him in the back seat. They made their way up the ramp, Frank glancing behind them.

20

Diane was worried. Jim hadn't spoken since showing Adeline and Frank the door, just occupied the sofa periodically switching TV channels. Grace had stayed in her room, playing quietly. It was dark now. Diane drew the curtains.

She'd learned to read him and sense when he'd lose control. Sometimes she could convince herself it wasn't his fault, living up to expectations had to be hard. His mother, at least her long dead shadow, influenced everything Jim and his brothers did. It was always, *What would Mammy think?* and *What would Mammy want you to do?* It made her want to scream sometimes. Ewan carried it with ease, comfortable with his status as Mammy's eldest and of course, he had an ego to match. The man was full of grand ideas, but depended on Jim for support and for the most part he was a willing functionary, carrying out Ewan's orders without question. At first she'd been shocked the way they spoke to each other, like they couldn't care less, but they were brothers, family could do that. Except it hurt Jim, which in turn, she discovered, hurt her.

'What do you want me to say?'

He said nothing.

'I didn't ask them to come, if we'd let Grace go down for a few days they wouldn't have had to.'

He looked up.

'Well they wouldn't, would they?' Diane read the rage in his eyes and felt a knot tighten in her stomach. If she could make him speak, engage him in some way. 'Why don't we go away for a while?'

'*This* fucking time of year?'

'We could get some cheap flights, go see Judith for a few days. She wanted you to go over for New Year anyway.'

'Me? So you can stay? You can piss off back down with him as soon as my back's turned?'

'That's not what I meant. I'll go with you.'

'Yeah, right, and that little bitch upstairs gets to tell Daddy lies.'

She stiffened at the insult.

'See, I know you. I know you better than you think. I see you.'

'No, please, not this again.'

He mimicked. 'Not again, Jim. Leave me alone, Jim. Don't say that Jim. Let's go see your sister, Jim.' He flicked the TV off. 'You know what, I think you wanted them to come. I think it was you that put her up to ringing her daddy. I think you want to break my heart and fuck me over.'

'Bloody hell, Jim. That's so unfair, why would I?'

He stared for a long time, chewing on spite, constructing, justifying. Then he began nodding and she knew it was coming, that she was locked into his process. She went cold, her bowels loosened and she could have shit herself there and then.

He was in her face. He raised his hand. She flinched, blinked. He laughed, then hit her anyway, a slap around her head. Her hair caught in his ring. He pulled and she swallowed her scream as the hair tore out, her one thought to keep Grace away. He pushed her, threw her almost. She twisted away from another slap. He half pinned her against the sofa, one hand on her shoulder, then it slipped across her throat. She fought then, fought hard. Reached into his face, scratched, bit, kicked, brought her knee into his balls and connected. She felt his grip weaken and he squirmed away. There was blood on his face, blood on her sleeve.

There was a surreal moment of calm. Diane getting her breath back. O'Keefe recovering on all fours. It didn't last long. He was up, standing over her. 'I'll fucking kill you.' She made it to the door. He kicked her hard in the arse and her leg went dead. He grabbed her hair, dragged her to her feet and threw her into the hall. He opened the front door. 'Out, you cunt. And stay out. Don't fucking come back.'

She felt herself propelled helplessly forward, landed groping at the lawn, snow and dirt between her fingers gasping for air. As she got to her feet, the door closed and she heard the latch click.

21

The woman pacing up and down by the shops with her arms folded, holding herself, limping and shivering, looked like every soap opera junkie you'd ever seen. Frank pulled in.

'What you doing?' said Adeline.

He got out the car.

At first Diane didn't recognise him. 'Excuse me,' she said. 'Please could you lend me some change for the phone?'

Christ knew how many people she'd asked. Frank put his arm around her shoulders. 'It's me love, Frank. Come and sit in the car.'

She forced the words out between sobs, her chest heaving. 'He's … got … my … daughter … please ... please …'

'Frank, we have to go get Grace.' Adeline rubbed Diane's back.

'What we have to do is call the police and wait.'

'For what?'

'For them to turn up and do their job. If you don't make it official, this carries on.'

'Just listen to yourself. I've got news for you, pal. This carries on with or without the old bill.'

Diane had her breath back. 'No police, there's no point. You call them and his brothers'll turn up. He won't give her up. He wants to hurt me.'

'Grace ain't even his.'

'Oh for God's sake Frank, just go. We'll work something out when we get there.'

Frank blocked O'Keefe's drive and left the engine running.

You wouldn't want a job like this, he thought. A thankless task you knew had every chance of heading tits up very quickly and which, even if you did pull it off, was likely to make you one serious enemy. Adeline didn't understand men like O'Keefe, or she did and didn't care. The usual rules did not apply. Carl had been reasonable – he was capable of nothing else – and look how he'd ended up. Frank had seen it all before. In years gone by he'd encountered a few of the real hard men of this world, the fanatics, and a hundred more who used violence easily. It gave them a hard-on. The smart thing to do was your level best to put distance between you and them. Right from the off it was pretty bloody obvious that O'Keefe had the same perverse logic that would make crossing him the least sensible thing you could do. But here he was, faithful old Frank, trudging up the man's poxy drive, with its bloody big Kraut motor, slipping in the slush on the worn-flat soles of his boots. He felt a long, long way from home.

Frank glanced back at the car. Adeline's face was pressed to the glass and Diane had moved across to the driver's seat. 'I'm a dog,' he said. 'A mangy old mutt. I do what mutts do. I do what they tell me, then come back with my tongue hanging out for more. I'm a fucking mutt.'

He walked up to the front door. His hand was almost on the bell, but he thought better of it, any kind of ruck with O'Keefe was only going one way. He edged down the side entrance, which at least gave him the advantage of being in the dark and out of plain sight from the street. He rattled a couple of loose fence-planks. Breaking and entering the back garden wasn't likely to be difficult if he could just squeeze through. It'd be bloody tight though. He tried the gate at the end of the drive. It was locked. For a split second he contemplated going over the top, but leaning over, he found he could easily reach and shoot the bolt on the other side. Too easy, he thought as he made his way, one step at a time, into the unlit garden. Grass overgrew the lawn, ragged at its borders. Frank picked his way to the shed. Breaking in was easier than the gate. He eased off the latch and was in. For a minute he stood silently while his eyes grew accustomed to the darkness. It was a tip, a bloody mess. Tools, spilled paint, rigid bristle paintbrushes, chemical stench, white spirit, rodent shit on the bench, the floor. He picked out a large flat-bladed screwdriver. He wasn't thinking about Carl, Adeline, or Diane anymore. There was just him and Grace and the house and O'Keefe somewhere in it. As he tried the locked kitchen door, as he navigated a thawed path between patio tubs with their stringy dead shrubs, as he slipped on the frozen mossy concrete and steadied himself, as he slid the screwdriver in between the patio door and its frame, levering against the lock until it broke, each movement took on an instinctive focus, the mechanics of the task triggering long-lost muscle memory. He held his breath as he stepped almost silently across the carpet in the dining room, taking in pictures on the walls, family mess on the table, a grease marked holly-pattern tablecloth, dirty dinner plates, beer cans. As he reached for the door handle, there was movement from the next room. The creak of sofa springs, a deep rumbling fart. Frank opened the door into the hall and tiptoed up the stairs, keeping his feet to the sides.

In the back of his mind he had known that once Grace was awake and alive to what was going on, he'd have to move quickly. Back bedroom, Diane had said. It was easier than that. The glittery pink kitty stickers on the door didn't leave much doubt which was Grace's room. Frank stood on the landing for a moment. Walking into a little girl's bedroom in the middle of the night without frightening the life out of her, how the fuck was he going to manage that?

He quietly turned the handle, closing the door behind him. He took in the room, walked across to Grace's bed.

'I saw you in the garden,' she said.

Frank kept his voice to a low whisper and hoped Grace'd take the hint. 'Did ya? Look love, it's a bit of a secret, but I want you to come with me to see your mum and I need you to be really, really quiet.'

'And don't tell Jim?'

'You've got it, don't tell Jim. That's the name of the game.'

'Are you a stranger? I'm not allowed to go with strangers.'

'Nah, I'm a friend of your dad's. Your Nanna Rose showed me this lovely Christmas card you wrote her and asked me to bring her little girl to see her. Your Mum's waiting outside in a car, I promise.'

'Will Jim stop us going?'

'Well he can't stop us if he doesn't know, can he? You got some clothes an' that, we can get you dressed nice and warm, quick and quiet.'

She eased out of bed. Her clothes were neatly folded on a chair. Frank was uncertain, trying to remember if nine year old girls needed help getting dressed. 'You alright, I won't look if you want to …'

Grace busied herself, daintily stepping into trousers, socks, sweatshirt, trainers. 'Do I have to brush my teeth?'

'No, you'll be alright, we'll do that in the morning.'

She slipped her jacket on. 'Please can you help me?'

He knelt and worked the zip.

'Can I take some toys?'

'Just keep it small, what you can carry.'

She filled a little rucksack and he helped her into it. She was ready. Frank knelt down. 'Listen Grace, you're doing really well, but when we go downstairs, I want you to be really, really quiet. We're not gonna say a word until we're outside, okay?'

She nodded.

As he opened the door, Grace ran back to the bed. Her training shoes drummed across the carpet. She reached under the duvet. 'Kangi.' She pulled out a small threadbare panda in an orange felt waistcoat. She cuddled him tight to her and reached up for Frank's hand.

They were half-way down the stairs when the living room door opened and a bleary-eyed O'Keefe emerged. A set of ugly red scratches across his cheek weren't doing his looks any favours. He stood watching for what felt like a long, long time. Frank kept moving.

O'Keefe said to Grace, 'I thought I heard you moving about love, I was coming to see if you were alright.'

Frank was first to the bottom of the stairs. O'Keefe still hadn't moved. Frank turned and took Grace's hand. He eased the chain off the front door and went for the latch. O'Keefe knocked his hand out the way. 'You really think you're going out that door with her?'

Frank reached for the latch again and once more O'Keefe batted his arm away. Frank let go Grace's hand and put himself between O'Keefe and the door. A punch to the back of his neck knocked his head forward. It smacked against the door as he pulled it open. He felt blood trickle across the bridge of his nose.

'Whatcha think you're doin' old man, eh?' Another punch, this time at his back.

Frank guided Grace out the door. 'Go on love, you go.'

'You, dead man, breakin' into my house. I'm not the sort to take that lying down, right? You're a fucking dead man. I will see you in the ground.'

Frank kept going, gentle words to Grace, quiet encouragement. 'See, look, there's Mummy.' Assuming O'Keefe would be behind him, Frank led Grace down the step, bracing himself for whatever was coming. He was surprised that they'd made it almost to the car. Adeline opened the back door.

Grace was nearly in. 'Where's Kangi?' Her voice broke and he thought she'd run back.

'Haven't you got him?' Frank looked across the lawn, the route they'd taken and there was the tatty bear, lying in the snow. 'You get in with your mum. I'll fetch him.' Adeline pulled her into the car.

Seven steps. Seven ordinary steps. He'd made it to five before O'Keefe appeared in the doorway with the shotgun. Frank picked up the bear, put him inside his coat. Behind him, Adeline was shouting, Diane screaming at him to move, to run. He heard the engine turn over and rev wildly. Taking a last look at O'Keefe as he loaded the shotgun, Frank turned away. O'Keefe let one barrel go, a wild shot that missed by a mile. Frank could see Diane behind the wheel wrestling the car into gear. Adeline was screaming for her to wait. Frank tried to run, his boot soles slipped in the snow. The car skidded, its wheels spinning on the wet tarmac, then the tyres gripped. O'Keefe fired the second barrel. Frank threw himself down, his mouth full of grass and snow, dirt between his teeth. He could hear O'Keefe re-loading.

22

He'd never forget it. That Saturday night in August 1978. Frank had been sitting on the sofa with Carol's feet up across his legs while they watched telly. He was just back from a short-notice job driving Mr Schiller down to his weekend place in Oxfordshire. Even with the windows open the car had been a sweatbox and by the time he made it back through the early evening holiday traffic, he was knackered. He was still in his shirt, although he'd loosened his tie. His suit jacket hung over the back of a dining chair. Carol leaned across and took a couple of Maltesers from the box on the coffee table. Her just-washed hair smelled of apple shampoo. She had a damp towel around her shoulders, a smudge of chocolate on her cheek. Frank sipped a cold Carling Black Label just out of the fridge. Arthur Scott and his Sealions had just finished on *Seaside Special*. The two big-haired birds from Baccara were jigging up and down and miming badly. Peter Powell bounced out in his poncy white bomber jacket to give Dionne Warwick the big build up. Then Frank jumped as someone hammered at the front door like they were trying to break the bloody thing down.

'You'd better get that.' Carol swung her legs off and closed the lid on the Maltesers.

Dave was on the doorstep, sweating, unshaven. 'I'm sorry, Frank, I wouldn't have come only … my boys, someone … some cunt's got my boys and I need you.'

Frank tried to control the sinking feeling in his stomach. He was blown, but he knew he couldn't close the door. He told Dave to wait and went back in the living room. 'Carol, I've got to go out for a bit.'

She kept her eyes fixed on the telly.

'Someone's taken Dave Price's kids. They don't know where they are, we're going out to look for them.'

129

'I heard.'

'I'm gonna have to go.'

'So you said.'

And as if to cap it all, as if to make the whole thing feel like a film scene, as Frank took his suit jacket off the chair and left, Dionne Warwick was singing *Walk on By*. As he put the jacket on over his crumpled work shirt, he knew he'd remember that too.

'So, you got any ideas?' Frank thought maybe the front room curtain twitched as he edged the Cortina out of its parking space; or was it just wishful thinking?

'What, you mean is there anyone who don't like me? Where d'you wanna fucking start?' Dave lit a cigarette, opened the window and spat out. 'Yeah, I've got a fair idea. Gary Stack, you know him?'

'Heard of him.'

'Well, he's been mouthing off ever since he came home from stir. Wally's heard him and I've heard similar from others. Some kid even told my Carl he was after me the other day, I should have found him and dealt with it then.'

'So what's the why?'

'For Stack? He reckons I owe him for his Uncle Lenny and he's got some idea there's a cash debt due to his family. Apparently, I took turf they'd been promised. Promised by who is anyone's guess. I dunno who he thinks he is.'

'So who's Uncle Lenny?'

'Lenny Baker, you never knew him. He was a local face, one of the Richardsons' occasionals until he disappeared after a night out at the Black Bull. Must have been, what, late sixty-seven. I was interviewed at the time along with a dozen others, but there was no evidence. Someone was giving some chat that I'd had an interest in putting Baker out the game.' He thought for a moment. 'To be honest, after Charlie and Eddie went down there were scores settling all over the place for a few weeks.'

'And did you – want him out the way?'

'It helped.' He smiled.

'And you think this bloke Stack's got the balls to take your kids?'

'Balls've got nothing to do with it. He's a head-case, like his uncle. He hurts people.' He lit another fag off the butt of the first. 'Turn left down here, I want to use the phone. You got some change?'

130

Frank watched him in the call-box, twitchy, sharp movements, flicks of his cigarette, the constant positioning and re-positioning of fags and lighter and columns of two and ten pence pieces on the directories. He held the phone to his ear as he thumbed through his little book of phone numbers. It was as if the box could hardly contain the build up of energy. When he sprang out, the door was thrown back on its hinges and he damn near ran to the car. 'We need to go round Wally's. I want him with us now.'

'You know where they are?'

'Yeah, I fucking do.'

Frank pulled into the cul-de-sac where Wally lived. A group of lads kick-chased a half-deflated ball across a threadbare patch of grass. They stopped to check out the car, then the ball got hoofed skywards and the game was on again. Wally came out carrying his black Adidas bag. He closed his gate behind him and got in the back seat. 'Alright, Frank, Dave?' He offered his hand.

'I will be when I get my kids back.'

'We will, mate.'

'Where to?'

'Walworth, he's on the Heygate.'

The Heygate Estate had gone up in the early seventies, replacing what was left of the two-up/two-down streets in Walworth when the war ended. Someone once told Frank, it was like some council dickhead had gone to Russia, thought, *them communist flats look nice, why don't we have some?* and built a load just off the Old Kent Road. According to the bloke Wally tapped up, Gary Stack's nan had taken a ground floor place with a bit of a garden next to the Claydon block, which, given as the old girl had passed on a couple of years later, had gone over to his sister for safe-keeping until he came out. It was what Nan would have wanted.

The flat was the last in a row with what looked like a vacant next door. An open staircase led up to the first floor flats and a row of front doors, washing draped across the balconies.

Dave wanted to bust straight in, but Frank persuaded him to let him take a walk round first.

'Don't be long.' Dave lit a fag.

'Five minutes.'

There was no easy way in the front. The walkways were littered with broken glass which made it noisy, but if you picked your path, it was a better entry point. At the back was a patch of sandy earth overgrown with waist-high weeds that passed for a garden. You'd easily take the door out. Frank looked up. There was a risk you'd be seen coming in either way from the first floor. They'd have to chance it and take front and back together.

When he got back to the car, Dave was wired. 'I'm not waiting. Not now.'

'Just listen a minute, he's dangerous, right?'

'I don't care how dangerous he is, he's got my boys.'

'Think, Dave.'

'Jesus Frank, what d'you want to wait for, fucking Christmas?'

Wally piped up, 'He's mental, and he wouldn't think twice about hurting them.'

'Exactly,' said Frank. 'It'll be dark in half an hour, then we can move in round the back unseen. It's an easier and a quicker entry. We're less likely to be seen and if we do it right, we'll be in before they know it. I'll take the back and you two come straight through the front.'

As night fell there were signs of occupation in the flat, light escaping around the edges of the boards, and then the door opened. It wasn't Gary Stack who came out.

'Lonnie. What the fuck is he doing here?'

Wally leaned forward for a clearer view. 'The little shit.'

Dave went for the door, but Frank pulled him back. They watched as Lonnie went past them to a car parked thirty yards down in front of another block. Dave slipped the safety off his revolver. 'Give us that,' said Frank. ' Just be ready.'

He kept low, using parked cars as cover until he was behind Lonnie. His heart raced. Lonnie was on his way back to the flat, carrying a cardboard box. With both hands occupied it'd be easy. Frank was on him before he knew it, hand over his face, the gun barrel pressed hard into his fat neck, foot in the crook of his knee to take him down. He tried to twist away, but Dave and Wally were with him. Dave's eyes were wide. He took the gun back, jabbing into Lonnie's face while Frank went through his pockets. 'Keys?'

'Ain't got 'em.'

'So how d'you get back in?'

'I have to knock.'

'So let's fucking knock.'

He looked to Dave, 'I'm sorry, Dave. I—'

'Don't worry, mate, just get us in and we'll talk then. I know it's not you.' Dave patted him on the shoulder. They lifted him, brushed him down, gave him back the cardboard box and walked him to the front door. He knocked, three short taps, a gap then another three. As the door opened, Frank shoved Lonnie to one side. Dave was past him as Stack turned and ran into the flat and through a side door. He tried to close it behind him. Frank put his shoulder to the door, it gave way and he was in. Stack sprawled on the floor, a kitchen knife spun and clanked against the radiator. Dave was at Frank's elbow. He levelled the revolver.

'Don't fucking move.'

'Dave, don't.'

In the corner of the room, partly screened by an old sofa, on a makeshift bed of seat cushions and grey blankets, Carl and Terry sat up, blinking in the half light.

Stack took his chance and made a lunge for the gun and missed. For a second he was up on his knees, his hands around Dave's leg like he was begging. Dave brought the butt of the gun down hard across his temple and Stack loosened his grip. Dave wrenched the gun back, kicked him in the stomach, knocking him down. He let go four rounds, one in his neck, two in the chest. Stack was almost dead by the time Dave shot him in the eye. Frank felt blood and muck spatter his face. Stack let out a thick sucking sound in his throat, then a high moan, then nothing.

They drove home in silence, Frank periodically checking his rear-view for police. Dave had his arms around the boys in the back seat, pulling them close. Their eyes met. Frank looked away first, no staring contest, not tonight. As they made their way down New Cross Road towards Lewisham, a car pulled out of a side-street behind them. Frank kept his eye on the clock, his speed a couple of mph over the thirty limit.

'You'd better come back to my place and clean up,' said Dave. 'Don't want to go home to Carol looking like that.'

'What about Wally?'

'He'll meet us there later.'

Last seen, Wally and Lonnie were humping a blanket-wrapped Gary Stack into the boot of Lonnie's car. There was a whispered conversation between Dave and Wally before they drove away. Frank didn't expect to see Lonnie again either.

Rose never gave him a second look, just grabbed hold of her kids as they came through the door and took them away. For a second Carl looked behind him and Frank managed a smile. 'Good lad.'

'Come through to the kitchen and get them clothes off, wash your face.' Dave pulled out a roll of black bin liners from a drawer. He tore one off and held it open. 'Come on, hurry up.'

Frank emptied his pockets of change and put his keys on the table. He pulled off his tie, unbuttoned the shirt and dropped his trousers. Finally he took his jacket off, checking the pockets, then folding it before laying it in the black sack.

'You don't wanna worry,' said Dave. 'Wally's got a mate down the crem, we'll get this lot incinerated.'

Dave tore off another bag from the roll. Frank held it open while he stripped. 'You think I was wrong to shoot the cunt, don't you?'

'Not now, Dave.'

'No, go on, say what you think.'

'You didn't have to do him right there and then, in front of the boys.'

'Right.' He poured them both a large scotch, downed his own and poured another. 'Drink up. Make you feel better.'

But Frank didn't feel better. As he drove home in borrowed clothes, parked the car and turned off the engine, Frank wasn't capable of feeling anything but sick to his stomach.

23

The only other passenger in the station waiting room at Newark was into his second long and winding anecdote. Carl tried to make sure his disinterest showed. This story was similar to the last in that it concerned a pick-up in a bar in Newcastle and was obviously bullshit. Carl had the guy down as being about his own age, only a good four stone heavier with his belly straining at the buttons on his trenchcoat. He couldn't have imagined a less likely candidate for a three in a bed session 'They was gaggin' for it.' The geezer stuffed his hands in his pockets and paused. 'Where was I?'

'You tell me mate.' If it hadn't been so bloody cold outside, and if his ribs hadn't felt so tight when he walked, he'd have left the bloke to his fantasies. He checked the mobile: no messages and another hour until the train was due.

'Yes, so she says, "Come on love, it's Christmas after all." So I says, "Aye love, an' I don't come gift-wrapped." So she says, "Big feller like y'self'd take a few rolls of wrappin' paper, eh?" Cos, y'know I am a pretty big bloke, but some women like that, right? And you would, right? So I mean, what was I gonna do? And then when she says we can go round her mate's place and make a night of it, the three of us ...'

Carl had his eyes closed, offering nothing. When he opened them, the fat boy's mitts were moving under his coat. He stopped abruptly, picked up the conversation. 'I been up seeing me brother and his wife for Christmas, he's got kids 'n' that so I thought I'd come back for New Year, leave 'em to it like.'

Carl walked around the waiting room, moving steadily, testing the borders of pain. He looked out down the platform. A couple of lads were hanging back out of sight of the CCTV for a smoke.

'You got brothers and sisters?' said Fat Boy.

'Sorry?'

'Brothers and sisters, you got any?'

The question took Carl by surprise. 'No, no I haven't.'

It always felt disrespectful and an incomplete truth to say he had no brother. But the whole truth was too revealing. It made him uncomfortable to say he'd had a brother and that he'd died, and they'd say sorry and you'd think: you weren't there, 'sorry' don't come close.

Terry had been drinking heavily when Carl found him sitting at the kitchen table a month or so after Dad died. There were two glasses, as if he'd been expected. Terry shoved the spare chair out with his foot. Carl sat and Terry poured, then went back to knotting and un-knotting a length of white cord he'd bought to fix the bathroom light pull.

'Cheers,' said Carl.

'Did Mum send you?'

'Not exactly.'

'She did, I know she did. She tell you what she said to me?'

'No, but I can guess. You should have heard what she said to me.'

The space between them had always been there, but with Dad around it hadn't seemed to matter; they had him in common. Now he'd gone Carl felt no sense of kinship. He looked at his brother's face, spit at the corner of his mouth, eyes cast down, winding the cord. When they were kids, aunties used to say they were alike, probably because it was what Mum wanted to hear, but the best they could come up with was that they shared the 'Price' nose. Barely true then, certainly not now. Terry's nose had been broken at least once in the ring and had a little left-sided tilt.

'She said you wouldn't help with taking over Dad's business like he wanted, that you were the eldest and you didn't have the heart for it so I had to. But she doesn't think I'll handle it because I'm not really – how'd she put it – the brains of the family.'

'Terry, Dad never said he wanted us to take it on. You think he was even up to thinking about all that crap?'

'Mum says he did.'

'But it's not your thing, our thing, just leave it. Let Wally or Uncle Ruby or someone do it. Anyway, you've got a job.'

'Yeah, Terry the doorman, Terry the barman, Terry the occasional bouncer. You don't reckon I can handle it either, do you?'

Carl shook his head. 'That's not it.'

'She thinks if I do it, you'll come onside. After all this time, she still thinks you'll look after me.' Terry had finished looping the cord around his finger, making an even spiral and pulling it tight until the fingertip crooked and went purple. 'And you don't, do you, Carl. Not ever. I'm getting Wally to get me a gun.'

Carl snorted, a shallow laugh.

'I'm not kidding. If you won't do it with me, I'm looking after myself. Some wanker comes for me, I'll be waiting.'

'Terry, you don't need a gun.' He poured another scotch and went to refill Terry's glass.

He put his hand out. 'No thanks, I'm fine.'

'What does Wally think – about you picking things up?'

'I haven't asked.'

'Terry he was with Dad for years, he ought to have a say.'

Terry shrugged, that bottom lip stuck out just a little. He released the cord and let the blood flow back into his finger. In that moment, Carl saw him for what he was, what he'd always been, a fuck up waiting to happen. Soon to be a fuck up with a gun.

Dad's old crew made a show of it for a few weeks, mainly for Mum's sake. But gradually they all fell away, went straight, found other, less dicey ways of making money. Terry was left with a couple of his own mates, chancers from the boxing club days, lads whose fists and baseball bats did their talking. They were pointedly not men to be respected. Dad's pubs and bookies and clubs gradually stopped paying. Terry and his boys'd go in heavy-handed, make threats, smash a few glasses. Invariably the next time they went back, either the law would be waiting or the guv'nor would have brought in his own crew.

Carl suspected Terry started using the drugs he'd been dealing around the time him and Diane moved into the John Evelyn – the last Dave Price pub in SE8 and the only one he'd ever owned outright. He remembered their last conversation more for what they hadn't said than for what they had. Terry hadn't said that things were going wrong, that he'd made a string of shitty deals that left him owing money, that he was planning a job way out of his league to get himself out of hock. Carl hadn't asked Terry if he was using and if he needed help, maybe a few grand to tide him over, get away for a few weeks. He could have found it. But they had a pint, chatted stiffly about football, about Terry needing to see Mum more and then went their own ways.

The fat boy had produced some sort of sandwich from his holdall. Carl turned away, the sound of enthusiastic chewing, his jaw clicking like a duff metronome, set him on edge. He clenched his fists, forcing his fingernails into his palms. Fat Boy was talking again, spilling salad. 'So, where you spendin' New Year?'

'Home.'

'Where's that?'

'London.'

'I'm goin' to London, whereabouts?'

Carl never had to answer. The door to the waiting room opened and Adeline came in looking like a tear-streaked angel. He stood up and they fell into each other's arms. He closed his eyes, ignored the pain and held on. She broke away, picked up his bag and took his arm. 'Come on, we've got a car.'

'We?'

'Yeah, I'll explain.'

Adeline reached behind her to close the waiting room door. 'Mate, you've got mayo on yer trousers.'

Grace was asleep in the back seat when he got in. She woke up as the door slammed. 'S'alright love, you go back to sleep.'

'Dad,' said Grace and snuggled into him.

24

O'Keefe walked around him, sometimes coming in close to make sure his threats were hitting home. The bloke had a sickly reek all of his own. Frank focused slowly. He was on the concrete floor of a store room surrounded by stacked pallets; boxes of crisps and pork scratchings, crates of import Coke, cartons of cigarettes and boxes of branded tonic water. He scanned across to the packing benches, a roll of plastic sheeting, a toolbox.

Behind him in a dark corner, that scrawny streak of piss Adam stretched out yawning on an old leather sofa. 'Want me to call Ewan?'

'Not yet, not till I've made this old man wish he'd stayed at home.'

'But Ewan said to ring him as soon as we got here.'

'*I know* what he said. Help me get him up.'

One either side, they lifted him to his feet. Adam held him as Jim O'Keefe tore off a sheet of plastic and laid it across one of the benches. 'Put his hand there, I wanna give him something to remember me by.'

They dragged him to the bench and Adam forced his hand open. O'Keefe took a hammer from the toolbox, smacked it down on the table. A flat metallic crack echoed around the warehouse.

'You got anything to say now?'

There didn't seem much point.

'Because I'm gonna break your fingers. And then I'm going down to that shithole boozer and burn the fucking place down with your boy and his family in it.'

Adam was shifting nervously. 'Just do it, Jim.'

But O'Keefe was still stinking drunk and he wanted more. 'You gonna say sorry?'

Frank said nothing.

Another glance at the door from Adam.

'Say it and I'll just do one finger. Last chance.'

Adam's hand tightened around his wrist. O'Keefe folded the plastic over and brought the hammer down. It hit his ring finger and little finger, but a combination of O'Keefe's loose aim and a last second pull back against Adam's weak grip meant the blow glanced more than connected direct.

'Again. Keep him still for fucksake.'

Frank's breath came in shallow gasps. O'Keefe brought the hammer down again and connected. 'Say sorry. Hold him. Again.'

Everything blanked except the thickening pain of his bruised and broken fingers. Then even that was lost for a few seconds. He felt himself lifted again, gritted his teeth as they pulled his arm out.

'Ready now? Say you're sorry.'

The door swung back on its hinges. It was Ewan. 'James, Adam, what in Christ's name are you doing?'

They carried Frank over to the sofa and dumped him down. He held one throbbing hand in the crook of his other arm.

'I told you to call me when you got here. I mean Jesus, James what were you bloody thinking?'

'This bastard came into my house. It's my right...'

'To bring him here, fucking *here*, and torture him?'

Adam piped up, 'We'll dump him down the dock road, we're not stupid.'

'Are you sure about that? Think about it before you answer, cos I've just had a twenty minute phone call from Rudi. That fat Dutch ponce wants some money from you for a deal he says you stiffed him on. That right? Cos if it is, I'd think again about the whole "stupid" thing.'

'Rudi's out of line.'

'So it's true. He's got friends Adam, y'know, the sort of European connections we don't have, seriously nasty people from places you've never heard of.'

'How much you owe him?' asked James.

'About twenty,' said Adam.

'Plus interest,' said Ewan. 'He calls it nearer thirty.'

Adam kicked the hammer, sending it spinning across the floor. 'I'm sorry, Ewan, really sorry, man. Just give me a couple of weeks and I'll sort it, honestly.'

Ewan grabbed the kid by his shoulders. '*We'll* sort it. Rudi wants his cash by the end of the week. First let's deal with the old man.' He nodded at Frank.

'So what about me, what about Price? That cunt owes me.'

'Like I said, let's drop granddad first.'

When you're on your own you drink; there's no-one to say no. But you lose your way. It's been a long road you were never meant to go down in the first place. You made some bad decisions, terrible decisions. And there's drink, and it's a stone cold truth, there's no glory at the end of that road. There's no God, no shiny gates, no love. There's just another drink. Frank's words kept pace as he walked, as if they were driving him on against the cold and the pain in his hand.

What began as an internal commentary as he walked had turned into a rambling one-way dialogue, a diatribe to keep his feet moving in a voice which occasionally lifted loud enough to compete with the rumbling traffic on the main road. 'This isn't good enough,' he shouted. 'Shit! Shit! Shit! Why does it have to fucking HURT?'

He'd long since lost track of time. The O'Keefes dropped him in a car park. Told him where the hospital was. He'd gone in and eventually been seen sometime during the night. The nurse gave him some pills for the pain, splinted his broken finger and bandaged his hand, told him he'd need to see his own doctor. They kicked him out and he walked.

He reckoned it must have been around 7.00 a.m. from the hint of a chill grey dawn as he turned onto the Humber Bridge approach road. A steady trickle of cars funnelled through to a single green arrowed barrier to pay before speeding away across the river. Frank walked back to the roundabout and raised his thumb. A mucky Peugeot pulled up. The passenger door opened. 'Where you going?'

'South.'

The Humber glistened blackly beneath them as they crossed the bridge. Frank looked out towards the open estuary and sat nursing his hand in his buttoned coat. Sporadically he felt a jolt of pain that sent beads of sweat across his forehead, a sickness rising from his stomach.

Brian the driver turned out to be a nice guy in need of some company. He was on his way home to his wife and kids, his Christmas having turned into one from hell. 'I got a call from my dad late on Boxing Day. My mum was ill. Dad didn't know if it was serious, but he'd called the doctor. I said I'd drive up to Scarborough, but the weather had been closing in and I waited for a couple of hours. I called again just before I left and they said she was worse. She's in hospital.'

Frank was gritting his teeth.

'I left me dad there on his own. When I left him he cried, y'know, like a kid. That's the first time I ever saw my dad cry. I didn't want to leave him. I said I'd stay longer. I offered, but he told me to go home to my family. Said Mum wouldn't want to keep me from my family, not at Christmas.'

There was a long silence. Frank was having a problem maintaining anything like focus. 'Did you want to stay?'

There was a pause. 'Not really. But it's not right is it? I should be there.'

'So go home, get some sleep, hug your wife, kiss your kids, call your dad later and tell him you love him. Tell your kids to tell him they love him and be there when he needs you.'

Frank closed his eyes and they said nothing else until Brian stopped at a service station just before the A1.

'I'm off here, but you should be able to get a lift south with a bit of luck. I'm going for a coffee before I head out west, you're welcome to come too. It's on me.' As they got out of the car, Brian noticed the way Frank carried his arm. 'What's up, are you ok?'

'No, I got my hand caught in a door. It's a bit ...' He pulled his hand out of his coat.

'Jesus Christ! Sorry. I mean, you need to get to a doctor.'

'I already have, I'll be alright. Seriously, it's fine.'

Frank had once spent some time with an old soak called Monty Adams, a bent and probably not very good lawyer. Monty used to knock off the Times crossword in about fifteen minutes. 'It's all about the formula, dear boy,' he'd announce on completion. Just one of dozens of largely idiotic sayings Monty issued on a regular basis. But one thing Frank remembered him saying was that he didn't believe in coincidence, only serendipity. So whether it was serendipity, coincidence, or sheer dumb luck, either way Brian's first-aid proficiency and insistence on re-bandaging Frank's hand, meant they were ten minutes later going into the Little Chef than they would otherwise have been. Which, in turn, meant they were sitting drinking their coffee when a dirty BMW X5 pulled into the car park and three seriously pissed off looking O'Keefes piled out. Frank took the hint.

'Brian, look I'm really grateful for the lift, the bandage, the paracetamol and everything. I'm really sorry about your mum, but it'll work out I'm sure. There's some things happen and all you can do is ride it out and come through the other side the best you can.'

Under the harsh glare of the lights Brian's complexion seemed even greyer. He shrugged away the kind words. 'Thanks, I was pleased to have the company.'

'Brian, sorry to have to ask, but could you lend me some money for a phone call.'

'Use this if you want.' Brian pushed a slim, silver Nokia across the table.

Frank had the feeling he could have hung on forever and no one would have picked up the phone in the John Evelyn, although it was early. He hadn't a clue what Adeline's or Carl's mobile numbers might be. There was only one other number he could remember and that was Rose Price.

She picked up on the seventh ring. He heard her breathing. 'Hello?'

'Rose, it's nothing to worry about, I came to your flat with Adeline the other evening, remember? We were coming to find Carl. I just wondered if he was back yet or Adeline?'

There was a long silence. Rose Price wheezed. 'You'll have to speak to my neighbour.'

He heard the phone go down, clattering on the table. In the distance the door latch and the old woman's sing-song voice calling, 'Lauren ... Lauren ...'

Across the table Brian looked at his watch. Frank ignored him.

Rose's phone picked up. 'Who is this?'

'Lauren, this is Frank Neaves from the John Evelyn, I came the other evening with Adeline and you let us in to talk to Rose. We went after Carl.'

'What's wrong, is he there? You've scared her half to death.'

'Listen, we ran into some trouble. I don't know where Carl is, but I reckon by now he should be back or at least on his way home, so is Diane and so is Grace. But I think Diane's bloke's heading that way with his brothers and they're not too happy. You just need to warn Carl when he turns up, leave a message at the pub or something and tell them to keep their heads down and don't open up.' There was a long silence. 'Lauren?'

'I don't believe this. You're saying these blokes are coming here?'

'I don't know for sure, but will you do it? Please, just make sure Carl knows.'

'I suppose so, what the hell have you done?'

Brian had his coat on and was getting up, ready to leave, waiting for his phone. Outside the O'Keefes climbed back into Ewan's car.

'What have *I* done? That love, is a bloody good question.'

25

The Sunday morning after Gary Stack's murder. A warm breeze had blown through the kitchen door, lifting the front page of the Express. Carol sat at the table, red-eyed. Frank took two slices of Sunblest from the bag and dropped them in the toaster. He twisted the top of the bag and put it back in the bread bin. He brushed crumbs off the plate Carol had used. He took a knife from the drawer and butter from the fridge. He put a spoonful of instant in a mug. When the toaster popped, he laid shavings of butter on the toast and made the coffee while it melted. He spread the butter and cut the two slices corner to corner before putting the knife in the washing up bowl. He returned the butter to the fridge. Carol followed each movement, scrutinising, saying nothing.

Frank wiped his hands on his jeans. 'I know I should have told you. Or just put him off, but it was his kids.'

Carol's hands linked around her coffee cup. 'It isn't just last night Frank.' She lit a cigarette. 'You lied to me and you must have re-made that choice to lie every day. Last night was just the cherry on the cake.'

'I'm not right in, love. I'm not – one of them. I've just been helping a mate out, I just ... advised.' Christ it sounded hollow.

'As if Dave Price needs another bloody yes man.'

'It's not like that, there's times I've kept him straight when it could have gone the other way.'

'So what, you're Henry Kissinger? Wake up, Frank. He's a shabby little villain with ideas above his station. He's no more likely to take notice of you than the man in the moon.' She studied the cigarette between her fingers. 'And you might have been mates once, but that doesn't give him the right to put his dirty paws on us.'

Frank noted the 'us'. At least there was still an 'us'.

'Well, I've had it after last night,' said Frank.

Carol touched the end of her cigarette to the corner of the newspaper. The paper browned and burned. 'If you go anywhere near him, Frank, that's it. I'll take Kate and we'll go. And I want a move, out to Orpington, somewhere like that, right out and away from all this.'

'I never wanted this.'

'I'm not having Kate growing up around lies, it just makes everything a bloody sham. It's horrible.'

He nodded, took a bite at the corner of a now cold slice of toast. It stuck in his throat. 'Carol, I've got to ask, if the old bill come round, I don't reckon they will, but if they do ...'

'You want me to lie for you.'

He shrugged. 'Just say I was here.'

'Doing what?'

'I dunno, watching telly.'

'What was on?'

'I don't know.'

'That's your alibi screwed, then. These people aren't fools, Frank, and neither are you, so for God's sake stop acting like one.' She got up, flicked the kettle on her way out.

The last wisp of smoke rose from the dead cigarette end. She was right, if the boys in blue dropped in for a chat, he was buggered.

Carol tossed the *TV Times* on the table. 'Read that and tell me what we watched after *Seaside Special* last night?'

After dinner, they took Kate to the park. Frank pushed her gently on her swing, Carol said, 'So, what did you do last night?'

'Stayed in and watched telly.'

'What did you watch?'

'*Seaside Special*, then *Starsky and Hutch*, then the first bit of Parky. I didn't like who he had on, so we went to bed.'

'Did you go out at all?'

'No.'

'A neighbour saw you drive away.'

'Must've been someone else. I was too tired, I'd been working all day. Driving my boss to his country place.'

Kate jumped off the swing and ran to join a couple of kids who'd just got the roundabout going. It was picking up speed as she jumped on. 'Careful, love, you hang on tight.' They walked towards her.

'The neighbour described the car, your car.'

'Was she pissed?'

'*Frank.*'

'Okay, I did pop out for a few minutes to get my lady wife some Maltesers. Look officer, there's the box on the table.'

'Which shop?'

'The off-licence on Brownhill Road, they had a special on and I bought the box because it had ten pence off.'

'Tight arse.'

'Can I go now, officer?'

'The girl in the shop doesn't remember you.'

'She wouldn't have, there was a bloody long queue and she had plenty enough to deal with. A box of Maltesers is hardly going to stick in the memory.'

She squeezed his hand. 'If I loved you a tiny bit less, Frank, I'd hang you out to dry for going behind my back.'

'It's not like I had an affair.'

'Good, I don't have to cut your balls off.'

The police had an un-marked car parked almost permanently outside the Black Bull for the first part of the week and Frank heard from Wally Patch that they were asking questions about Stack. Far-fetched as it seemed, word was going round that Stack had been a grass for a CID bloke. Wilder still was the rumour that snatching the kids had been a set-up to tease Dave out of his comfort zone; a warning, the precursor to some elaborate old bill sting.

'Rumours,' said Frank. 'It's all bollocks.'

'Probably,' said Wally, not convinced.

Frank stayed close to home. He went to work, kept an eye on the papers. Wednesday's *South London Press* carried news: '... of a significant breakthrough in the search for Lewisham-based Gary Stack, missing presumed murdered in a bloody gangland feud.' That evening the phone rang. Carol took the call, handed Frank the receiver. 'It's him.' She stood close enough to listen.

Dave's voice was barely above a whisper. 'Frank, look mate, I thought I'd better give you fair warning, you might be getting a visit from the old bill. I've just got back, been there all bloody day. There's a DS on a bit of a mission. Wally reckons he had Stack lined up as a grass, if he wasn't already.'

'So has Wally been in, then?'

'Nah, just me so far.'

'So what makes you think they're coming here?'

'They just might, that's all.'

'You didn't tell 'em anything.'

'No, course not. Just that your name was mentioned and I thought you should know.'

He put the phone down. Carol had gone pale. 'You look how I feel.'

'Sick.'

'Something like that.'

'Thing is, Frank, you just about stopped short of accusing him of grassing you up and he didn't bite.'

'He wouldn't, just wouldn't. It goes against everything.'

Carol went back to the kitchen. The radio was on while she was cooking tea. She put Kate to bed, stayed upstairs reading her bedtime stories longer than usual. Frank sat and watched the news and waited for the knock at the door. When it came, he already had his jacket on. Carol came downstairs. He kissed her, said he'd see her later. He might have been off to work, or down the pub if it wasn't for his stomach churning and police cars double parked in the street outside.

They were an hour into the first interview before Frank realised his cobbled together Saturday night alibi wasn't going to make a blind bit of difference. Detective Sergeant Fraser was a bleary-eyed misery-guts, lighting one Rothmans' king size from the butt of the last. He couldn't have cared less if Frank knew that *Starsky and Hutch* had come on after *Seaside Special*. He kept his questions coming in a low blunt monotone without appearing to give a damn about Frank's answers.

'So you've said you weren't involved in the murder of Mr Gary Stack?'

'Right.'

'And you're sure you don't feel like changing your mind on that?'

'No.'

'Where were you on the evening of Saturday the twelfth of August?'

Frank sighed. 'I was at home, with my wife, watching television.'

'You work for David Price, yeah?'

'I know him and occasionally I act as a driver, just now and again, that's what I do. I'm a driver. I don't work *for* him.'

'But he pays you?'

'He pays my petrol and a little bit for my time.'

'You pay tax on that?'

A silence.

'Never mind, eh? Who gives a shit if you get a few extras on the QT. So, Frank, you drove Mr Price to the Heygate Estate, Walworth on the evening of Saturday twelfth of August.'

'No, I was at home with my wife.'

'You weren't, you were a stone's throw from the Old Kent Road. You were seen.'

Frank shrugged.

'What's that supposed to mean, that shrug. I'm right, but you're not saying?'

'It doesn't mean anything.'

'Means you was on the fucking Heygate.'

'No.'

And so it went on, hour after hour. Not quite the third degree, but relentless.

As Frank had thought it through countless times in the years afterwards, he always reached the same conclusion, the bastard was playing for time, going through the motions. His mind was already made up. Frank stopped in mid-sentence. 'Why are you bothering, I mean what the fuck are you getting out of this? You're not even listening.'

A uniformed copper knocked and came in the interview room. He handed Fraser a note. Fraser stubbed his fag out, put the chewed lid back on his biro and left the room. He returned a few minutes later with a brown paper parcel and an air of self-satisfaction. He laid the parcel on the table and undid the string. 'Recognise this, Mr Neaves?' He unfolded Frank's suit inside a clear plastic evidence bag.

'It looks like a suit.'

'It's a blue suit with bloodstains on it, which we've just confirmed are the same blood group as the late Mr Stack. It's your blue suit.'

'Is it?'

'It's made to measure Frank, a one-off fit, made especially for you.' The cheerless bastard winked. 'Joey Silverman told my DC so. He's even got the measurements all written down in a little book with your name next to 'em. See what I'm doing? I've got you, your suit, Stack's blood. What we call a chain of evidence. So let's have another go, where were you on the evening of Saturday the twelfth of August between eight o'clock and midnight?'

Once the trial date was set, Frank got word that Dave was offering to pay for his legal representation. He might as well have saved his money. They took him from his remand cell in Brixton to a holding cell at Southwark Crown Court. His barrister, a panto-ponce in wig and gown called Aubrey Dawson-Winters, waltzed in and gave him a ten minute briefing, the basis of which seemed to be: keep your chin up, old boy, and don't swear at the judge.

The whole show passed in front of him like a play on the telly. He heard his name spoken. He was a family man, they said. A former soldier who'd served Queen and country and who'd seen service in Cyprus and Germany. All very nice, but hardly a cast-iron defence. Especially when balanced against the prosecution's argument that as a soldier, he had an intimate knowledge of firearms. Without Stack's body, Dawson-Winters was confident the prosecution wouldn't have enough to make the murder charge stick, but one after another, they produced witnesses who'd seen him out that night, who put him on the Heygate Estate. None of the eye-witnesses mentioned seeing Dave Price, or Wally Patch, only him.

Fraser walked to the stand, hoisting his trousers and running his thumbs around his belt. He gave a slow explanation of the significance of the bloodstained suit for the jury as a court clerk paraded the suit along the row of jurors, lifting its plastic cover as if they were investigating a dry-cleaning accident. They leaned forward to get a closer look at the stains. It was all circumstantial, Dawson-Winters argued, but the jury weren't buying it. And when the prosecution produced a living, breathing, lying through his teeth Lonnie Chambers as their eyewitness and he testified he'd seen Frank pull the trigger, he knew he was going down. He glanced to where Dave had been sitting, but his place in the gallery was empty.

There was barely time to draw breath. The jury took an afternoon to return a guilty verdict. The judge sentenced him to fifteen years and boomed a final theatrical pronouncement to *take him down*. Frank felt a chill in his insides. He was taken back to the holding cell and left alone with his guts cramping up. They started churning ominously and he asked to be taken to the toilet. The copper pointed to the bucket in the corner.

'No, seriously mate, you really don't want me to try and go in that. I need a proper bog.'

'Fucked if I care.'

'You will if I stink the place out. Honestly, my stomach's doing somersaults.'

The copper posted himself outside the toilet door. Every couple of minutes, Frank made himself heard. When he came out, they cuffed him to a screw from Brixton – a dumpy sod with bad breath – for the journey back. They sat him down in the back of the airless prison van. As they drove out through the car park, there were a few faces lined up at the kerbside. A couple of camera flashes. He kept his head down. Once they were out into the traffic, he looked up. The world was going about its business, the afternoon slipping by, another day gone; home for tea.

He was processed in Brixton that evening, but told that he was likely to be moved within a few days. He asked if he could contact Carol, arrange a visit. The screw said he would be entitled to one visit a month – in a month.

Carol didn't come, not that month or the next. Frank wrote and the letters went unanswered. Six weeks later they moved him to Maidstone. It could have been worse. He continued to write to Carol once a week. And to Dave, and then when no one wrote back, he wrote to Jacqui. Within a week he had a letter back. She said she'd speak to Dave on his behalf. She was sorry. What happened shouldn't have. It was wrong and they all knew it. She signed off: *I can come and visit if you want, tell me if you need anything brought in. Take care, Jacqui x*

It was another four months and another half a dozen unreturned letters before Dave visited. He arrived half an hour late for the hour's visiting session and sat across the table fiddling with his Dunhill packet. 'Feels like we should 'ave a pack of cards or something.' He glanced around the hall, seemed overwhelmed by the place, the echoes, bare bricks and the low hubbub of conversation.

Frank couldn't make his mind up whether Dave was antsy about being recognised or wanting to make sure the other cons had clocked him.

'Oi, I'm here, Dave, hello?'

'Yeah, sorry mate. Jacqui said you wanted to see me.'

'Cos you wouldn't have made the effort otherwise. I've been here six months.'

'Come on, Frank, it's a bit dodgy me being in a place like this.' He looked behind him. A bloke from B wing acknowledged the nod.

'Right. Dodgy for you, seeing as I'm in here for what you did.'

He had Dave's attention.

'You wanna keep it down, Frank. I'm here.'

'Look, I've spoken to a few people and I want to appeal against the sentence. The evidence, it's all circumstantial apart from Lonnie and I reckon they could easily discredit him. And that suit, Jesus Christ—'

'I know, I can't see it somehow. Maybe Wally screwed up.'

'Thing is, it could easily get turned over on appeal, but I need some backing for a decent solicitor. There's no way I can do fifteen years of this.'

'Sure, but Frank, y'know I already paid once for that Dawson-Winters bloke.'

Frank couldn't believe he was being so bloody tight-fisted. 'So can't we find someone better? Come on, you must have contacts.'

'Right, yeah. I'll do what I can. You managing alright otherwise?'

'Other than being locked in here. Yeah it's all tickety fucking boo. There's something else I need you to do, it's important. Dave, I need you to go and see Carol.'

He laughed. 'She hates me. Looked at me like shit all the way through your trial.'

'I want you to tell her, convince her that it wasn't me who killed Stack.' He dropped his voice. 'I want you to tell her who did.'

'You're kidding, right? There's no way. She'll go straight to the old bill.'

'No she won't, not if you tell her it was for the kids, that you didn't have a choice. And that you're helping me with an appeal. I don't want to lose her, Dave. She won't see me or answer my letters, nothing. She thinks I killed a man and I need her to know I didn't. So just go and have a chat, yeah?'

'If you reckon she'll listen.'

The alarm bell gave two short rings. Dave was looking to leave.

'It's five minutes,' said Frank.

'Right.' Dave was back to eyeing up the talent like the best man at a footballer's wedding. 'So, you doing alright then?'

'You already asked me that.'

'Right.'

'What about you, business booming?'

'Yeah, well, to tell you the truth, I'm looking at knocking a lot of stuff on the head, letting some of the pubs go. I need to take things under the radar. It's not like it was, Frank, ten years ago we had the patch to ourselves, but it's not like that anymore. We had our turn, our wild years, but I've been thinking it's time to wise up a bit, y'know? You always said the smart move was to know when you're past your best and get out with what you can. It ain't far off.'

Frank took a Dunhill from Dave's pack and lit it. He sat back, smoked, said nothing.

'We had a crack though, didn't we.' Dave checked the clock. 'Had a laugh, some good times, made some decent money. I'm thinking of sticking to the kind of business that don't bring the Flying Squad on the doorstep like the man from the Pru.' He laughed quickly.

'So what, you run out of favours?' Frank stubbed the cigarette out. '*You* had good times, Dave. *You* had the best of it, the money, the birds on the side Rose never knew about, the flash nights out and a bit put away. Well, a lot put away unless you were stupid with it. I didn't get that, none of it. I made those deals work, I gave you the good sense you never had.'

'And I made sure you were alright.'

'Well I'm not fucking alright, am I? I'm in here.'

The bell went for the end of visiting. Dave stood up, pocketed his cigarettes and matches. 'I'll talk to Carol.'

'And the lawyer, yeah?'

'Sure.'

It was the last time Frank ever saw or spoke to Dave Price.

Frank's second visit came unexpectedly a week later on a morning when you could, at a stretch, imagine the crocuses making an appearance in the park, when the sunshine coming through the cell window after breakfast made you feel better in spite of yourself. The senior prison officer, a bloke called Gidding, pulled Frank out from the line of cons making their way to the worksheds.

'Neaves, you've got a visit.'

'I'm not due,' said Frank, panicking suddenly because he hadn't been allowed a shower in nearly a week and knew the rank odour of week-old clothes and a cramped three-man cell clung to him.

'You don't want to go, fine.'

'Course I do, Mr Gidding, have I got time for a wash and shave?'

Gidding laughed. 'On your bike, she's waiting. Governor's office.'

'She?'

'Your wife.' He laughed again. 'Remember, the silly slag you married?'

153

Carol looked pale. Her hair had grown out and her hands were deep in the pockets of a new coat, smart, well-tailored, charcoal grey. There were fine lines around her eyes; he didn't remember those. 'Hello, love,' said Frank.

Gidding interrupted. 'The Governor says you can use his P.A.'s office. Sally's on a break and he's in a meeting. I'll be next door.'

'What's going on?' Frank sat in one of the chairs in the waiting area and motioned to Carol to do the same. 'All this Governor's office shit. Is it Kate, she's not ill?'

'She's fine Frank. She's healthy, physically.' Carol took her hands out of her pockets and took a seat. 'I needed to see you.'

'Christ, I've missed you. Did Dave talk to you?'

'Yes, he did. I listened to what he had to say out of respect for the fact that you'd asked him to come round.'

'And?'

'Then I threw him out of the house and told him to take his shitty bloody money and give it to the cats' home.'

Frank knew Gidding would be eavesdropping. He lowered his voice and moved closer. 'I wanted you to know I hadn't killed that bloke. That's what he was meant to tell you.'

'Well, he didn't say that, but he'd have been wasting his breath if he had.'

'Carol, I swear to you I didn't.'

'I know. I always knew. I told you that at the beginning.'

He looked down at his feet, the clumsy black work shoes, the too-long prison issue trousers, frayed at the bottom. 'So why wouldn't you come? I wrote, did you get the letters?'

'Yeah, I got them. She took the stack of letters from her bag and put them on the seat between them. They had not been opened. 'I don't want letters, Frank, I want a husband.'

'You've got one.' He reached out to touch her hand. 'Always.'

She pulled her hand away. 'No, Frank, I'm not waiting. That's why I've come here and why I needed to see you and tell you myself. I want you to know you'll be getting a visit from a solicitor. His name's Saxby and he's going to ask you to sign some documents. It's what he needs to start divorce proceedings.'

'I don't understand.'

One of the secretaries came past, put some papers on the P.A.'s desk and took her time doing it. Carol waited for her to go. 'I need to make a clean break. For me and Kate.'

'I know you must be pissed off ...'

154

She snorted. 'Pissed off? It doesn't even come close. I mean Jesus Christ, what was it Frank, the money? We didn't need money, we were doing ok. So what, was it him with his bullshit, make you feel like you were his best mate, one of the boys? Because to be honest, I can't think of anything *less* manly than not having the balls to be straight with your wife. You lied to me for months, years. And now you're in here for a murder you didn't do. No Frank, I'm not pissed off. I'm way past pissed off. I've been in bits for months, that's why I never came, I didn't think I could stand it. But I've realised, this is your time, not mine, and I'm not doing it with you.'

Ever since he'd been inside, Frank had always kept this vision of the future, a mental snapshot of how things had been and could be again. It had grown increasingly vivid and held him steady for the last few months. He took a deep breath, but couldn't keep the tremor out of his voice. 'I don't want to argue with you.'

'So will you sign the papers?'

'I love you, Carol.'

'I don't want it, Frank. What I want is for you to agree to see the solicitor and sign the papers. One lot will be for the divorce, the other signs the house and the mortgage over to me. I want to put it up for sale.'

'Carol, please?'

'Well, you ain't gonna need it. And I don't want it. I don't want to be there and I don't want Kate growing up there.'

'If I do this, can you keep in touch, let me see Kate?'

'Tell you the truth, I haven't decided and I'm not making promises I don't know if I'll keep. She knows where you are and she knows what for. I won't lie to her. She can make up her own mind when the time comes.'

Gidding put his head around the door. 'The Governor's due back in about ten minutes.'

Carol pulled her things together. 'It's fine, we're finished.'

'I love you.'

'I'm sorry.' She put her hand on his arm. 'It's no good to me.'

Gidding called a screw to show her out. The last Frank saw was the charcoal grey coat disappearing down the corridor.

'Come on, Neaves, I'll take you back. D'you want these?' Gidding picked up the letters and flicked through.

'What do you think?'

Frank took on his first three or four years inside the way he had his national service: go where they tell you; shut up when it's shutting-up time; eat, sleep, crap and watch your back. You took it one day at a time and closed out the future, because there was no future. Only Maidstone's relentless routine: up at seven, into the dining hall for breakfast at seven-thirty, worksheds eight-thirty, dining hall for twelve, then back to the cells until two. Worksheds again until four-thirty, then back to the cells with lock-up at nine. Half-day Saturdays, no work on Sundays.

The promised visit from the lawyer Saxby took place late on a Friday a couple of weeks after Carol's visit. He laid the papers out across the visitors' table and drew pencil crosses where Frank had to sign. The room was empty. Saxby lit up a menthol fag and handed Frank a pen. He signed without reading. Back in his cell that night, Frank smoked dope for the first time. It helped. He gave up writing letters. The new lawyer Dave had promised never showed up and the more time passed, the less chance there seemed that any kind of appeal would do more than raise his expectations and screw him up. He had no visitors, which was fine. Occasionally Jacqui would write with news and offer to come and see him, but he always turned her down. He had insulated himself and wanted it kept that way.

It was a letter from Jacqui just before Christmas 1987 that put the first dent in the fug. Dave had died. He had been ill for a while, although a lot longer than he'd admitted to anyone. By the time he was formally diagnosed, the cancer was inoperable. They offered a course of chemotherapy, but with such slim odds Dave had turned them down. He'd rather die with his hair on, he told them. He'd hung on for another two and a half months, the last couple of weeks morphine dependant. He died with Rose and the boys there. Jacqui thought Frank would want to know. And that she had sent a wreath in his name to the cremation service at Hither Green, although she hadn't attended herself. Frank folded the letter, slid it back into its envelope and left it in the shoebox with the rest of his personal things. It was fourteen hours until lock-up and the first opportunity for a smoke.

Frank had been allocated a job in the workshop repairing furniture for re-sale or use in the prison. That morning he was working on seat cushions for a set of four waiting room chairs. He'd stripped the worn fabric away, a snotty municipal green, and was cleaning up the chair frame when he became conscious of someone standing over him. It was Gidding on one of his *see and be seen* tours of the workshops. 'Get your letter this morning?'

'Yeah, I got it.' Frank carried on working, sanding off a patch of hardened glue.

'A good mate of yours was he, Dave Price?'

'I knew him.'

Gidding nodded. 'A lot of people did and I expect quite a few'll be happy to see him gone.'

Frank blew away the fine wood dust. 'There aren't many of us who make it through without pissing someone off somewhere down the line.'

'Well, you'd know.' He walked on.

Frank didn't know how he made it through to the evening. At lock-up he rolled his first spliff, felt the thump in the back of his head recede. He smoked a second, then a third and slept without dreaming.

There was a regular crew of around a dozen working in the furniture shop. The prison made a few quid to put back into tools and materials and you could opt for some poxy qualification, but Frank wasn't interested, preferring to get on with the work rather than kid himself he'd learn anything worthwhile. He didn't have much time for chat, but on the odd occasion if a job was a two-hander or it needed a bit of extra muscle, he'd call over the dark-haired lad, Chris. It put them on nodding terms in the dining hall and on the landings.

Some time after Gidding's visit, a change in personnel saw a couple of new blokes coming into the workshop. There was an older bloke, George, who Chris shook hands with on arrival and introduced to Frank, and a skinny tosser with a broken tooth, Sean, who within five minutes was sounding off that he'd been to hot to handle in Wandsworth. He seemed to know his way around and had a few mates already in the workshop, judging by the backslapping going on. There was a bloke called Kev Ellis and another lad they called Shandy. They did bugger all work all morning, but as Frank was packing up for the dinner break, he caught Sean checking him out. He came over. 'Frank Neaves, right?'

Frank shrugged.

He jiggled from foot to foot. 'Yeah, it is you. Knew I could place you. I'm Sean Stack, you remember my cousin, Gary?'

Frank went cold.

'I'll be seeing you.'

157

That was that. So much for a quiet life. He didn't know where or when they'd come, only that they would. In a place where entertainment was at a premium, watching for a score to be settled was the best show in town. Stack was younger, stronger, looked nastier and he had mates. Frank was on his own. He thought about making the first move, get it over and done with on his own terms. He also thought about saying something to one of the screws, but they were unlikely to act and in any case, you'd mark yourself out as a soft touch and that wasn't worth thinking about.

When it happened, it was quick and Frank saw it coming. There were usually two screws supervising the workshop, Foster and Lane. On the morning Foster was called away to the senior P.O.'s office, Shandy put a chisel to his thumb and when Lane went for the first aid kit from the office, they barred the door, locking him in. Stack pulled a sharpened screwdriver and was on him fast. Frank avoided the first wild slash; the second tore through his sweatshirt and opened a gash in his forearm. He stumbled back, turning sideways on and Stack slashed him again across the small of his back and his arse. Then suddenly Chris was behind Stack, grabbing at the screwdriver, holding onto his arm and wrenching it round behind him. Frank butted Stack in the face, blood spewed from his nose. Frank piled three, four, five punches into his stomach, then one to the jaw. Stack's mates let Lane out of the storeroom. Frank was staggering, breathless, blood dripping down his arm, his trousers ripped and bloody. Stack was in a heap. Chris let his arm go and the screwdriver clattered to the floor. He kicked it away. A dozen screws arrived, batons drawn.

'Thanks mate,' said Frank.

'No problem,' said Chris. 'Uncle Costas says *yia sou*.'

Frank was patched up in the infirmary, half a dozen stitches in his arm and another five across his arse. No lasting damage, so the M.O. said. Stack was put into isolation, pending a psychiatric report. Some dickhead told him he'd lose less remission if he told them he was driven to it by voices. Not the brightest. Chris was up there too in solitary for a couple of weeks, but he was looked after.

Frank was still recovering when they told him he was being transferred. He'd lost his remission and they reasoned it was a risk, keeping a bloke with his record in Maidstone. The request went in and was confirmed within a week. Gidding oversaw the paperwork.

'You're on your travels, Neaves.'

'Looks like it.'

He smiled. 'Enjoy Hull, I'm sure you'll be welcome up there, London lad like you.'

26

Diane drove south on the A1 from Newark keeping to a steady seventy, the engine note constant, her hands tight on the steering wheel. Just before Peterborough she slowed behind an articulated lorry. It threw up muck from its back wheels, smearing the windscreen and working the Focus's wiper blades way past their usefulness.

Grace was sleeping, sometimes giving little sighs and snores. Carl lay back against the headrest, closed his eyes and let the wave of relief that he was going home wash over. Adeline leaned round from the front passenger seat. 'We had to leave Frank behind.'

He sighed heavily. 'What happened?'

'He went into their house and it all kicked off ...' She nodded towards Grace. 'He brought her out and Jim O'Keefe came out after him with a shotgun.'

'He shot him?'

'We don't know,' she said pointedly.

'I wasn't hanging around to find out,' said Diane. 'I know what he's like.' Her eyes were fixed on the road ahead and she accelerated to leave the lorry behind. 'When we get back we'll have to find somewhere to dump the car. I don't want to leave it anywhere they can trace it back to us.'

'Frank said we were gonna take it back to the yard,' said Adeline.

'I think you'll find things have changed a bit.'

'I know.'

'Right, so where d'you want to ditch it?'

'We can take it on the estate and leave the keys. It'll be gone or torched by morning. And if not, I'll mention it to a couple of people I know.' Adeline leaned round again. 'So what about Frank?'

Diane's voice hardened. 'I know he's your friend, but there's sod all we can do about it now.'

Carl looked out of the window, staring straight through his reflection. 'I just want to go home, get Grace home.'

No one spoke again until they were on the south side of Rotherhithe Tunnel.

The pub was cold, the flat upstairs even colder. Carl managed to carry Grace up to her room without her waking. He swept the soft toys on the floor and put her into bed. He left the door ajar and put the Christmas tree lights on so that if she woke she'd see them first. He went to the window and waited until Adeline and Diane came into view walking back down Evelyn Street. They weren't speaking and when he went downstairs to meet them, only Diane came in.

'She's gone home. Thank Christ.'

Carl let it go. He poured two large brandies. They sat at a table in the empty pub.

Diane looked tired. 'Why did you come, I mean after all this time, what made you decide it would be a good thing to do now?'

'The call from Grace, I s'pose. She said he wouldn't let her have my presents and that he wanted her to call him "Dad". She told me he frightened her.' He paused. 'And that he frightened you.'

'You know Adeline was working for Adam, selling drugs. And they were sleeping together last year. Jim reckons she did Adam for a lot of money.'

'And what, that explains him knocking you about and threatening our daughter?'

'I *can* handle him most of the time, you just need to know when to—' She broke off in mid-sentence and looked away. He looked up, nodded for her to continue. 'No, I just realised what I was about to say. I'm not thinking straight, too bloody tired. I really need to sleep. Can we sort things out in the morning?'

'Sure, you get up to bed. I'll kip on the sofa.'

'That's got a familiar ring to it.' She was halfway out the door, then came back and squeezed his arm. 'I'm pleased you came. I just don't know if it was the right thing.'

Carl sat for a while, listening to the sound of the empty pub, its ghost voices echoing in his memory. He finished his brandy and Diane's, locked up and made his way upstairs. He laid out the blankets and pillow on Grace's floor and slept there.

The phone's persistent tone filtered through into Carl's dreams, but not enough to bring him fully awake. He stirred only when Grace's voice came through. 'Dad, the phone's ringing downstairs.'

His mouth was cardboard dry and he had difficulty speaking. 'Okay, I'll get it.' He lifted himself out of the blankets and made it half way across the landing when the phone stopped ringing. He went downstairs and dialled 1471 for the last caller ID and didn't recognise the number. His imagination saw only O'Keefe coming for Diane, for Grace, for him.

He made Grace's breakfast and took it to her in bed on a tray. He made Diane a coffee, knocked softly on the bedroom door and went in. He sat on the edge of the bed and woke her gently. 'Welcome home.'

Diane eased herself up against the pillows. 'Where's Grace?'

'Watching a film. She wouldn't go back to sleep once the phone rang.'

'I didn't hear it. I was asleep.' She glanced at the bedroom clock. It was nearly nine. 'Who was it?'

'I don't know, I didn't get to it in time.'

They both knew. Diane took the coffee from him and put it on the bedside table. 'I'm sorry, Carl.'

'What for?'

'Leaving, coming back like this, all the rotten stuff in between.' Her expression changed, softened a little. 'Grace has really missed you.'

'And you?'

'Now and then.'

It was a start. He hugged her then broke away suddenly. There was a rattle at the front door downstairs, someone knocking. He looked out of the window and saw Lauren step away into view. 'Something's up with Mum, I'd better go down.'

Diane was already half out of bed. 'Carl, wait a second.'

'What?'

'I just wanted to say, I couldn't come back and live here – at the pub.' She paused. 'But maybe I could come back. If we wanted to try again. We can talk about it.'

'I'd have to convince Mum, about the pub.'

'I'll take that as a "no" then.'

He shrugged. 'Stranger things have happened, most of them this week.'

If there was one thing certain to make Grace kick off, it was having to give up her pink blanket and a place on the sofa in front of *The Wizard Of Oz* to wash and dress to go to Nanna's house. Carl sat with her and negotiated a compromise. He would take her to Nanna's, Lauren and the DVD would come too, *and* she would definitely be allowed to stay up past midnight for the New Year. He promised. Grace ran a victory lap of the living room before Diane steered her towards the bathroom.

'You coming to Mum's?' said Carl.

Diane shook her head. 'I'll face your mother when I'm ready. I've got to go see Mum and Dad anyway. They ought to know, some of it anyway.'

'So, I'll see you later?'

For a moment she became distant, frowning.

'Carl, he might not come. Frank might be wrong. Lauren didn't say he definitely would and it might not even have been them he saw. But if it was, if he does turn up, please be careful. Just don't wind him up.'

'*As if?*'

'You know what I mean, just say yes to everything and don't give him an excuse to start anything. He'll be alright if Ewan's there, I'm sure, just let him say his piece, have a bit of a rant and go.'

It was as if she could will the outcome, but it was naive at best and Carl wasn't about to be convinced.

When Mum opened the door, Grace rushed in giving off squeals of delight at the Christmas tree, the decorations, the strings of cards, but mostly at the tin of Quality Street on the dining table. 'Can I, Nanna?'

'You can choose three.'

Grace raked through the tin.

'Grace, d'you want to go next door and do some painting with Lauren for a bit?'

'No, Dad, I'm watching the film with Nanna. You said.'

Lauren helped herself to a purple sweet and whispered in Grace's ear. He couldn't hear the exact words, but it had something to do with dressing-up and make-up boxes and Grace let Lauren take her hand.

'What are you two up to?' said Carl.

'Secret.' Grace's giggles disappeared into the hallway. 'Back soon, Nanna.'

The door closed and there was a long pause, finally Mum said, 'So you brought her back?'

He nodded, had a fleeting thought about Frank, but said nothing.

'Not without a fight, by the looks of it.'

He gave a shrug. 'Actually it was more of me taking a kicking than anything. Thing is though, Mum, I think Diane's bloke's coming down here, that's what the call was about first thing. Diane's left him, for now at least and he's … gone off the deep end.'

'What you gonna do?'

'Go back, check my stock and get ready to open up tonight. Couple of busy nights in the offing. Should have a pub full, pretty rare these days.'

She touched his arm. 'You be careful, son.'

'Course.'

'You did well, bringing our girl home.'

There was a space for: *I didn't think you had it in you,* but she held her tongue. Carl thought for a moment, his eye drawn to the photograph of his father that took the centre of the mantelpiece. 'Mum, once this is sorted I'm gonna sit down with Diane and talk about what we're gonna do.'

'I knew you'd 'ave 'er back.'

'I might and I might not, and I'm not talking about it now. I just want you to know things'll have to change a bit.' He kissed her on the cheek and said he'd see her later, that he'd be back around three to pick Grace up.

Carl couldn't manage more than a couple of bites of toast. He switched on the TV in the office and watched a re-run of the first Roberto Duran and Sugar-Ray Leonard fight. You either loved the game or you didn't – Dad's words. Carl loved the game. Duran was fierce that night, arrogant, hard as nails. An overblown lightweight stepping up and doing the business. Leonard, renowned as a stylist, worked hard to score. The commentary cranked up from the first round, '... that's Leonard coming forward and Duran backing off'. The co-commentator cut in, 'Leonard is not backing off. He wants to trade with Duran'.

Carl started to fidget. The post arrived and the clattering letterbox made him jump. This wasn't the way he wanted it to be, sitting, waiting. He turned the television off, put his overcoat on and stepped outside. Sleet hit the pavement, melting into grey sludge as he waited and gave a silent prayer for every car that wasn't them. He tried to convince himself they wouldn't be coming, but it wasn't long before a black BMW four by four pulled into the car park. Carl counted off the seconds. For a full minute after the engine was turned off there was no movement, then Ewan and Adam got out from the front. A few seconds later James stepped out, walked round, opened up the boot and pulled out two baseball bats. Carl felt like a boulder had dropped through his guts.

Ewan walked up and said flatly, 'Alright if we come in?'

Carl thumbed towards James and Adam carrying bats. 'Is that necessary?'

'Depends.' He led the way into the saloon bar. The brothers followed.

Carl thought about doing a runner.

Adam went straight behind the bar and pulled out a bottle of Jameson, poured himself a drink. 'You want something?'

'Bring the bottle,' said Ewan. He sat down, waved Carl into a seat at the table. He unbuttoned his coat. 'When we put you on that bus at Doncaster, we had an agreement, right? You'd go home and I would do my best to sort things out with my brother, get you and your daughter some time together. Now don't tell me you don't remember that?'

'I remember.' He looked across to Adam, leaning on the bar, visibly itching to do damage.

'Then you sent some old bloke to break into my brother's home and take her.'

'I didn't know about that. I never sent him.'

Ewan shrugged and leaned forward, his elbows on the table. 'Then there's this business with my brother's drug dealing, an independent little sideline with some bitch called ...'

'Adeline.' Jim O'Keefe spat the name.

'She works for you, yeah? She turns up with the old man and now I find she's been making money off my brother's back, taking the piss. Either way there's a *price*.' He smiled.

Carl wondered if that had taken him the entire journey from Hull.

'And the price is fifty thousand pounds.'

Jim O'Keefe rolled his bat along the bar and caught it as it dropped.

Ewan opened his hands. 'So?'

'You know I don't have anything like that sort of cash.'

'So we'll take the pub. Sign it over to us. We'll take it anyway. Or burn it to the ground.'

That he *had* thought about. 'This is mental.'

165

'Your choice.' Ewan stood up.

His brothers went to work. Adam smashed glasses, tipped out crates of mixers and bottled beers, swung at the optics until there wasn't a bottle left intact, then disappeared into the back office. Jim walked around the bar and smashed every framed picture and photograph off the walls. A signed, framed black and white of Henry and George Cooper hit the deck. Carl stepped forward, but Ewan held his arm and pulled him back. Jim stamped on the glass and ground his boot, ripping the picture to shreds. One by one he took out the lights. He fronted up to Carl and pulled a blade, then walked around slashing at seats. Carl heard footsteps upstairs. 'Is he up there? What the fuck is he doing up there?' He broke away from Ewan's grip.

He found Adam in Grace's room, standing on the bed with his cock out, pissing on the duvet.

'Get the *fuck* out.'

Adam grinned, shoved his prick away and buttoned up, then swung his bat, taking out a shelf of books and toys.

Carl went to the cupboard under the kitchen sink. He threw bleach bottles, cleaners, dusters, light bulbs and unused vases and ashtrays behind him. At the back of the cupboard was an old blue metal toolbox. He dragged it onto the floor, worked the combination padlock on the lid, opened it out and reached inside for the rag-wrapped parcel. Dad's gun.

Adam was behind him when he stood up and turned round. 'Get out of my flat.' He clicked off the safety, raised the gun in both hands. Adam took a step back, the grin slowly falling away as he retreated across the lounge, stepping carefully over the trashed Christmas tree.

Ewan and Jim were waiting by the street door when he directed Adam through the bar. Carl called out, 'This animal pissed on my daughter's bed. Is that the sort of people you are?' His voice hardened. 'Eh, is this who you are?'

'Adam, come over here.' Ewan stretched out a hand to his brother, then turned to Carl. 'You do need to find that fifty grand, or look for somewhere else to live. We'll be back tomorrow and you'll find out exactly who we are.' He ushered his brothers out into the street.

He couldn't face clearing up. Too much was broken. He was going to call Diane, but thought better of it. He put the gun in his coat pocket, went upstairs, stripped the clothes off Grace's bed and loaded the washing machine. He set the tree upright. The lights didn't work. He salvaged as many of the presents that hadn't been trodden on or ripped apart as he could.

Carl stopped on the landing outside Mum's flat and kicked the snow off his shoes. Mum's front door was hanging off its hinges. Lauren's door opened a crack. 'Your mum's here,' she whispered. 'They both are. Some blokes came and kicked it in about half an hour ago.'

This was just extras. A little added twist of the blade. 'Where is she?'

'Watching *The Wizard of Oz* with Grace. Grace was here, Carl. She doesn't know.'

He stuck his head around the door. His mum at one end of the sofa with Grace in blue gingham, hair in plaits, curled up beside her. 'Nan knows all the words, Dad.'

Carl nodded, smiled. Rose stared at the screen, mouthing Tin-Man dialogue.

He called Diane from Lauren's, didn't mention the O'Keefes. But when she saw Rose's front door, she twigged. 'Grace, where is she?'

'She's here and she's fine.'

They went into the hall. 'I knew this would happen.' Her hand went to her forehead. 'You should've stayed away, I should have stayed and dealt with it. What did he say?'

'They want money, a lot of money. More than I've got and it's not about you, not any more. They've trashed the pub.'

Her hands were shaking. 'So, what now?'

'I need you to take Grace over to your mum and dad's for tonight.'

Diane's face fell.

'I'm sorry, I know the poor kid's getting bounced from pillar to post, but I need to try and get the pub sorted for opening tomorrow night and she can't come back with it as it is.' He lowered his voice. 'Seriously, they've really gone to town on it and I don't want you there.'

'Oh, Christ,' said Diane.

Carl put his hands gently on her arms, hugged her. 'It's fine, just a bit of a rough ride. He's not right for you or Grace. Come on, say hello to Mum, she'll be chuffed to see you. Give her something to take her mind off things.'

167

'That's not funny.'

'Best I can do.' From somewhere, he found a smile and followed her into Lauren's front room grateful for the distraction.

Later, when the others had gone, Carl sat with his mother. Rose was a world away. After a long silence, Carl reached out and touched her hand. 'Mum?'

'What?'

'Did you hear what I said? They want fifty grand, maybe if I can get some of it together I can get them to back off. Mum, are you listening to me?'

The television was on silently, a John Wayne western, but she wasn't really watching. She was much further away than that. It had been his biggest fear since the episode in the supermarket, that she'd cloud over and gradually disappear from him. He felt a pull of guilt that he'd even mentioned the money or that she'd become involved in any way, but there was nowhere else to turn.

'Didn't you say there was some money Dad left in an account somewhere on the quiet? Maybe I could borrow that, and I'll get it back when I can.'

'That went years ago,' she said as if it was common knowledge. 'I gave most of it to Terry and there was never anything like how much you're asking for. I'm gonna 'ave a cuppa tea, want one, son?'

He was left mulling over what the modern equivalent of putting the wagons in a circle might be while she rattled around in the kitchen. She called in above the clatter, 'It was good of that friend of Lauren's to come and fix my door. Bloody yobs.'

Carl stood in the kitchen doorway, 'That wasn't yobs, Mum, that was the O'Keefes.'

'I don't care who it was, they're still yobs.' She turned to him, suddenly sharper. 'And that's how you ought to treat them. You don't pay people like that. You'll end up a nobody if you let that kind push you around.'

The tray was laid, tea in the pot, cups, milk in the china jug. Rose wandered off and Carl assumed it had been left for him to pour and carry in. When she came back, she handed him a photograph. An old black and white snap of a group of faces in a pub somewhere by the looks of it. He recognised younger versions of his mum and dad.

'That was the first do we had in there. Just after your dad bought it. We 'ad a long table down the middle and Jeff, he was yer dad's manager at the time, he got some caterers in. You can't let 'em 'ave it son, you'll 'ave to find a way. Cut us a bit of that cake out the tin while you're there.'

He set the tray down on the table in front of her chair. She broke off pieces of the fruitcake. 'I like this one,' she said. 'It's got whole pieces of nut in it. Don't you want yours?'

'In a minute.' Carl took a deep breath. 'Mum, it's not that I want to give it up, but I can't take these blokes on. They're hard men.'

'You did alright, brought Gracie home.'

He said nothing.

'You'll have to find a way.' She bit down on a piece of brazil nut. 'You wouldn't be thinking twice about it if Diane hadn't stuck her oar in. She never did want to live there.'

'No, Mum, neither did I.'

'You'll find a way.'

He'd been waiting for something, a signal that she'd understood the shit he was in, but it wasn't coming and never would. She still lived there, in that place where those ambitions stirred up by his dad held sway over them and he had no choice but to buy into the whole dead fantasy of it all. Carl sat back and finished his cake. Mum turned up the sound on the telly.

I call that bold talk for a one-eyed fat man.
Fill your hand, you sonofabitch!

27

Frank's last hitched ride was with a bullet-headed Scot who had air of regimental fucked-offness about him. He picked Frank up at Potters Bar. Gruff monosyllabic responses to Frank's opening chat made it clear there would be no conversation. Frank noted the kitbag on the back seat, but couldn't make out the stencilled lettering. He put his seatbelt on and as they hit the first section of congestion near the A10 junction, he closed his eyes. The pain in his hand was winning through as the painkillers faded, otherwise he might have slept. Instead, he planned.

He was certain the O'Keefes would have made it down before him. What they'd do when they got there was anyone's guess, but they'd want a piece of Carl. And James O'Keefe had a dent in his ego that'd need straightening. Even if Diane wouldn't go back, and there were no guarantees, he was unlikely to do the dignified thing and let her go. So whether Carl headed home to the pub or to his mum's, or was still on his way, he'd be in no state to handle what was coming. And he'd have Grace and Diane to think about now.

The stop-start speech-free drive dragged on. Every junction slowed the traffic for miles ahead. The Scot tutted, muttering a dozen curses under his breath when the build up near Lakeside brought them to a standstill. The going was easier the other side of the QE2 Bridge and to make up lost time and prove his macho credentials, he hit 85 m.p.h. on the A2. Slowing near Eltham, the rain-spattered screen made a red blur of the brake lights in front and the traffic once again bunched to a halt.

'You can get out here,' said the Scot abruptly.

Frank dithered, his thoughts elsewhere. 'Sorry, what?'

'South London. Out, here.'

'Sure, cheers for the ride, happy New Year.'

Frank was back on the pavement. The lights ahead changed and his ride took off. He turned his coat collar up and started walking in search of a bus stop.

The five pound note the blessed Brian had pressed into his good hand that morning bought a 124 ride to Grove Park Station. No one was checking tickets. Commuter trains heading into London and out to the suburbs were half-empty and after a short wait on a deserted platform, Frank had a carriage almost to himself for the two fare-dodged stops to New Cross. He felt like he'd been away for weeks. It had been like this before, belonging, but not belonging, coming back a different man from the one who left. Home, but not home.

ROUND THREE

28

After fifteen years inside, Frank had expected to feel different coming out. He had a few backslaps from blokes as he walked his landing for the last time. Then he was processed through the system, a re-acquaintance with personal effects, his wallet, watch, the cufflinks that felt like they belonged to another man. He signed out and stepped up into an airless van and it finished just like it started. The last man he saw was an unreconstructed shit called Groves who, when he opened the door of the prison transit, told him to fuck off and don't come back.

Frank found himself back on the streets a free man with a travel warrant from Hull to King's Cross and seventeen quid in his pocket. It was summer, 1993. As part of his exit interview they'd given him the address of a hostel in Hither Green. All he knew then was he needed the next train south, a bath and a change of clothes. The damp, musty smell of his suit filled his nostrils and caught in the back of his throat.

The journey had been a blur. The Humber, curling alongside the track, then patchwork fields of wheat and towns bathed in sunshine; the suburbs giving way to smoke-blackened tunnels. He'd taken the tube to Charing Cross and jumped the couple of stops to New Cross. Home, but not home. He'd walked by the old house, knowing Carol was long gone and that it would break his heart. The shirt stuck to his back in the sunshine. He felt as though he wore his story on his face, on his clothes, in the way he carried himself and the instinctive glances over his shoulder.

He jumped a 21 bus to Lewisham, then walked up to Catford and Dave's house. A woman he didn't recognise had opened the door, shielding a toddler behind her legs. 'Sorry to bother you love, I'm looking for the Price family,' he said.

'We've been 'ere for nearly five years, they went ... hang on, I did 'ave an address for the post.' She closed the door and left Frank waiting on the doorstep. Minutes went by. Her shadow ghosted across the hallway a couple of times and he wondered if she'd forgotten him. Eventually the door opened again. 'I can't find it.'

He folded the suit jacket over his arm and rolled up his shirtsleeves to walk, stopping in at the Ram. He stood at the bar while the barman served the punters around him. There was no one he recognised and he couldn't drink more than a few sips of his pint before he felt sick. He rolled a cigarette with the last of his prison baccy. The rest he'd left with Dan, his last cellmate. The lad had been short on decent conversation beyond the back pages of the Sun, but he'd kept things clean and Frank had shared with worse, a lot worse. He phoned the hostel from the pub and a disinterested voice told him they were full and asked him the name of his probation officer at the prison. 'Mickey Mouse,' he said, and hung up. He took off, wandering aimlessly, taking in the dusty streets, the clothes, the stuff in shops. He nipped into an off licence for fags, asked for ten B&H and thought the woman had tried to charge him for twenty.

For something to do Frank rode the buses, listening to conversations. Then, as much by luck as judgement, the bus he'd been riding to nowhere particular took him past Jacqui's Launderette before pulling up at the stop fifty yards further on. He stepped off and strolled back in the afternoon sunshine. She was in there, singing along to the same transistor radio she'd always had, folding a small mountain of towels in random faded burgundy shades when he walked in.

'Alright, Jac?' He heard himself say, 'I don't know where to go.'

Jacqui turned the mug, offering the handle, 'Take it Frank, this is bloody hot.'

'Sorry, thanks.'

'You want a biscuit?'

'No. Can I sit down?'

'Course love, hang on.' She slid the towels along the bench, gathering them into a bale which she dropped into a waiting laundry bag.

'So where you been?'

'Just around. I went by Dave's house. I thought ...' He stopped himself. What *had* he thought? That they'd take him in, give him money, welcome him home? 'I dunno, they've gone.'

'Rose moved out after Terry died, reckoned there were too many memories in the house. Carl's got the John Evelyn in Deptford, you know it? She's in some flat in a lowrise on the Pepys Estate. To be honest, I don't see anything of them and that suits me.'

He sipped the tea, scalding his lips. The disconnection felt absolute. 'It's all ... different, all changed so much.'

'You could say that.'

One of the big tumble dryers stopped. Jacqui raked around inside, pulled out a couple of shirts and fed twenty-pence pieces into the slot. 'Tell you what, Frank, you wait here and I'll drop this lot into *Shanice's.*' She heaved the bag of towels onto the bench. 'I won't be a couple of minutes, it's just a few doors down, then I'll close up and get you something to eat, okay? We can catch up properly.'

'Yeah, cheers.'

'Don't look so worried. You'll be alright.'

She put a stack of twenty-pence pieces next to him. 'And if that one stops while I've gone, just take out the dry stuff and feed the bloody thing again.'

Jacqui took him upstairs to the flat. Frank slept in the chair. She made them steak and chips for tea. He couldn't eat it all and she suggested a drive up to Greenwich Park, a walk in the wide open spaces. She parked her little blue Renault near the hospital and, as they made their way up the hill towards the observatory, she did her best to fill in fifteen years of news starting with Terry Price. 'He was in trouble as soon as Dave had gone. I don't know how the hell they didn't see it coming.'

'Still a kid, or was he?' Frank's memory had him not even into his teens.

'Twenty-two, not that you'd have known it. Last time I saw him he had this old shiny suit on like something he'd found in a charity shop that fit where it touched. He had a shirt with three day's worth of grime round the collar, Christ knows how Rose let him go out like that. If he'd taken a bit more care of himself, he could have been a handsome lad.' She paused. 'Like his dad.'

'How did Rose cope?'

'I couldn't understand it Frank, still can't, and Christ knows I've thought about it often enough Terry never had the nous to take over Dave's business. At least what was left of it. Even if Dave had lived he would have had problems. He'd already admitted to me he knew he couldn't keep it going and he was planning an out. But apparently he never told them kids so Terry ... that kid tried so hard it breaks my heart. And Rose pushed him, she bloody pushed him all the way.' She stopped by an empty bench. 'Can we sit down, d'you mind?'

Frank sat forward, his elbows on his knees and drank in the evening sunshine and the gentle breeze on his skin. There were blokes he met inside who had every detail of their first night out planned. It was all families, wives, girlfriends, parties, tarts, mates, pubs, beer, coke, clubs, football – the things that kept them going. They'd give you the blow by blow of the ride home, the clean clothes, the first kiss, the cool fresh sheets and a loving woman. Frank had never thought further than being out, never daring to see himself alone in a shitty room somewhere. He'd have a bed if he was lucky and a messy reconciliation with the outside world. He closed his eyes and listened to the familiar music in Jacqui's voice.

'So what's it like to be out?'

'It's good, really good.' He smiled. 'Thanks.'

'Did you manage alright?'

He shrugged.

'Come on, if I had your file in front of me, what would it say?'

Frank thought for a moment. It seemed like an odd thing to ask. 'I don't know. Something like, given the dodgy company, he's an honest man who practiced clean living under difficult circumstances.' He leaned back, felt Jacqui's skirt brush against his leg. 'Once I was up north I was on me own really. There was a couple of blokes I got to know a bit, they came and went, but I didn't make much of an effort. No one liked me very much, but that's alright, I wasn't bothered. I wasn't in there to be liked. I used to read a lot. What about you, how've things been?'

'Yeah, up and down. The usual. I still miss Dave if I'm honest.'

'I bet.'

'I know people always thought I was 'avin a thing with him.'

'You don't have to explain to me, Jac. It's none of my business.'

A bloke on a bike wheezed past, pedalling up the hill with a look of pained determination etched across his face.

'I never was, never wanted to after he chose Rose.' She sighed deeply. 'I've just about had enough of being round here though. I'm selling up and moving away. A two-bob launderette's not the place I want to spend the next twenty years.'

'Good for you, got to move on.' Frank leaned forward again and wondered if he had twenty years left in him.

'I've got a buyer. This bloke reckons he'll turn the shop and the flat into four separate apartments.'

There was a long silence.

'So you don't see Rose any more?'

'The last time I saw her was just after Dave died. She comes in the launderette, puts her hand on my arm and says, "It's been a long time Jac," in this whispery voice. Oh it pissed me off. I'm sorry, but it was such a bloody put on. Then she puts this big polythene bag on the counter, Chiesmans of Lewisham. I hadn't seen one of those in years. Then she says, "This is the suit he wanted. He made me promise to bring it to you and for you to make it nice. He liked a nice crease in his trousers. I'll send someone to pick it up. Would Thursday be alright?" And that was it. Never got an invite, never got as much as a phone call from her since. Oh, I did buy him a silk tie, a nice one from Selfridges. That was my part in it. Carl came and picked the suit up and as far as I know, they cremated him in it.'

Frank's first night of freedom in fifteen years finished on Jacqui's sofa – which she stressed would be a strictly temporary arrangement – *a few days, a week at the outside.* It was fair enough. They talked long into the night. Jacqui had Terry on her conscience.

Dave hadn't been dead six months and Terry turned up at the launderette one afternoon. 'He had this sports bag,' said Jacqui. 'I had a fair idea what was in it without having to open it. "I need you to sort this," he says. He was having to shout over the noise of the machines so I only caught odd bits of what he was saying, but it didn't make much sense, something about a mess and cleaning. I made a joke of it, "Get your mother to do it," I said. He just stood there. I thought he was gonna slap me. "She sent me to you."' She paused. 'He was desperate, Frank.'

'So what was in the bag?'

She shrugged, 'Money? Clothes? Gear he'd used on a job? Who cares? I never had anything to do with Dave's business. It was *her* again, a lifetime of thinking the worst of me and now her boy's in trouble, so get someone to sort it out.'

Frank looked up. 'So what did you say?'

'To Terry? I talked to him, tried to make him feel like a human being, reminded him of the old times, told him he didn't need to try and be like his dad, told him to let it all go and make his own life.'

'And?'

'He pulled a knife on me and threatened to use it if I didn't wash his filthy gear. I showed him this.' She pulled her hair back and revealed the scar he'd first seen a lifetime ago. 'He backed off. I told him, "Your dad's gone so fuck you and fuck your family." And that was it.'

There was a pale light beginning to appear at the curtains. 'They found him down by the river a couple of weeks later. An overdose apparently, but who knows? Half the time I think I should have done something. He'd come to me for help and I hadn't. And then other times I'm pretty sure there was nothing I could have done, earlier maybe, in all them years but not by the end. I'll live with it.' She glanced up at the clock, 'Jesus, have you seen the time?'

'It's alright, I won't sleep anyway.'

She yawned. 'I've got to go to bed, get a couple of hours at least.'

'What time you opening up?'

'Half-past eight, every weekday. Like bleedin' clockwork.' She kissed him on the cheek. 'Welcome home, Frank.'

For those first few days the routine held him together. He'd take up the sheets, blankets and pillows from the sofa and leave them folded on the spare chair. He'd wash, shave and dress. By the time Jacqui got up, usually around seven, he'd have a cup of tea waiting. There was a day towards the end of the week, she was up early.

'I haven't made the tea yet.'

'It's fine, I'll do it.'

He stood awkwardly in the kitchen.

'You just gonna stand there and watch?'

He moved away, took his place on the sofa. Jacqui came through and put the tea in front of him. 'So what are you doing today?'

'I dunno, go for a bit of a walk, have a look round, see what's changed.'

'Like yesterday.'

He picked up the mug, held it in both hands. He could feel the heat through the china warming the bones in his fingers.

'You want me to have a word around, see if there's someone who can offer you work?'

The thought of putting himself forward for some shitty job turned in his guts. He shook his head. 'I'm not ready, not yet.'

Jacqui sat down and thought for a moment. He could see her working something out. 'Why don't you go and see them?'

He looked up, 'Carol and Kate?'

She nodded slowly, 'Yeah, you got the address, give it a go.'

'I don't think so.'

'If not now, then when?'

'When I'm back on my feet. A few weeks, maybe.' He nodded, convincing himself.

At that moment the phone rang. Jacqui held up a finger for him to stay put and answered. When she looked away for a pen, Frank took the opportunity to head into the kitchen. He washed his cup up, rinsed it out and was drying it when she followed him in.

'Don't walk away from me, Frank.'

'The phone, you—'

'Don't walk away from it. You want to wait until you're back on your feet? I don't think you can get back on your feet until you get this over with. She can tell you to piss off or welcome you with open arms, either way you'll know where you stand. Then you can make some decisions.'

He folded the tea towel over the radiator, but said nothing.

'That was a mate of mine on the phone, he's seeing a bloke he knows later, he thinks there's a chance of some driving work. He's got a courier company, you could do it easily. And then we'll go about finding somewhere for you to stay that isn't my sofa.'

Frank felt a tightness in his chest.

She put a hand on his arm. 'Come on, Frank, don't make me put you on the streets.' She smiled. He didn't. 'I'm joking.'

He was on the train just out of Grove Park when the heavens opened. It had been threatening all morning. The cloud was low, the atmosphere thick and heavy, thunder crunched in the distance – just God moving the furniture. He felt the beginnings of a headache. The rain was hitting the platform hard and bouncing back as the train pulled into Bromley South. Frank got off for the connection to St Mary Cray and went under cover. He'd just missed one, it'd be another twenty minutes or so.

He unfolded the directions Jacqui had written down earlier, tracing the route across the pages of her A-Z held together with yellowing sellotape. She'd handed the book across the kitchen table at one point and a folded sheet of notepaper slipped out. He held it in front of him. It was Dave's writing. Directions from Stamford Hill, through Edmonton to Palmer's Green. Frank felt lost for a moment. 'Well that's one meeting he won't have made. He couldn't navigate a dodgem.'

Jacqui took the note and set it aside. 'Ravensbury Road, you got it?'

He had it. Now here he was turning the corner and making his way along a broad sweep of low post-war terraced houses set back and down a few feet from street level. The downpour had stopped, the pavements drying quickly in the hot dead air. He checked the address again, not that he needed to, following the numbers up into the nineties. Suddenly he was conscious of blind spots in his peripheral vision. He slowed as he walked down the sloping drive to the front door, clenched and unclenched his fists, trying to release the tension. He should have phoned from the station. Too late now.

'I should have called, I'm sorry but I was down this way and—'

'You should have called.'

Carol stood on the step, her hand on the door. She had a wedding ring, not his.

'Can I come in?'

'No.'

'Is Kate in?'

A smile. 'She's at university, Frank. In her third year.'

'Good, that's good. Can I come in, just for a minute, to say hello, catch up an' that?'

'No. I can pass your address on to Kate if you tell me where you're staying.'

'With a friend, I've only been back a few days. Y'know, just trying to put things back together.'

'There's nothing here to put together. It was another life, Frank.'

'No, I know, but Kate – I thought I could see her now. I really want to make up for ... everything.' He knew it sounded stale, a corny thing to say, but the words weren't coming easily. He couldn't focus and the pain was beginning to pulse over his right eye. He looked up at Carol and a thick dark patch closed down areas of his vision entirely. She was talking, asking his address, but her features were swimming away. He was saying something about staying with Jacqui, kipping over the launderette, making a crack about cleaning up his act. Carol said she'd tell Kate he came round and pass on his address, then leave it up to her. 'It's the best I can do. You'll have to ring if you want to contact me in future. I'm in the phonebook.'

'Sure, sure, I'm sorry.'

'I don't want you here, please don't come again.' She closed the door.

He had no distinct memory of the journey home beyond an awareness of walking towards the station, being unable to read the indicator signs, wanting desperately to be home, in darkness. Waiting on the platform, then vomiting onto the tracks.

Jacqui put him in her bed and pulled the curtains. She asked no questions.

Jacqui let him stay another week. It was as if she was determined to bring him back piece by piece. Today it was Mickey, a friend of a friend working out of a Limehouse industrial estate and looking for a driver. He turned out to be a big bloke, wide face with little coal-dark eyes, blond crew-cut, younger than Frank had expected. Somehow, he'd thought running a courier business would demand a degree of experience. Mickey shuffled invoices, tossed them into a red plastic tray. 'So, this Jacqui woman reckons you're a good driver.'

Frank nodded.

'Done the knowledge?'

'Nope.'

'Lot of blokes here are doing the knowledge. You might want to give it a go.'

'I'm just a driver.'

Mickey looked him up and down. 'Eighty quid a week. The van's outside and I want it back here and washed at the end of every shift. If I need you at weekends there's no extra. It's eighty quid flat. I'll give you a month's trial, which means you're out on your arse with no notice if I say so. We start at eight. If you're late, you can piss off. I need blokes I can rely on. Where you from?'

'I've just moved into a flat in Deptford.' Frank had the feeling that was the wrong answer.

'I'm from the East End originally. We've got a place out in Essex now, me and the missis and my girls, detached, four bedrooms, double garage, full-sized snooker table in the extension. South Woodham Ferries, you know it?'

Frank shrugged. 'Should I?'

Mickey sniffed. 'Just do the job and don't piss me about.'

Frank had been out six weeks and thanks to Jacqui he had a wage – Mickey had taken him on full-time – and a place that was his own as long as he paid the rent. He had a bed, a chair, a second hand telly from the market and a transistor radio. He had an alarm clock that he didn't bother to set; he never slept past 6 a.m. On Saturday afternoons he'd buy a few bits of shopping, a few cans and half a bottle of scotch if he could afford it, then walk back through the park, lay back on the bed and listen to the radio. On Sundays he'd catch a 47 to London Bridge and walk around the City until he was too tired to walk any more.

One evening towards the back end of September, Jacqui dropped by. She looked around at the bare walls, sparse furnishings. 'Looks alright, really. Be better once you get a few more things in.'

'I know I ought to try and do a bit more with it, but I'm grateful, really, there's no way I'd have a place if ...'

'Frank, shush, it's alright. It's a pleasure to help you out, no strings eh? Come on, let's go out, I want to talk to you and it might as well be over a pint.'

Of all the places they could have gone, the John Evelyn was the last Frank would have picked. He'd stayed away from the place and pubs in general, retreating, avoiding contact. Jacqui walked through the doors and up to the bar. 'Alright Kev, is Carl in?'

'Upstairs with Di, I think.' He winked.

'Give him a shout would you? Thanks love. And a pint of best and a Bacardi and Coke, no ice, when you're ready. Ta.'

They found a place in a corner away from the other drinkers. A young woman in a spectacularly low-cut top came round with raffle tickets in a pint mug. Jacqui put her hand in her purse. Frank turned to look at the photos on the walls and framed bill posters of boxing promotions from way back. He was sitting, almost exactly if his memory was right, in the place he'd found himself countless nights penned in between Dave and Roy, or Wally, or Ruby. Easy nights when the beer and the Johnnie Walker kept coming and nobody paid.

'Alright, Jacqui?' Carl pulled over a chair and folded his skinny legs under the table. 'Not seen you in a while.'

'How's your mum?'

'Yeah, alright. Still misses Dad, we all do. You should pop in and see her sometime.'

'I think we're a bit past that, son, don't you?'

Carl shrugged, 'I s'pose.'

'No love, sorry I've not been in, but I've been busy with a few things. You remember Frank Neaves? Frank was a good friend of your dad's. He's just moved back round here.'

'Oh, nice one,' said Carl. He nodded appreciatively, but apparently without making a connection.

If Carl did recognise him, it must have been as one of a sea of faces, old mates and acquaintances of his dad's, but then his expression changed. He tapped the table with his fingertips. 'No, I remember, we took you to Joey's for a suit. Joey Silverman's ... and you had that blue Mark III Cortina with the vinyl roof.' He went quiet, but Frank could see the sequence of memories running on. He wondered whether they went as far as that night on the Heygate Estate.

'The thing is,' said Jacqui, '... is that I've sold the launderette and the flat and I've bought a place near Margate and I wanted you to know. Both of you. I'm due to complete first week in October.'

Frank felt her watching him.

'Well someone bloody say something. How about, *well done* or *we'll miss you* or *nice one Jac, you deserve it.*'

'It's good news,' said Frank. 'Really good.'

Carl looked like a kid who'd been told he couldn't go to the party. 'Keep in touch, eh?'

'Oh for Christ's sake, it's only Margate. Well, Cliftonville, as it goes, it's just over an hour away. Carl, can you get me another drink please. Frank?'

'Yeah, go on.'

'Bacardi and Coke and a pint of best. And put a smile on your face when you come back.'

Frank waited until Carl had gone. 'You didn't want to tell me without someone else there, did you?'

'No.'

'You thought I'd want to come with you.'

'Do you?'

He hesitated for what seemed like a long time, too long.

'See Frank, that's an answer that needed to be there already. You shouldn't have to think about it. I want someone who wants to be with me, Frank, I've waited long enough and I'm fine, happy with my own company if that's the way it goes. You ... you're still somewhere else, stuck in some other time. I'm doing this to go *to* something not run *from* it.'

'Is it really that easy? What's the secret?'

Their eyes met briefly, Frank looked away.

'No secret Frank, just no fear.'

29

Sleet pelted at Frank's back and dripped down his collar as he walked along a bolted, locked and shuttered Deptford High Street and turned into Evelyn Street. He stalled at the kerb. For all those years the past had nagged away, needling him on a daily basis. He'd served his country and his family faithfully and Dave Price faithlessly. It didn't matter which belief system he chose to justify his decisions, what mattered was that now, with the memories piling up, he'd gained a perspective, seen the possibility of a life lived with meaning, purpose, a choice and a future.

The pub looked to be in darkness. A sign on the door said, *Closed due to staff illness – open New Year's Eve as usual.* Lauren had got his message through. He headed for home, stopping on the way at the Happy Shopper. There were a few kids hanging around freezing their arses off, hoods up, sleeves pulled down and bunched in their fists, stepping from foot to foot. The shop's outside light flashed on and off like a tramp's disco as Frank counted what was left of Brian's cash, hoping there'd be enough for milk and tea bags. The dodgy bulb finally gave out and the kids mooched off into the night. As he looked up, the O'Keefes' truck rolled by, picking up speed as a police patrol car cruised the other way.

He doubled back to the pub.

Carl was sitting in darkness in the saloon. His was the only table not in bits or kicked over. Frank found the light switch, but only the bar backlight came on.

'They did the light bulbs,' said Carl. 'Baseball bats,' he added.

Glass crunched underfoot as Frank walked across the carpet.

'They went round Mum's as well, looking for me.'

'She alright?'

'Shaken up, I s'pose. Didn't say much really, not to me. I've left her in with a neighbour for now. If you want a drink, I think there's still a bottle in the office under the desk.'

'You want one?'

'Yeah, I do.'

Everywhere Frank went there was a trail of debris. Behind the bar was a puddled cocktail of booze from demolished optics. The narrow passage was littered with papers and more broken glass. In the office he tripped over Carl's telly, bust open on the floor with the screen smashed. The video player was in bits. He found the crate with a couple of intact bottles, a Courvoisier and a Bell's. He took both. There were a couple of glasses in the washer. Carl poured himself a large brandy. Frank set a chair upright and sat down.

'What happened to your hand?' said Carl.

'All got a bit hairy when we picked Grace up, Jim O'Keefe got a bit handy with a hammer. You seen your little girl?'

'Yeah, she was with Mum. Thank Christ she wasn't here when this lot happened.'

'I'm sorry, son. About all this. They did your telly and video an' all.'

Carl shrugged. 'I'm whacked, Frank. I feel like I could sleep for a week and still need a kip.' He massaged his temples. 'They're coming back.'

'When?'

'Tomorrow. Ewan gave me a choice, either I sign the pub over to them or he wants—'

'Thirty grand.'

'Close. Fifty actually, what made you say that?'

'Educated guess. Adam's in trouble, some dodgy deal with a Dutch geezer. The bloke's connected with some Euro-bollocks firm, dealers, smugglers. Thirty thousand quid takes Adam off the hook, apparently. The rest is for Diane, time and trouble, I guess. And this,' he looked around the wrecked bar. 'I 'spose it kills a couple of birds with one stone for 'em, given that you've got back what Jim had.'

'I don't care, I'm not paying. And they're not having this place. Diane's finished with him, she ain't going back, so there's nothing more I can do. You know Adeline was dealing for Adam?'

'She told me while we were away.'

'She ripped him off.' He twisted uncomfortably in the seat. 'Diane reckons that's where the fifty grand comes from. She

185

reckons Adeline had a thing with Adam and broke it off. It's been winding Jim up for months apparently.'

'You're not blaming Adeline for this?'

'Who else?'

He felt himself stiffen. 'Let's get this straight.'

Carl shot him a look, then looked away.

'No, listen, this is your pub. I know you never wanted it, but it is. So if you choose to hide in a backroom, then you won't bloody know half of what's going on, right? You aren't gonna know when one of your barmaids is earning a bit on the side. Or when your missis is having a bit on the side. So don't you dare judge her.'

'No, Dad.'

'Bollocks.' Frank hesitated. 'Don't give me that shit. You want to carve up the blame, take your own share first. You ring her, you talk to her and get her in and help clear this place up. Now I know this is hard, really hard, but you're on a hiding to nothing taking these people on. You'll have to try and sort something out.'

A puzzled look came across Carl's face. '*I* can't talk to them or deal with them, Frank. In the end, all you're ever left with is a geezer who's harder than you, who'll go further than you. I've got Grace home, that's what I wanted.'

'Except she can't bloody come home, can she?'

'She will.'

'So what happens when they come back tomorrow?'

Carl had an expression, a kind of blank non-comprehension and for a moment he looked at Frank as if they were strangers. From his coat pocket he took the revolver and laid it on the table. 'It was Dad's, from the army.'

Frank picked it up and weighed it in his hand. It was heavier than he remembered, blacker and colder. 'It's mine. Came all the way back from Cyprus in the bottom of my kitbag.' He opened the chamber, it was loaded, all six. 'You ever fired it?'

He shook his head. 'Terry did once when we were kids, aimed at a baked bean tin in the garden and nearly took next door's window out. Other than that it's been in the toolbox under the sink since I moved in.'

Frank put the gun back on the table. 'You know you can't use it.'

'Why not?'

'You just can't, son. It's a whole other level you start waving one of these around and you don't want that.'

'One minute you're saying I've got to sort it out and then you're telling me I can't use this. Sod it, I wasn't asking you, Frank. This is my place and it was my old man's place.' He got up, stiffly. He stretched and winced, held his hand to his ribs. He went to the window, the streetlight's fuzzy yellow glow shone through the frosted glass across his face.

'In ten years time, there won't be a local here,' said Frank. 'It'll be like everywhere else they've tarted up, new flats, different kinds of people. They ain't gonna want an old-fashioned boozer and they won't give a sod about you, your family, what you were, who your dad was.'

'No, they'll want a plastic theme bar they can drop in and score a few pills, some coke and a bit of blow, which is what the O'Keefes'll give 'em. And kids puking in the street and knifing each other for taking the piss out of a pair of trainers. Box fucking fresh.'

Frank shook his head. 'Sounds like you've decided to make a stand against the whole world.'

'Only the O'Keefes as it goes, the world can wait till the New Year.'

'And you'll use this?' He motioned to the gun.

'Yes.'

'Well you've picked a right fucking time.'

'I didn't pick it.'

Frank had a faint recollection of two small boys, hiding behind a sofa watching their old man shoot a bloke in the face. Kids, just kids who should never have had to go through that. 'Take it from me, son, it ain't worth it. I've seen the load you carry around with you for your mum, your dad, for Terry, but you don't have to prove anything to anyone.'

'You don't think so?' He shook his head and slapped Frank on the back. 'Nah, thanks for everything, but goodnight, Frank.'

Outside the night was bitter. Frank looked up and down the empty street and back at the pub. The light came on upstairs. It looked like Carl had chosen his moment to start being his father's son.

30

A full scaffolding had been constructed up the side of the house in Frank's absence. He made his way up the stairs. A wrapped box stood on the floor by the door to his flat. He bent to pick it up and felt a freezing draught from under the door; surely he hadn't left a window open. The box was bottle-weight, from Adeline – *I'm sorry for everything, please call when you get back so I can explain. A xx ps – whatever the time.*

Frank put the key in the front door and pushed. There was some resistance from the post on the mat. He gave it a shove. He put the light on and picked up the local free rag, takeaway menus, junk offers and what looked like a Christmas card. It was from Jacqui, she said she missed him, that he ought to get down and see her soon. There was a phone number and her address, same as last year. He opened a brown envelope, typed, addressed to Mr F Neaves, with the word TENANT in bold black letters. As he was tearing it open, he looked up to see that the sash window had been left open, but not by him. It was jammed apart five or six inches to give an anchoring point for the scaffold poles braced against the inside of his room. That bastard Hilton had let himself in and wedged it open to build his poxy scaffold. There was no way to close it or keep the rain out. The carpet under the window was sodden. His bed was damp and the whole place was like an icebox.

'Hilton, you shit,' shouted Frank. 'You tight-arsed, scheming piece of shit.'

He finished reading the letter by the light spilling from the street. It was a formal eviction notice, politely worded, but the score was the same in any language, he had less than a week to get himself and his possessions out.

For a few moments, the developers' flags across the street had been hanging limply, silently. But now, as he re-read the eviction

188

notice with the words jumping off the page, the wind picked up and that incessant bloody pinking started up with it, louder than ever through the open window. He tossed the post away, went to the kitchen and pulled out the sharpest knife, a short-bladed black handled bastard that had occasionally taken bits off his fingertips. He went downstairs, striding across the street. He looked up at the happy-face corporate bollocks emblem. This close, the stiff nylon lanyard hitting the one note flagpole over and over sang like a bell. Frank cut the cord. It whipped away. He grabbed the loose end and pulled it through, bringing the flag fluttering down with it. He did the same with the second cord.

Those first few moments of silence, when even the traffic on Evelyn Street seemed to pause, felt like the most beautiful thing he had ever heard. As he looked up, one or two faces appeared behind glass. A window was yanked up and a bloke shouted down, 'Nice one, mate, nice one.'

Frank went back upstairs. Jesus, he was cold. He opened Adeline's box and pulled out a bottle of Johnnie Walker Black Label. 'Good girl,' he said, and poured himself a large one.

He ought to have been exhausted, but as he stepped it out towards Lewisham, he felt a surge of energy. In the old days, when it came to Dave Price's business, he sorted things in his own quiet way. No fuss, no bother. You tried to make it easy for people, give them a way out and most took it, but there were always people like the O'Keefes, mouthy, tooled up when there was no need; always with their mates, their brothers, cousins, *their* mates. It never bothered him, why would it? Whatever they thought would put them one up, he'd thought it first. If they came mob-handed, Frank made sure Dave had his people better-placed and with the appropriate means at their disposal. They got the job done quickly and efficiently, and went home to their wives, their families and their Ford Cortinas until the next time. Only this time, the next time was thirty years later and it was Carl who stood to lose everything if he couldn't even up the odds.

It was nearly midnight by the time Frank walked up a well-kept path and rang the bell.

Wally Patch came to the door still laughing from something on the telly. He brushed against a string of Christmas cards that sagged on the wall behind him. The laughter stayed in the corners of his mouth for as long as it took to recognise Frank on the doorstep.

'*Frank*, do it outside. Not in here.'

189

'Do what?' Frank gently pushed the Johnnie Walker in Patch's chest. 'Happy Christmas. Can I come in?'

The years had been kind to Walter, aka 'Wally', aka 'Waltzer', Patch. He'd grown into his old man's name for a start. His close-cropped hair was better for being silver, even the glasses suited him. His fading tan told of a fairly recent holiday. But when he sat down at the dining table and poured the scotch, it was the scars across his knuckles that told the story of the Wally Patch Frank knew.

'Good to see you, Frank.'

'Is it?'

'It is now I know you're not here to, well ... y'know, settle scores.'

Frank shook his head slowly.

'Well what then? It ain't for old times' sake.'

'I've spent the last few days up north with Carl Price, trying to help him out of a bit of a situation he's got himself into.'

'*You?*'

'Yeah, me.'

'I thought you was—'

'Was what?'

'Pickled.'

Frank laughed. 'The long and the short of it is this bloke Carl's ex has been shacked up with, him and his brothers have come down here and they want to take the pub off him. Or take him for a few grand he hasn't got. I can't do any more on me own than I've done already and I need to put on a bit of a show, let them know it's not just one bloke they're dealing with. He needs protection.'

Wally raised an eyebrow.

'Yeah, I know,' said Frank.

Wally fumbled with the lid of the Johnnie Walker, sending it scooting across the table. Frank trapped it with his good hand.

'I'll be honest Frank, anything I owed that family I paid off a long time ago. It's a no.'

The flat refusal was unexpected. 'What about the others?'

'What others?'

'Dave's boys.'

'You're kidding, right? Roy Wills and Ruby are dead, Ruby went years ago. The two Tonys are fuck knows where and my brother Stan's been in and out of St Thomas's so many times in the last year it's like he's on a conveyor belt, so forget him.'

'What about Ruby's boys?'

Wally laughed. 'Alan's an out and out Trot, social worker, community bullshitter.'

'What about Lee?'

'That would be Inspector Lee Murray of the Met's "don't give a fuck" squad.'

'Shit.'

'I know.'

'And you won't help?'

'Not a chance.'

'Not even as a favour?'

'I'm sixty-eight years old, Frank. This ain't fucking 'ollywood.'

Frank helped himself to more scotch. 'When you saw me at your front door just now you thought, here's Frank come to settle things up, right? What did you think I'd 'ave to settle with you?'

'I dunno, it all went a bit bad back then with Dave an' everything, the way it ended. With you going down, I mean.'

'And you been waiting for me all this time?'

Wally shrugged. 'It's not like I think about it every day.'

'But you knew what it all cost me and you felt bad about it. All those years wasted, losing Carol, never seeing Kate grow up, and you thought I'd want some kind of reckoning.' He stumbled over memories, trying to make them fit.

'It doesn't mean I owe you this.' Wally dropped a sprinkle of baccy into a Rizla. 'I wish what happened to you hadn't happened.'

For a moment, it was like he was back inside, feeling the burning injustice of those first few months. 'I want you to tell me what happened.'

'Don't you know?'

'You tell me.'

Wally looked over Frank's shoulder as if he expected Dave to come walking through the door. Frank reached back and pushed it closed. 'This is between you and me.'

Wally nodded. 'You know what Rose was like, Frank, probably still is. Doesn't matter what it takes, she makes sure she gets her own way. Once Dave had done Gary Stack, and Fraser knew it, there was no way she was letting him go down. But I honestly never knew that she'd kept your suit as an insurance policy. I thought I'd burned the whole lot down the crem. She gave me the bags and shoved me out the door and I chucked 'em in. I didn't go through 'em.' He pinched the loose strands of tobacco and lit up.

'She kept it – on purpose?'

'Yeah, I thought you'd have sussed it out.'

Frank felt a stillness come over him. 'Go on, what about Lonnie?'

'Right, yeah, Lonnie who I was supposed to shoot. You always said that leaving bodies around the place'd bring the old bill down hard. And we weren't that kind of firm, were we? I mean none of us was back then, it was only the headcases who really went out to do someone in. And *I'd* never killed anyone, so to just knock the bloke off on Dave's say so, even if he had deserved it, Lonnie was never the full shilling.'

'He did alright at my trial.' The words seemed to stick in his throat.

'Rose coached him. They went over and over it. She knew that if he couldn't convince the jury it was you, then Fraser would 'ave 'ad to call Dave. And he'd either 'ave given evidence against you, or gone down himself. So she gave Fraser the suit and a line to Joey Silverman. Joey had no choice and then there was Lonnie as an eye-witness. Dave paid Fraser off as per their usual, then gave him you.'

Wally's dining room went spinning. Frank put his hand on the table. 'Can I have a glass of water?' Frank drank it down, Wally went back and re-filled the glass and Frank gulped it down again. He closed his eyes. 'I thought it was just bad luck.'

Wally went to the toilet. Frank wiped his eyes, and tried to focus on the photos along the sideboard. Wally's family, holidays, black and white snaps of old faces he half-recognised. He saw himself at one of their ladies' nights at the Dock Labour Board social. Carol doing her best to crack a smile for the camera, clearly hating the whole thing. He remembered what he'd have to do in return for her dolling up for one of those dos.

When Wally sat down again he leaned across the table and put his hand on Frank's arm. 'The Prices were no good, mate. They always looked after their own and the devil take the rest of us. If you're doing their dirty work again, let it go.'

'Carl's not like them.'

'You reckon?'

He nodded, slowly.

Lorraine shuffled into the dining room in a pair of too-big reindeer slippers, 'I fell asleep on the bloody sofa, I'm going to bed babe, you gonna be long?'

'Not long,' said Wally. 'Sweet dreams.'

Lorraine leaned down, kissed Wally and shambled into the hall. 'Don't forget to lock up.'

'I won't.'

Frank waited for Lorraine to make her way upstairs. 'Has everyone known, all these years?'

Wally shrugged. 'People think they know things, but most haven't got a clue. That was always your thing though wasn't it, making sure no one knew how much you was involved. Only Dave, Rose and me really knew what you did for him, making sure he never got stiffed, setting things up, clearing up his mess, but then it's all easily forgotten. I doubt Carl even knows. Rose won't have told him.'

Wally poured one for the road. He was making noises about going to bed, offering the sofa, but Frank needed the walk home.

'You got a car?' said Frank.

'Yeah, but I can't drive now after this lot. I can call you a cab.'

'Tomorrow, I need you tomorrow.'

'It's New Year's Eve, Frank, we're going down Tunbridge Wells, spend it with Karen and the grandkids.'

'So you can drive me daytime. I want a lift, couple of hours, half a day at most.'

Wally took a long indrawn breath. 'Couple of hours is all I've got.'

Frank nodded. 'That's all I need.'

An hour later and Frank found himself outside Adeline's flat, knocking softly while a skinny cat darted from the recycling bins to fast-food litter in the street. He heard keys jingling and felt himself being observed through the spyhole. She was in her pyjamas and invited him in sleepily. 'All I had was Baileys, Christ knows why I bought it, and some dodgy Metaxa Kev brought back from Mykonos which I think was in a raffle. I've 'ad it for donkeys' years. What I'm saying is I can't offer you a proper drink.'

He lifted the Johnnie Walker. 'Me and Johnnie've been doing the rounds.'

'You want a glass?' She took an involuntary step back against the doorframe, her hair falling down across her face.

'Please. I got the note. You said to call in when I got back. If it's too late, I'll bugger off and get home.'

There was a bed made up on the sofa in the living room, a fleece blanket and a pillow. Baileys and Metaxa bottles on the floor. Frank picked his way through, took his coat off and sat back in the spare chair. Adeline came in with a couple of tumblers and a bottle of Coke. 'I'll join you, if you join me. Come an' sit here.' She patted the sofa seat next to her and poured him half a glass.

'Cheers.'

She leaned into him. 'I'm sorry we left you behind, Frank. I wanted to come back, not that it's an excuse, but I did.'

'It's alright.'

'What happened to your hand?'

He turned it over, the bandage now a grubby mitt with the two outside fingers splinted and swollen. 'Adam O'Keefe held me down while brother James threatened to hit it with a hammer unless I begged forgiveness for going into his house and taking Grace away. I declined.'

She put the glass down and held him, burying her face in his shoulder. 'Oh Jesus, I'm sorry, so sorry.'

'It's not down to you. You didn't make me go.'

'Yes, I did.'

He relaxed back into the sofa and took Adeline's weight against him, he smelled her hair. She'd washed it that evening and the shampoo smell was fresh, clean. Apple. 'Have you heard, they did the pub over?'

She froze. 'What, they came down here?'

'This afternoon. They turned the place over, smashed up Carl's telly and did what used to be called demanding money with menaces. They're coming back, well it'll be tonight now. They want fifty grand to make up for what they reckon Adam lost in this poxy drug deal, and as compo for what we did taking Diane out of an abusive relationship with a drunken psychopath and bringing Grace home to Daddy. Cheap at half the price.'

'It was nowhere near that, what the hell are they talking about?' The penny dropped. 'That means Carl knows.'

'If he didn't already. And if he didn't, he should have. I want you to go into work tomorrow like nothing's happened. Just help him, be around.'

'I can't.'

'Yes you can. He needs you to be there.'

'What's he gonna do?'

Frank hesitated. 'He thinks he's gonna front up, take them on and tough it out.'

'Him and whose army?'

'Well, I was trying to find him one as it goes, that's where I was tonight, but it's not happening. They're all dead or dying or just living their lives. Carl thinks he's got the family reputation to uphold, Rose has drilled it into him since he was knee high. It's a non-starter ... as if he thinks taking a stand now makes up for not being the man his Dad was, not being there to look after his brother, never being able to make his bloody mother happy. Take your pick.'

She brought her feet up onto the sofa, covered them with the blanket. 'What was he really like, Carl's dad?'

There was a long silence. Frank couldn't pin it down, he thought he'd known as well as anyone, but in the end maybe only Dave himself, and maybe Jacqui, had any idea who Dave Price had really been. The rest of them all got their own Dave Price, the one he showed you, who'd get you to do his bidding. Finally, he said, 'He was a face.'

'And you, were you a face?'

'No, never. I was anonymous once I got with Dave. Started out wanting it that way, ended up being the only way I knew. In prison it suited me even more and now, well, who wouldn't want to be a nobody if all you do is prop up the end of the bar?'

'Doesn't it bother you?'

'It didn't. Until tonight.'

In the distance a siren wailed. Adeline nestled into him and pulled the blanket over them both. Frank drifted into a dead sleep with her arms around him. The glass fell from his good hand to the rug and nestled there.

Frank didn't sleep more than a couple of hours. The pain in his hand was worse, stiffening up to his shoulder. He eased Adeline back onto the sofa and went in search of painkillers. He unwound the bandage releasing his fingers, bruised purple and swollen. He scrawled her a note, left it on the kettle and let himself out quietly.

When he got home, the first grey light was coming up across Deptford Park. The last day of the year. For a while he sat stiffly, the cold clamping his thoughts. He made a coffee, took his time and managed a wash and a shave. He was slowly doing up the buttons of his shirt when a movement outside the window distracted him. He grabbed the knife from the table and went to the window. Harry Singh was scaling a ladder up the scaffolding, hauling it up behind him at each level with what looked to be his tools in a plastic carrier tied through one of the holes in his cardigan. He waved at Frank through the window. 'You alright, Frank? I'm fixing the roof.' He pointed upwards. 'No more rain in the bathroom.'

'You'll fucking kill yourself. Go down.'

'Mr Hilton, he wants me to repair guttering first, so I got the tools. No problem. I told him I'll do the roof when it stops raining.'

The scaffold poles strained against the inside of the window frame. Frank could imagine the whole lot just pulling through the wall. 'Take it easy, mate. Just be really careful.'

'What you think, I'm flying trapeze act?' Harry laughed and climbed past the window. As the ladder went up out of sight, he yelled down, 'Happy New Year.'

31

Frank called Wally from a phone box and told him to meet him in an hour at Rose Price's.

At first, Lauren was reluctant to let him in. She stood in the doorway. Frank stepped back. 'You know they're coming back. They won't give up.'

She thought for a moment, then stood aside. 'Rose is in the living room. Go easy though, she's not too good this morning.'

Rose was propped up in a chair, an oversized cushion behind her, a small table at her side with a TV remote and a freshly made cup of tea. It was almost a replica layout of her own living room, only with Lauren's brightly coloured throws covering the three-piece and a tasselled scarf draped over the lampshade. The rain slapped at the window, driven by a relentless east wind.

Lauren led Frank through. 'It's a visitor for you, Rose.'

She sighed wearily at the intrusion. The television was on low, a burbling daytime talk-show.

'You want me to turn the telly off?' said Lauren.

'I'm watching it.' Rose's voice was cracked.

Frank turned the set off.

'I know who you are,' said Rose.

'I never doubted it.'

Lauren stood at the door.

'You don't need to stay.' Frank unbuttoned his overcoat, sat on the sofa. 'Rose might want some of what I've got to say to stay between me and her.'

'No, you stay,' she said, finding a slightly stronger tone.

Lauren perched on the corner of the sofa closest to Rose. A string of decorations hanging over the gas fire dropped.

'I spent last night at Wally Patch's,' said Frank.

The old woman's eyes flitted around the room. 'I 'aven't seen Wally in years. He's another one who let us down in the end.'

'Is that right?'

'Yes it is.' She thought for a moment, addressed her comments entirely to Lauren. 'You know in those days you could see their heads turn when we went into a place. Dave was respected. When we used to have parties after the pub on a Saturday night. Dave's boys'd be there; Wally, Ruby, Roy, all them lot and their wives. And we'd have a few drinks, some eats, a bit of a party, dancing an' that.'

'Did Lonnie used to come along, Rose?' asked Frank.

She picked up the cup, brought it to her pursed lips, sipped noisily. The cup clinked heavily back in the saucer. 'The name doesn't ring any bells.'

'He was the bloke you and Dave put the fear of God into so's he'd swear blind I'd killed Gary Stack. Remember now? Lonnie was the bloke who made sure I went down for murder.'

Frank hadn't for a minute thought she'd crumple. As frail as she appeared to be, he couldn't see her falling into a weeping mess and admitting to what they made Lonnie do, what they'd done to him. But she leaned forward and extended a finger. 'You let us down, an' all. You're another one. I remember you and your missis, Carol right? You were always on the outside, never wanted to be part of anything, the pair of you. Dave always said you'd be the one to grass him up.'

'What, so you thought you'd get in first?'

Afterwards, weeks afterwards, Frank would look back at that moment; the world as Rose had chosen to remember it unravelling. She was an old woman, but in years not so much older than himself. All her lies and resentments were in that bony accusing finger and the cracks and creases of her skin. It made her ugly, pinched and dreadful.

He ran his fingers through his hair and said, 'Tell you what I'll do Rose, I'm going to tell you some things. Think of me like a priest. I'll make it easy, you don't even have to say your confession. I'll tell it to you, alright?'

She said nothing.

'You and Dave set me up. You and him let me work for you, back you up, help you out, clear up one godawful mess after another, and when I needed your help, you sold me down the river. Your husband was in hock to that copper, Fraser, right? So when Dave shot Gary Stack dead, shot his face off in front of your kids and covered us all in Christ knows what, you took our clothes to get rid, remember that?'

'Yes,' she said quietly.

'Except you kept my suit back from the incinerator, that was you, Rose. And when Fraser came calling like you knew he would, you dropped me in it. Wally told me he was supposed to do Lonnie as well, poor old loser Lonnie, everyone's village idiot. But he didn't did he, so what did you do?'

Rose glanced at Lauren whose eyes stayed down. 'Lonnie was a bloody fool.'

'Who'd do whatever the last person he spoke to told him to. What you and Dave told him to. So what was it, grass Frank and we'll set you up somewhere nice? Where'd he go, Spain? Margate? Worthing?'

'Stanmore.'

Frank laughed. 'Fucking Stanmore. I do fifteen years inside and Lonnie goes to Stanmore.' He paused. 'See, I could tell you what it cost me, what I lost, but I don't think you'd give a damn either way, would you?'

'You look after your own Frank, that's the first, the only thing that matters.'

'Jesus, I *was* one of your own, one of Dave's own. And you don't believe that crap anyway, how could you? You pushed Terry into taking on Dave's business when you must've known he never had it in him. How was that looking after your own?'

'Everyone said that, but he would have been alright ...' She stalled, took a laboured breath and put her hand to her chest. 'Lauren, get my pills will you. The little white ones.'

Lauren raked around in Rose's bag. 'They're not here. Must still be next door. Hang on and I'll fetch them.'

Frank stood up, walked to the mantelpiece and picked up a photo. Lauren and Grace in a seashell-frame. 'What you did to me was unforgiveable. What you made Terry do was worse.'

Rose's turn seemed to have subsided as quickly as it came on. 'He'd have been alright if they'd stood by him. If his brother had stuck by him.'

'Then you'd have lost two sons, Rose. Simple as that.'

'What do you want, Frank? Want me to say I'm sorry? Or you just dragging up a load of old stories?'

Lauren came back in with pills and water. Frank waited until she'd finished fussing and took a seat on the sofa, close up. 'What I want is this: I'm gonna go now, but I want you to call Carl, ask him to come over here and tell him that you want him to do whatever he thinks is the right thing with the pub, give it all up if needs be. But most of all, I want you to tell him to walk away from this business with the O'Keefes.'

'That's his father's pub.'

'He's doing it for you, Rose. Let him off the hook. You owe me and this is what I want.'

There was a long silence, interrupted by the rain at the window.

'Lauren, you got a phone?' She took the hands-free from its dock. Frank punched in the numbers. It was ringing. He gave it to Rose, her hands trembled and she gave him a look like murder.

32

Wally was keeping warm in the car outside, engine running. He looked up at the flats as Frank got in. 'She alright, then?'

'She will be.'

'Look Frank, I've got to be back by two.'

'You will be.'

'So where we going?' He put the car in gear.

'Over the river. Aim for Seven Sisters and I'll give you directions when we get closer.'

'Bit of a mystery, innit?'

Frank settled into the passenger seat and put his seatbelt on. 'One of many.'

The rain was still belting down and judging by the slush puddles the cars were racing through it must have grown a degree or two warmer overnight. He was still feeling chilled to his bones. They didn't speak much. Wally slid a Small Faces CD into the player. 'Lorraine bought it for me for Christmas. I've still got me records up in the spare room, but I haven't got a record player and well, it's easier on CD. Do you a copy if you want.'

'Not a lot of point, Wal, nothing to play it on.'

'Right.'

The cafe's shutters were down. It was looking increasingly like no one was home. Wally pulled back his sleeve to check his watch, must've been the third time in five minutes since they'd parked up off the main drag in Palmers Green.

'I don't know why you keep doing that,' Frank growled. 'There's a clock in the dashboard. You coming?' He un-clicked the seatbelt.

'It looks shut.'

'Stretch your legs, then?'

'Frank, I gave up going into places I couldn't be certain of coming out of a bloody long time ago.'

'There *are* no bloody certainties,' said Frank.

All the way over he'd avoided thinking about what he was going to say, or even considering that the place might be closed. He was half-surprised to find it still there. As he crossed the street between parked cars, there was some movement from inside. A dark-haired unshaven bloke in a good-looking leather jacket came to the door, looked out both ways, then lit up a cigarette. He smoked for a minute and flicked the butt into the gutter. Frank held back, then went in a few seconds behind him.

There were no customers. The cafe's wood panelled walls were hung with photos of lads' football teams in yellow and green kits. A framed and signed print of an altogether more grown-up bunch of lads in a similar kit hung behind the counter. Underneath it read: *Akritas Chlorakas*. A pot of fresh coffee bubbled gently on a hot plate and above it on a shelf, half a dozen bottles were lined up. A serving hatch through to the kitchen was closed, but Frank guessed this geezer wasn't about to knock up a bacon sarny.

He nodded. The bloke ignored him, sipped his coffee and turned the pages of a newspaper.

'Kalis pera,' said Frank.

'Sorry mate, s'a private club, members only.' He didn't look up.

'You got the New Year's Eve shift then? Unlucky.'

He gave off a kind of grunt, a wordless fuck off.

'Can I 'ave a coffee, black. Please?'

'See that sign up there? Says members only. Says it so's we don't get people like you comin' in askin' for moussaka and chips. And coffee.'

Frank registered movement, a passing shadow behind the serving hatch. He put his hands in his pockets and walked up to the counter. 'I was a member once as it goes, sort of honorary, when Danny Georgiou and his Uncle Costas looked after the place.'

This time he looked up.

'And I don't think they'd 'ave denied a bloke a cup of coffee on a cold day. Member or not, especially if he'd come all the way from New Cross.'

'Costas was my grandfather, God rest 'im. I'm Antonis Georgiou.'

'In that case, Antonis, I met your Dad once. Lakis, right? In fact he wanted to shoot me, but we got over it.'

Antonis closed and folded the newspaper. 'Who the fuck are you?'

'Frank Neaves. I used to work for a man called Dave Price a long time ago. Now I'm working for myself.'

No recognition. The name meant nothing. 'So, what d'you want here?'

'Black coffee, when you're ready.' He moved to the nearest table and pulled out a chair. 'No rush.'

Antonis disappeared through the back door. Frank heard voices. He took a deep breath.

Danny Georgiou had certainly made the best of his years if his ample belly was anything to go by. And once the sense of disbelief had fallen from his face, the craggy smile alone was worth the journey. Frank stood.

'Frank.'

Danny held his arms. 'Jesus, you look terrible. Antonis, get Frank's coffee. And a brandy. No, bring the bottle.'

They sat. Danny shaking his head with disbelief.

'What?' said Frank, smiling.

'You took your fucking time.'

Wally was drumming at the steering wheel when Frank came out twenty minutes later. He crossed the street to the driver's side, gesturing to Wally to open the window. The combination of sweet black coffee and Five Kings brandy had warmed him nicely. Wally took the blast.

'Jesus, Frank. If I'd known you were on a bender I'd have brought a sleeping bag.'

'I'm gonna make my own way back. You get off.'

'That's it? What about Carl?'

Frank walked away. 'Cheers for the lift, you have a good New Year, mate.'

33

Pale squares on the walls where photographs had been, hastily re-stitched upholstery, some borrowed chairs and inventive bodge jobs on other bits of furniture. Frank followed Carl round. Adeline was behind the bar, loading up the Gordon's optic. 'This is the last, I've got one of each, Bell's and Smirnoff and Martell, the others are all bent and bloody useless. Alright, Frank?' She smiled.

He nodded.

Linda emerged from the back room dragging the hoover behind her. 'It don't bleedin' matter how many times I go over it, there's still bits of glass goin' up the tube.'

'Leave it now, it's fine,' said Carl. 'You finished upstairs?'

'Just got to change Gracie's things over.'

'Right, well do that then get yourself off home and put your gladrags on.'

Linda waved.

'See, Frank, we've pretty much got it sorted. We'll be ready to go by six and then ...' He shrugged. 'What will be, will be.'

It was all very blitz spirit, all very admirable. Carl's manufactured enthusiasm put Frank in mind of an officer he'd once had. An overgrown schoolboy who walked them into a minefield and insisted he'd walk them straight out the other side rather than call the sappers to see them through. Frank couldn't quite believe Carl had put the word out to the regulars. As if they'd have some kind of collective power over the O'Keefes, who more than likely would come back tooled up to the nines. 'Come over here and sit down a minute.' Frank took Carl's arm, led him to a chair. 'You sure about opening up tonight?'

'No question.'

'And what about you, you alright in yourself?'

'Yeah, fine.' There was a weariness in him, as if stopping to sit down had allowed him time to think. 'I saw Mum earlier. She told me to do whatever I thought was best.' He looked to Frank for a reaction, but got none.

'Where's the gun?' asked Frank.

'Where I can get to it.' A nod towards the bar. 'What's on your mind Frank?'

'In all the years I was away, I never spared a thought for anything but coming out and making a home somewhere with someone, I still had Carol in mind I s'pose. I wanted a bit of a life. But mainly it was this idea of a home, somewhere that's your own. And after a while when I realised that was never going to happen and I wound up here, I thought it'd do. And it has, but it's not the be all and end all, or it shouldn't be. Not for me and especially not for you.'

Carl folded his arms. 'Where's this going? The pub isn't the be all, not now I've got Grace and, well, Di and me might—'

'Exactly, so why put it all on the line? You know these jokers are two-bob hardcases not worth the shit off your shoes.'

'I'm not backing down. You said I had to come out the back room, that's what I'm doing.'

'With a gun under the bar?' He paused. 'Well, granted, you wouldn't be the first. But what if I said there's another way to handle this? I mean, you ain't relishing the prospect of going toe to toe I take it?'

'Course not.'

'So you'd think about an alternative?'

He opened his hands.

'Let me deal with the O'Keefes tonight.'

'And what, you'll do 'em in a drinking contest?'

'You don't want to do this, Carl. I don't buy it, I can see you're shitting yourself, trying to come on like ... like your dad. But they'll come through that door knowing what you've got under the bar, and they'll be ready. And you'll be on your own and all your punters, your people, Adeline, Kev, they'll all be in the firing line. You won't win.'

'You know that for certain?'

'I'm telling you, there's no way. Not a chance, but there is another way that'll mean you seeing the back of them for good.'

'I'm listening.'

'I want you to sell the pub.'

He laughed. 'You been saving your empties, Frank? Cost you more than that.'

Frank gave him a moment. 'Name the price.'

'What?'

'Name it.'

Carl's mouth hung open slightly. He rubbed his hand against the bristles on his face.

'Maybe you *could* front up to the O'Keefes,' said Frank. 'I can do it better. Up to you.'

'But you said yourself, they'd never respect you. You've spent the last five years propping up that bar. A week ago you were asleep on it.'

'Yeah, well, it's been a strange week.'

'Even if I went along with it, you'd need the deeds, there'd be a load of paperwork and it's ...' he looked up to the clock above the door, still bust at twenty-past one, 'I dunno, about four o'clock on New Year's Eve afternoon, where you gonna find a lawyer?' He stalled when he caught Frank's expression.

'His name's Sampson and he's in the silver Merc parked outside. Have a look if you like. With your say-so he can sort it this afternoon.'

Carl went to the door and looked out. 'You really have got it all worked out, haven't you?'

'I think so.'

34

Frank felt lightheaded as he walked down Evelyn Street that evening in a freshly pressed suit, clean shirt, borrowed tie and with a good shine on his shoes. It was just before nine. The traffic was light and moving easily and the rain had recently stopped, but still rolled the cigarette butts along the gutter. From some of the houses there were signs of parties already in full swing, some spilling out into the street. He stepped into the road to let a group of youngsters pass, three girls arm in arm and half a dozen lads ambling behind. They bellowed a *Happy New Year.* Frank forced a smile. There was a clean white bandage on his bad hand. He shoved both hands in his coat pockets and walked on. What was the worst that could happen? The O'Keefes could turn up mob-handed with a few mates and an arsenal of hi-tech hardware on board, but he thought not. Ah, fuck it. *There's no early retirement in this business. If I could've I would've.*

Frank went through the John Evelyn's double doors. The O'Keefes were early, Jim O'Keefe's arse was perched on Frank's stool at the bar. Not a good start. Linda and her old man and half a dozen other regulars sat around tables in quiet conversation. Most had stayed away. Adeline put a just-poured pint down on the bar and Jim picked it up.

'Ha, old man, how's yer fingers?'

Frank nodded to Adeline. He lifted his bandaged hand and managed to uncurl and lift a single middle finger. 'Yeah, fine, thanks.' He pulled out a barstool further along the bar, took his overcoat off and folded it across the next stool.

Ewan and Adam were sitting at a table. They were all waiting for Carl. Adeline whispered, 'We haven't seen hide nor hair since he disappeared with you.'

Ewan looked at his watch uncomfortably. 'Adam, just go outside and have a walk round will you.'

Adam put on a pained expression.

'Just do it. And don't be long.'

As he stood, Adam's jacket clunked against the table edge. So at least one of them was carrying.

'Can I have a pint, please?' said Frank.

'Yeah, course.'

Adeline waved his money away. 'That's one of quite a few I owe you.'

'You don't owe me anything.'

'Touching,' Jim cut in. 'She letting you fuck her, too? You'd better enjoy that pint. You'll have to find somewhere else to drink after tonight, or you could always sit in the park with a can of Tennent's.'

Frank tapped his wrist and nodded to Adeline. 'You got the time?'

'Ten.'

Instinctively, Ewan looked at his own watch. 'So where is he?'

They turned to the door as it opened. Adam came back in and found himself unexpectedly the centre of attention. 'Nothing.'

'You didn't see him out there did you?' said Jim. 'He'd be the bloke shitting himself.'

'Carl's not coming,' said Frank.

Ewan stepped up. 'You think because my brother fucked up your hand, you've got a call to wind me up? Not wise.'

Frank reached into the inside pocket of his jacket and produced a thin sheaf of paper, folded three times. He flattened it out and passed it to Ewan. 'What that says is that as of tomorrow, the first of January, this pub no longer belongs to Carl Price. It belongs to Daniel Andreas Georgiou. It's legal. That's a copy, which you can keep. Either way, Carl has nothing to give you, so you might as well go back where you came from.'

'You really have taken against us for some reason, old man, you've bloody pissed me off. What happens if I break the rest of your fingers?' Ewan pulled an automatic from his coat and forced Frank's bandaged hand onto the bar. As he brought the butt down, Frank turned and connected with a short straight left. Ewan staggered back, wiped blood from his nose.

Frank kicked his stool away. 'No more.'

Adeline fumbled under the counter for Carl's gun. James O'Keefe was already through the hatch and behind the bar. He grabbed her arm, backed her up and took the gun. 'See? You can't fucking count, can you? More of us than you. You had one gun, now I've got it. Which means ...' He lifted his jacket to show the automatic in his waistband, 'I've got two. And along with the one in my brother Addy's coat and my brother Ewan's, that makes four. Four-nil. But fuckit, who's counting?' He smacked Adeline across the face with the back of his ring hand. Her lip tore and blood dripped down her chin.

'Enough pissing about.' Ewan levelled his gun at Frank and shoved him towards the door. 'You, outside and we'll sort this without an audience. If Carl's shit out, that's tough on you. You won't need your coat. And you lot ...' he pointed to Adeline, Linda and the others, '... stay right here. Anyone comes through that door will find themselves – *involved*, understand? Move, old man.'

As Frank pulled the door open, he stepped back. Carl entered first and behind him came Danny Georgiou, Christos, Lakis, the lad Antonis, and half a dozen others, all Danny's boys and for one night only, Frank and Carl's boys. Lakis' sawn off in his ribs persuaded Ewan to give up his gun. Adam, giving it the *come on you cunts* one second, found his nose broken, pouring blood the next, with Christos emptying the mag from a flashy 9 mm he hadn't been able to hold onto. He held it up swinging by the trigger guard for Danny to see. 'Boy thinks he's a gangsta.'

Danny shook his head.

Jim O'Keefe had grabbed Adeline as Carl came through the door. He held her, one arm around her throat, the other holding the gun, which he jabbed hard into her ribs. She'd been forced forward and was gasping for breath, her face reddening. As she struggled, his arm tightened. 'You owe us, you cunt. You give us the money or we take the pub, right Ewan?'

Frank turned to Ewan. 'Tell him to leave her, right now.'

Ewan said nothing.

Frank took Lakis' sawn-off and shoved it in Adam's neck. 'How much did she take off you, boy?'

'Thirty-grand.'

Frank kicked the back of his legs, forcing him to his knees. 'You lying shit, you never gave her thirty-grand's worth in the first place. How much?' He pulled the hammer back.

'Seven, it was seven. Ewan!'

'Ponce.' Frank pushed him aside. Jim O'Keefe let Adeline loose. She fell back, pulling bottles off the shelf. Antonis was up, sliding across the bar on his arse. He shoved O'Keefe out the way, lifted Adeline and helped her to a seat, soaked a clean cloth and held it to her mouth. 'We'll get you sorted, no problems, eh?'

Danny's boys persuaded Jim and Adam outside. Adam went easy, Jim went through the door cursing and then went very quiet. Frank, Carl, Danny and Adeline were left with Ewan.

'This was my dad's pub,' said Carl. 'Always will be. It's protected, you understand? My friends know you. They know where your business is, where your family lives, who your contacts are. You want to keep any of that safe, you stay away from here.'

They put the O'Keefes in the back seat of Ewan's BMW. One of Danny's boys drove with another in the front passenger seat looking back with the sawn-off to keep things honest. A second car followed.

'How far they gonna take 'em?' Asked Frank.

'Home,' said Danny. 'All the way.'

From the houses behind Evelyn Street came the sound of a countdown. *Ten, nine, eight, seven, six, five, four, three, two, one.* '*Happy New Year*'s and Big Ben chimes rung out around the streets, fireworks exploded in the night skies over south London and beyond. 'You gonna invite me in your pub for a drink, then?' said Frank.

The party in the John Evelyn that night went through until daylight. For a while there was music, with the locals and Danny and his boys vying with each other for floor space. Carl made a couple of calls and Lauren and Rose came down, Danny's boys making such a fuss of the old girl, that she let a smile cross her lips as well as a couple of large whisky macs. As good as his word, Carl brought Grace along for a while and Diane found herself behind the bar once more, dispensing drinks and the occasional withering glance towards Adeline, who'd stopped the flow of blood from her cut lip and was practising self-anaesthesia with a bottle of Martell. She hardly left her seat and so saw the whole night unfold, but missed the moment when, with Antonis' arm around her shoulders, Frank threw a look that was pure heartache.

As the night wore on, they closed the doors. There were a few of them left and they began yarning. And as these things do, stop me if you've heard this one before, the stories turned to Dave Price.

The room was quiet as each of them told a story, first Danny, then Carl, then Rose, then they turned to Frank.

'Jacqui told me this one.' He glanced at Rose, her eyes dropped. 'She told me how when she wanted to open that launderette with the money her dad left when he passed away, and she didn't have enough, she went to the bank. And the bank turned her down, so she went to Dave for the rest of the money and everyone told her she was getting in bed with the devil. Yeah, Rose, you remember that one?'

Rose nodded slowly.

'So he gave her the rest of the money and said she could pay him back once a week, every Friday, and they agreed a rate. He told her she'd 'ave the only protected launderette in Catford. So she paid him, every week until the loan and the bit of interest had been paid off. Then, when he died, he asked Rose to get his suit cleaned before they, y'know, took him away in it. And to make sure that Jacqui cleaned it and got it looking right, fair enough. And when she went through the pockets, she found an envelope with her name on it. Inside was a letter, a page from a notebook and a cheque for the entire amount she'd borrowed off him. The letter said how frightened he was, how he never wanted his boys to do what he did, how he was worried about how Rose would handle being on her own, and how, all things considered, he felt bad about taking her money all those years, but he needed an excuse to keep seeing her. So here was the money back, and he'd kept a tally in the notebook of every penny for nearly twenty years. Thing was, Jacqui spent the best part of her life slaving in that launderette to pay what she owed. It meant she gave things up. She could have done, I dunno, whatever she wanted. But he kept her there where he needed her. That's what he did, that's what Dave was like. He made you do things you didn't want to do. Didn't mean you didn't love the bloke, but that's who he was.'

As soon as he left the table Frank regretted what he'd said. It wasn't the time or the place and maybe he'd let the whisky work his tongue. But it can't have been so bad; a minute or two later Danny was telling a dumb story about his cousin in Limassol, probably made up but it was making them laugh. Frank took his seat at the bar and lit a cigarette. In front of him the whisky was trying to put the hex on. From his pocket he pulled a tenner with a note attached: *Is this really the emergency you think it is?*

'Is it?' Adeline was by his side.

He smiled. 'Tomorrow, maybe.'

'Managed to kill the mood a bit there.'

'I know, sorry.'

'S'alright. I never met the bloke, he's got nothing on me.' She smiled and winced, put her fingertips to her lip to see if it was bleeding again. 'Reckon it'll leave a mark, a battle scar? I just wanted you to know, Antonis has offered to give me a lift home in a little while. He could drop you off as well if you like.'

'Nah, I'm hanging on here for a bit.' He shivered at the thought of his flat's permanently open window. 'Until Danny goes, anyway.'

'Antonis says he's going to ask Danny if he'll let him be manager here once Carl moves out. I mean, it won't be for a few weeks yet, but ...' She tailed off.

Frank nodded. 'It's a good idea.'

'So you'll still be able to send your IOUs through. It's been good, Frank. Getting to know you.' She put her hand on his and squeezed. He felt its pressure there long after she'd stopped squeezing, long after Antonis put his coat around her shoulders, long after she'd gone.

It wasn't the way he'd planned it, not exactly. There were *seeyas* and *nice ones* and *Happy New Years* as he walked out, felt the dawn air hit his lungs and made his way up Evelyn Street. The street-sweepers were out, picking up soggy rockets, bottles and odd shoes from the gutters. Here and there the night's casualties wandered in search of a bed. Frank crossed to the middle of the street and walked the white line, keeping it straight, sober as hell.

35

A warm breeze blew across Deptford Park as Adeline walked to Frank's flat with the sun on her back that Sunday afternoon. No one remembers dates around here, but they're pretty sure it must have been around June time. As the weeks went by, Frank had been coming into the pub less and less. The stool was always kept there, of course, and the bowl at his elbow would be filled if he wanted. But it had been a few days, maybe a full week since anyone had seen him.

She stood on the step, looked up and pushed the bell to his flat. When there was no answer, she pushed them all. A disinterested voice tried to give her the brush off. She kept pressing until he buzzed open the front door. She walked up the stairs, shivering in the cool passageway. Frank's door was ajar. She pushed it open, 'Frank, you in?'

The kitchen cupboards were empty, the fridge turned off at the wall socket. The chemical smell of cleaning fluids clung to the work surface and the cooker top. In the living room, the single chair with its saggy arse cushion had been smoothed out. She opened the stand-up wardrobe and wire frame hangers clanked against each other.

There was pub talk. Some said he'd gone to work for Danny Georgiou. Antonis pulled a pint and shrugged, the first he'd heard if it was true. So maybe Danny had set him up with a place in Cyprus and he'd retired there? You couldn't see it. So, had he gone to find Carol and Kate? They didn't think so, more likely if he'd gone looking for anyone it'd be Jacqui – he'd talked about her now and again, but not so much lately. Behind Adeline's back, they wondered if the O'Keefes had come back and taken a quiet revenge. Until someone pointed out they'd hardly have cleaned his flat for him and taken out the rubbish. When Carl dropped in for his

Sunday evening pint, as he did these days when he'd taken Rose home, he was as much in the dark as they were.

In the end it was all speculation. Just pub talk, another story to tell. All they knew was that Frank had left town. He had the right to be whoever and go wherever he wanted. Adeline just hoped he'd walk back in one day, park his arse at the bar and tell them stories about his wild years.

Lightning Source UK Ltd.
Milton Keynes UK
UKOW051214300412

191734UK00001B/6/P